Hap for you

Luci Beach

lucibeachbooks@gmail.com
LuciBeach.co.uk

Copyright © 2018 Luci Beach
All rights reserved. No part of this book may be reproduced in any form on by an electronic or mechanical means, including information storage and retrieval systems, without permission in writing from the publisher, except by a reviewer who may quote brief passages in a review.

Cover Design by Gabriella Regina

ISBN: 9781691289592

First published 2018
First paperback edition 2019

Published by Luci Beach Books
LuciBeach.co.uk

Happy for you

Luci Beach

NOW: Flatmates Forever

You don't expect the ex-love of your life to text you on a random Friday while you're sitting in a damp Croydon kitchen. Particularly when you haven't heard from him in years, and you didn't think he'd ever contact you again.

Especially when that's because you broke his heart.

I'm not opening the message. Not now, anyway, and not here. My flatmates are in the middle of their usual weekly moans about work and I'm supposed to join in. It's what we do every Friday night.

"Knickers, knickers, knickers!" Louis complains. "It's all about knickers! Nobody appreciates me. I'm a proper photographer. I'm an artist!"

"Of course you are," Tilly says, ever the people-pleaser. She works in HR and she's very good at her job, even when she's not at work.

"An artist for a has-been fashion catalogue! Selling *knickers*!" He barely pauses for breath. "An artist forced by monetary necessity to shoot a load of vanilla underwear shots!"

"I once tried strawberry-flavoured underwear." Tilly sips her drink. "It smelled weird. Sickly-sweet."

Louis leans across the breakfast bar and aims a glower at her.

"Anyway, where we work is... Well, it's..." Tilly tries, but even she can't think of a good way to defend the Something For Everyone catalogue. "Ciara is happy there." She emphasises my name so much that the 'key' sound at the beginning goes on for ages. *"Keeeee-ra is happy there."*

"Don't drag me into this," I say, though I'm secretly relieved. I need distraction, something to stop me not-looking at my phone and not-thinking about Max. Why is he texting me? What does he want?

"*Keeeeee-ra* isn't happy anywhere." Louis swigs his cheap wine.

"Hey!" I protest.

"You're one to talk," Tilly tells Louis. "You're going out with a supermodel and you're still miserable!"

I really haven't been paying attention tonight. "What's going on with you and Tomas?"

Louis sighs in the direction of his phone. "Our texting ratio is terrible!"

"Your *what*?"

"His *texting ratio*, Ciara," Tilly echoes. "He gave a massive explanation five minutes ago. How did you miss it?"

Louis obviously doesn't mind repeating himself. "We're currently at three of my texts to every one of his! It's absolutely not good enough."

Tilly laughs. "It sounds even more pathetic the second time. Who keeps count?"

"I do. And that's before I compare our pay packets. His modelling career has really taken off.

He's off to Paris for that advert soon, the coffee company one. He's going on glamorous adventures with attractive, professionally caffeinated people!"

"Paris isn't that far away," I soothe, nudging the wine bottle in his direction. "And isn't it just a short thing, anyway?"

"Three months!"

"That's not very long," I say.

"But you know what those advertising people are like – throwing their cash around. It could even be longer! He's leaving me behind! It's a tragedy of epic –"

"I'll tell you what makes me sad," Tilly interrupts. "Dougal. All the joy's gone out of my life. I've lost my soulmate."

"Ages ago," I remind her, gently pushing the bottle away from Louis and towards her instead. Tilly's boyfriend ran off with her then best friend. How clichéd is that?

"It was three months ago."

"That's a very long time," I say.

Louis glares at me.

I change direction quickly. "Anyway, Dougal didn't deserve you."

"Oh, I know that. I meant Jess. She was my best friend. I miss her, and it's all Dougal's fault we had that big fight!"

Louis rolls his eyes. "Jess is to blame, too."

"Yeah!"

"Yes, for seeing someone with such a stupid name."

"Yeah." Tilly sighs before the penny drops. "Wait – no! I went out with Dougal first! Did you seriously just say that? I dare you to repeat it!"

"Fine. Dougal has a stupid –"

"Louis. Tilly. Stop it!"

They look at me sheepishly.

"You know what, though?" I realise. "It's probably good that you're fighting. It shows you care. It's better to argue than never communicating in the first place." I don't look at my phone.

"Tell me about it!" Louis says. "It's what I've been saying all night. It's like Tomas just can't be bothered!" He waves his phone at us. "Still nothing! You know what? I'm texting him right now. I'm demanding a grand gesture. I'm writing it in all-caps!"

"All-caps?" I give an impressed whistle. "Wow, you really mean business."

"A grand gesture?" Tilly asks. "What are you on about, Lou?"

"You know, like in romantic films," I explain for him, as he's busy caps-locking at Tomas. "A big declaration of love!"

"Oh, well then. People don't do things like that in real life! So there's no need to text-shout at your lovely Icelandic boyfriend." Tilly sniffs. "He's basically just a man, after all, and you lot are famous for squashing your feelings."

"I'm sorry – what?" Louis is back from his texting trauma. "Like women don't? And *just* a man? What exactly do you mean by that?"

Tilly and Louis start an argument about toxic masculinity, where they're both basically agreeing but they don't seem to notice.

"Stop!" I look at them both. "Flatmates forever, remember?" It's a cheesy thing we started when we moved here a few years ago and immediately started bickering over bathroom-hogging and borrowed milk. We repeat it at least once every few boozy Friday nights and it always cheers us up.

"Flatmates forever!" Tilly chimes in, holding up her glass. "In it together!"

"In it together!" I raise my glass and stare at our missing musketeer. "Louis?"

"In it together," he grumbles. Then he smirks. "Until something better comes along."

We all laugh.

"Never!" Tilly declares. "Well, maybe."

"Probably."

"Definitely!" Louis says, but we know he's joking. Except when he adds, "But we'll always be friends."

"Yeah, we might all be miserable, but we'll always be happy for each other!" Tilly adds, clinking her glass against mine.

I let myself glance at my phone. The text from Max is still there, lurking behind my screensaver.

Tilly and Louis pick up their argument again, leaving me with my thoughts. I think about Max and what went wrong between us. I think about Louis and Tilly and all their complaints tonight.

I realise I'm on to something.

I can't wait to share my discovery.

I wait patiently for a gap, and then I say, "You know what, guys? I think I might have the answer!"

They break off their discussion and stare at me.

In the silence, I announce, "I think I know the secret to happiness!"

☼

NOW: Operation Happiness

There's a bit of a pause in which I wish I could shove the words back into my mouth.

"Happiness," I repeat slightly less triumphantly. "The secret? To happiness?" I mean, who wouldn't want that?

My flatmates stare at me in the dim glow of our shared kitchen. The gas ring we've lit for extra heat – and because Louis calculated that switching on the hob is cheaper cranking up our ancient boiler – flickers in the silence. It had better be creating an atmosphere rather than showing signs of breaking altogether. Our landlord takes about a year to ever fix anything. Afterwards he rewards himself by raising the rent, and there's no way any of us can afford any extra on our current salaries.

Eventually, Louis deadpans, "Uh-oh, here we go."

At least Tilly is on my side. "What is it, then? Tell me!"

"Thanks, Tilly. It's good to see someone appreciates me." I glare at Louis. " So this is what I'm thinking. You've been saying..." I point at Louis. "...you're sick of being ignored by your boyfriend."

"Tomas hardly ever reacts to my shares," Louis grumbles again. "Once I posted a –"

"Yes, I know, he's the worst boyfriend in the world. And Tilly's best friend acted like she didn't care about Tilly's feelings."

Tilly jiggles on her stool. "Just hurry up! I want the secret to eternal happiness and I want it now!"

"Do your worst," drones Louis.

I'm ready to tell them, if only they'd shut up. "Well, as you know, I think about this stuff a lot. I'm part of a project that's all about happiness."

"Oh, the one where you meet up with sexy Max?" Louis gives me a knowing smile.

My heart jumps. But he can't know about the text. I suppose I've mentioned Max in the past. "Um... So, anyway..." I try to remember what I was going to say. "I've realised it's simple. We only need one thing."

Louis raises one wry eyebrow, which is his trademark. Tilly and I call it 'the wry-brow'.

Tilly urges, "Go on, go on!"

"OK, this is it." I take a deep breath. "We need to... banish indifference."

Tilly's face clouds over, the traitor. "We need to *what* now?"

"You know. Indifference. Get rid of it. It's the worst emotion anyone can have towards me. Or you. Or anyone. The worst thing in the world is when people don't care!"

"What?"

"We need to replace indifference with... I don't know." I haven't exactly thought this through. "With passion!" I'm aware this isn't making sense, so I try for honesty. "I need to make everyone love me," I finish with what can only be described as a whimper, after all that. "Um, yeah. I'm going to make it my new project. Operation Happiness!"

"I already love you," says Louis, and I instantly forgive him for all his previous annoyingness.

"Wa-aaaait!" Tilly says, making the word go on for about a year.

We look at her.

"I know what has triggered this!" She announces.

"Do you?" She can't possibly.

"Yes! It all makes sense now!"

"Huh?" Louis and I say together.

"It's so obvious!" Tilly beams. "Ciara is in love!"

☼

NOW: Trash and Treasure

I nudge my phone – I can't help it. But Tilly doesn't know much about Max. Neither of my flatmates does.

Also I'm not in love with him. Not anymore.

"Is that a fact, Ciara?" Louis asks. "Who's the lucky guy?"

"I... er..."

"It's Chester, of course!" Tilly declares.

Louis gives a dramatic gasp. I almost join in. Tilly seriously thinks I fancy *Chester?*

"You mean Chester from work? Chester, Temporary Project Manager of Mystery?" Louis fakes a swoon. "Ciara, I had no idea!"

"What? No! I –"

"Don't try to deny it," Tilly says, "I've seen you eyeing him up over the side of your cubicle!"

How can she have seen something that never happened?

Louis sits up straighter. "Ooh, ooh!" Nothing is guaranteed to cheer him up more than romantic intrigue, especially if it's on his own doorstep, or by his work cubicle. "Fabulous! You two are perfect for each other!"

OK, now I'm finally distracted from my phone. "What? No way! What makes you think that?"

"Oh, yes! You're all... enigmatic."

"I'm not!"

"You are! You're like the Mona Lisa. The *Moaner* Lisa!" He laughs at his terrible joke for a couple of seconds, even though technically he's been the one complaining all evening. "And he's all... well, just a total mystery, really. Where did he come from? Why did he get his own office? And what exactly does he do all day?"

"Nothing." Tilly sounds bitter.

It's true. Our new colleague already has a reputation for not being seen to do much. Nobody knows what his role is, beyond his job title. He just pops up near us occasionally, writing in an expensive-looking moleskin notebook. In fact, I think that's where Tilly might have got the wrong idea about me and Chester. I think I was glaring at him as he was standing beside me, scribbling into leather-bound pages.

"No, no," Louis insists. "He does *something*. Something intriguing. Maybe Ciara can get close to him and find out!"

"And maybe Ciara can't," I say.

"Oh please, Ciara. Do it for us," Tilly begs. "For the gossip. And because it's about time you got yourself out there again."

"Out there?"

"You know. Dating. On the scene."

On the *scene*? What has Tilly been drinking tonight? (Actually, I know the answer to this. It's a bottle of cheap Prosecco from the nearest convenience store. We always pool the money from the Swear Jar/Forgot-to-Wash-Up Jar and buy whatever we can to liven up our Flatmate Fridays.)

Louis springs to my defence – the angel. "Ciara doesn't have to do anything she doesn't want to."

I nod. "Thank you."

"Except this. Go on, Ciara! Please seduce Chester for us and get us all the gossip!"

Louis is a total devil. "Seduce him yourself!"

"He's straighter than straight! It's obvious! And anyway, what would my Tomas say?" He preens a bit. "I could never do that to him."

"You've spent all night complaining about him," Tilly points out.

"True," Louis says. "But Chester's good-looking. He has a posh notebook. What's not to like, Ciara?"

"Why are you picking on me? Why not Tilly?"

"Not my type," Tilly remarks.

"Well, then! Maybe he's not my type either."

"I don't believe you! And I think he likes you!" Tilly bounces on her uncomfortable kitchen stool. "People like different things," she adds thoughtfully. "One man's trash is another man's treasure."

"Is that a Granny Newman expression?"

"Yes!" Tilly exclaims. "How did you know?"

Louis and I exchange a glance. We know. Tilly always brings Granny Newman into our conversations. Tilly's gran has the perfect phrase for every occasion.

"You mean one man's meat is another man's poison?" Louis unleashes his wrybrow.

"Yes, that means the same thing! Granny Newman says the trash and treasure thing, though."

"Probably just as well," Louis remarks.

"Why?" Tilly is wide-eyed.

"One man's *meat*?" He sniggers.

"Ohhh! Can you two stop..."

"Me? What did *I* do?"

"Stop what?" Louis asks.

"You know what! Don't drag my Granny Newman into your gutter, Louis. And Ciara, stop trying to deny your feelings. Chester is perfect for you and you know it. You should go for it. As part of this new Project Happiness thing, or whatever you called it."

"Operation Happiness. You really think so?" I'm starting to wonder now. Chester has an intensity about him that's sort of attractive, if I think about it. And he doesn't seem to have any friends at work. It's like he doesn't care what anyone thinks of him.

He doesn't care. He's indifferent. And my mission – my new project – is to banish indifference. So why not start with him?

It's actually not a bad idea.

Tilly's obviously detecting a chink in my armour. "You can try to win that Employee of the Quarter thing he introduced at our last meeting? That will get his attention. Plus there might be a bonus?"

"*Bone*-us!" Louis can't resist.

"Thanks for that." I nod. "OK. You know what, Tilly? I'm going to make Chester notice me. Professionally, I mean. For Operation Happiness."

Tilly's eyes sparkle. "You're going to make him love you?"

"Professionally."

She gives me a knowing look before her face falls. "But haven't you got that week off in three months? Right before the next big print deadline? You're going to have a tough time making him love you – professionally – when you're off on holiday at the absolute worst time of year."

I groan because I keep trying to put it out of my mind but Tilly's right. Sometimes it's annoying that she knows so much about my personal stuff, like when exactly I've booked leave. Although I suppose sharing a flat would mean she'd know anyway, sooner or later.

"It's not a holiday, though," I remind her.

"Of course not." Louis smiles. "It's serious business. A week in a luxury hotel with sexy Max!"

What? Again? My hand moves instinctively to my phone. But he can't have seen the text. I haven't seen it myself.

"It's a social study," I remind him. "And it's in an adventure park this time, not exactly luxury. Also, why do you keep calling Max sexy when you've never even met him?"

Louis shrugs. "You said he was."

"I'm sure I've heard you say that," Tilly agrees. "More than once."

What, are *they* studying me now too? And I might have thought that about Max, but I definitely haven't said it to them. I've barely mentioned him, except maybe once, ages ago...

I remember, and give a frustrated growl. "Guys. I told you that he used to play the sax! As in 'saxophone'. Max plays a bit of everything. I think it's mostly guitar now." As far as I know.

"See, you just said it again. He's a sexy saxophonist!" Louis gives a lewd laugh and Tilly joins in.

"Guitarist," I correct.

Tilly giggles. "He plays a bit of everything!"

"Honestly, how old are you both?"

They cackle in response.

"I have no feelings for Max."

Tilly stops laughing for long enough to pat my leg. "Don't worry. We're just teasing."

"But it's true! He's just someone I'm in a social science experiment with."

"Ooh, yes!" Louis chuckles. "An experiment in luurve!"

"Chester will be so jealous!"

My flatmates collapse into more childish laughter.

"But she has no feelings for Max!" Louis mocks.

"Ah! She'll try to make him love her anyway!" Tilly joins in.

My heart thuds. "Of course I won't!"

"But you have to, Ciara!" Louis manages between snort-laughs. "Because *everyone* has to love you! Not just Chester. Banish indifference! That's your path to happiness, and all that jazz." He mimes playing a saxophone – badly. "Jazz! Saxophonist! Get it?"

I touch my phone. I can't help it.

"You've been giving that thing strange glances all night!" Tilly says. "What's going on?" She leans across the breakfast bar and reads the display I've just stupidly lit up. "Ooh, talk of the sexy devil! It's a message... from Max!" She smirks at Louis. "A sext?"

Seriously? She couldn't be more wrong. The last, extremely short text exchange Max and I had was about three years ago and it ended with me writing: *See you at CHAPS*. It translated as 'don't contact me again and I mean it'. He didn't send me a single message after that.

Until tonight.

That's it. I can't stand it any longer.

I jump off my wobbly stool, grabbing my phone from under Tilly's smirk. "I'm going to bed! I need to get away from you babies!"

"You mean you need to sext with Max!" Tilly calls out.

I don't dignify that with a reply as I stagger away to the sound of Louis calling, "Sex-ophonist!" and Tilly practically exploding with hilarity.

☼

NOW: Contemplating Max

What my flatmates don't know, because I've never told anyone except my closest childhood friends – or at least, not the full story – is that Max and I have actually had a relationship.

I mean, obviously we have, because we've been in a social research project together since we were babies.

We were born on the same day in different towns, and our mums were approached by researchers who were starting what they called a 'cohort study' – a long-term analysis of development, or whatever else researchers want to focus on. All they were looking for was a sample of subjects with the same birthdate.

Initially, the aim of the study that my parents, Max's mum and various others were roped into was general: to do with our growth and development, plus anything else the researchers decided to look at. They called us The Sevens, as the aim was to contact us every seven years to collect basic data like weight, height and the ability to kick our legs ferociously.

That's all that happened when we were babies, at least. But somewhere between birth and our seventh birthdays, a new group of researchers arrived to work with The Sevens project. This lot had secured funding to study us in a particular way.

They wanted to examine exactly how contented we were, relative to our background, family income, education and other criteria. The new researchers decided they wanted to bring a subset of us together all in one setting, to take us out of our normal surroundings and eliminate external factors during some phases of data collection. They could then compare our data with the overall, full set. It was supposed to level the playing field for some of us, I suppose, at least temporarily. It was also a kind of reward for taking part in the study – a free week's holiday for participants.

They re-named our sub-group the Cohort for Happiness: A Prospective Study, which promptly got nicknamed CHAPS.

And now, every seven years, us happy 'CHAPS' get together for a fun – and, most importantly, all expenses paid – week of observations, tests and questionnaires. We go to different locations each time but they're usually pretty fun places – adventure parks with accommodation, or hotels set up for managerial team-building exercises. In the early days, we used to attend with a parent, too. It was always great for me, getting Mum to myself and leaving Dad to juggle my two big sisters. It was harder for Max's mum, who was on her own and struggling to manage with time off work. But now that we're grown-ups, we go on our own. This year, for our fourth meeting at the grand old age of twenty-eight, we've even been offered the chance to book family rooms and attend with our own children, which some of the CHAPS delegates must have already. It's strange to think how much we've grown up.

So I've known Max since I was little and I've spent a lot of time with him on and off, which I suppose should make us a bit like brother and sister.

We're absolutely not, though.

When I say we've had a relationship, I do in fact mean the kind that Tilly and Louis have been cackling about in our gas-lit, crisp-packet-strewn kitchen.

It's been over for a long time, though. I think it's fair to say it ended badly. In fact, I could probably upgrade that assessment to 'disastrously'.

Because I broke his heart.

So why is he texting me on a random Friday night, just over three months before we'll be forced into each other's company by a sense of duty, a touch of curiosity and the desire for a free week away?

I toy with my phone as I contemplate whether to open the text now or wait until morning. There are obvious advantages to a delay, not least of which is the alcohol I've consumed. I want to have my wits about me if I'm going to reply to Max, especially after the last text I sent him.

On the other hand, I didn't drink much. And staring at Max's name on my phone screen is sobering me right up.

I open his text.

☼

NOW: The Text

Hi Key. How's life? It says. *Are you still in London? Would be great to chat to you.*

Well. That doesn't give much away. It could be anything. He could be confirming where our next meeting is – something that he seems to struggle with despite the mountain of CHAPS paperwork that's sent our way every few years. When we were twenty-one, he nearly missed the whole week after misreading the dates. He only made it because I reminded him. And he was still a day late, due to having a gig. Max is a professional musician who's on the road half the time. The last I heard, he was playing with a band called Four Part Cure who were pretty big in a couple of Northern European countries, including Belgium and the Netherlands. He's probably swanning about in some gorgeous square eating chips with mayonnaise right now.

I look at his text again. He called me 'Key', his nickname for me. I can't remember the last time he used it.

I press the 'call' button impulsively and then it's too late, because he answers immediately, as if he's been waiting for me.

"Ciara." No nickname. "How are you?"

Hearing his deep, full voice makes my heart beat faster, which is ridiculous. There's nothing between us now, and what there was died long ago.

"Max." I might as well get straight to the point. "What's going on?"

☼

NOW: An Accountant in Australia

Instead of answering my question, he says, "Ah, you know," and before I can say I really don't, he asks me a hundred questions about my life. He distracts me so completely that more than ten minutes have passed before I realise he hasn't told me a thing about himself. Max has always been like this. I used to welcome it – he really is a brilliant listener. You can spend a whole evening with him and leave feeling like you've unloaded all your troubles. That is, until an uneasy feeling dawns on you that it's all been a bit one-sided.

"So your sisters are mega happy and successful, your mum and dad are planning an exotic second honeymoon cruise, Olive is saving the world as a scientist in Cambridge, Sophie's a health food expert and you work on underwear for a catalogue?" he sums up.

"Yeah, that's about it. Everyone else is having the time of their lives and I'm selling knickers."

He laughs. "It sounds pretty cool to me. You always did land on your feet."

I squirm because I feel a bit guilty when I think about how different our lives have been. Max and I could probably be the poster children for being born on opposite sides of the tracks. In fact, we probably have been held up as examples of exactly this in at least one research paper.

I want to force the conversation around to him but I know it won't be easy.

I go for the direct 'barrage of questions' tactic. "Tell me about you. How's your mum? How's the band? Do you still live in Belgium? Are you OK?"

"Carol's... not great. Four Part Cure split up. I moved in with a girl..." He coughs. "I took some courses. I, er, retrained. For a while I worked as an accounts assistant in Australia."

I'm stunned. "You're an accountant in Australia?" He moved in with a girl?

"An accounts assistant, and I've left Australia now, but –"

"I'm a copywriter in Croydon."

"That's awesome."

"Yeah. Except it isn't. I spend my days describing underwear, remember? I'm the opposite of awesome!"

His laugh is throaty. "Ciara."

Oh god, the way he says my name. It's like a hug.

"That's my name," I grunt, trying to sound annoyed but probably reminding him of my seven-year-old self.

His voice is soft. "You're always awesome. Everything you do is awesome!"

There's a huge pause.

Not everything. I remember the last time we were properly together. But I am not going to go there – oh no. Not now, and not ever if I can help it.

Besides... he moved in with a girl. And why not? Good for him. He deserves to be happy. I can be happy for him.

"So hey..." I make my voice all bright. "You still haven't told me what this is all about. The mysterious text you sent me?"

"Oh, yeah. Well..."

I wait, clutching the phone and hoping it's nothing bad.

"It's just... I'm kind of in town."

"In Croydon?"

"No. I mean, I don't really know where that is. But I'm in London."

"Yeah, well, Croydon's on the outskirts of London."

"The outside of London?" I can hear the smile in his voice. He's quoting my words from when I was seven. "Like where your parents live?"

"A bit like Northwood, yeah, but the other end of London. It has more shops and it doesn't even pretend to be on the tube."

"Great. It's just..."

I'm not going to like this. I know it.

"See, I got here early for CHAPS."

"CHAPS is in three months!"

"I know, but I had to come back to England and the CHAPS meeting place is near London this time, so I thought I'd maybe hang around, busk a bit..."

"Now that you're an accountant? Like, doing tax returns in tube tunnels?"

He laughs again, but this time it sounds sharp and nervous. "Yeah, no. I mean, I was only an accounts assistant anyway, but I lost that job... and the girl... and I had to move away."

This sounds more like the Max I'd expected. *He lost the girl*, I notice.

"And I still play the guitar. Some things never go away. I mean you never really... forget. Like, riding a bike, or whatever..."

Riding a bike? "Are you trying to tell me you need a place to stay?" I blurt, mostly to put a stop to his nervous waffle.

"Um, yeah. That's it, I guess. Just temporarily, you know. For three months, until CHAPS, and then I'll sort something else out. I wouldn't ask but I'm really stuck and I thought of you and... it doesn't matter."

I grip my phone harder. "You're asking to stay with me?"

"No, no! Oh my god, Ciara, I hope that's not what it sounds like! I only thought you might know someone, or something. But never mind." He fills the silence that follows with a gush of, "Look, I swear I'm not asking to crash at yours. I just thought you might be able to help. You know the city better than I do, that's all."

Well, that's a relief. There's absolutely no way he could stay with me, after everything that happened. It could never, ever work.

"London's so expensive, even the hostels," he continues. "But I'll find another solution. It was only that I thought... I don't know anyone in London, I'm all alone. And then I remembered that I know you."

"Max, honestly, don't worry about it." I try not to be hurt by those words – I'm his last resort. Of course I am – what else would I be? I hide another sigh. "Look, my flat is tiny and I share with two of my colleagues, so there's absolutely no space. But I'll ask around at work. There are always people looking for flatshares and renting out rooms and stuff." That was how I ended up moving in with Louis and Tilly in the first place – it was the result of a coffee machine conversation.

"OK, thanks," Max says. "And it's great to talk to you again. Ciara..."

It's as if he wants to say something, but instead there's another long pause.

I fill it. "Bye, Max. I'll give you a call sometime, OK?"

It takes me ages to fall asleep.

Every time I close my eyes, my brain replays scenes from my past with Max.

☼

CHAPS: Seven Plus – part 1, 1997

My most boring seventh birthday card arrived in the post at my house, but the envelope didn't say 'Ciara Ryan', my name. Instead, it was addressed to 'Max Renzo'. This was the main reason I talked to him for the first time. I was curious about Max.

Max was exactly my age, like every child at CHAPS. We were all born on 3rd January 1990, which was the official start date for the special project my mum had signed me up for when I was a tiny baby. CHAPS was the nickname for something called a 'social study', and it meant that some scientists were checking whether we were happy or not. It was fine by me. I got angry with my big sisters and sometimes had fights with my best friends, Olive and Sophie, but mostly I was a happy girl. Anyone would say so.

We were seven when the CHAPS people invited us to stay in a holiday park for a week, but even before that, they tried to be nice. That was why we got birthday cards every year. The pictures were dull blue with lots of sky and sea, sometimes livened up by a whale fin or a jumping dolphin. They were signed with printing instead of proper writing, like no human had ever touched them. The computer or robot that sent them always made mistakes with the names and addresses, and I kept getting cards with Max's name on. I figured out his name must be right near mine if you put all the CHAPS children in alphabetical order, so maybe the robot was quite clever after all.

The day I first spoke to Max, I was in the soft play area at CHAPS with my mum and a girl called Amelia who always wore really neat, pretty dresses like a princess. Amelia's mum was there too. The mums were talking about mum-things and Amelia didn't want to play, so I wandered off for a bit, towards the cafe area where they had interesting sweets. I'd spent a long time making Mum promise me she'd buy me some later. I thought I'd start choosing what I wanted.

"Max! Max!" a fierce woman in the cafe was calling loudly. Her hair was three different colours and she had inky pictures on her arms.

I followed the direction of her shout and spotted a lone, sad-looking boy at the very top of the play equipment.

"Max! Get down from there!"

Max? Could it be the Max from my birthday card?

I headed off to climb up the tower towards him. It involved a complicated cycle of twisting through netting and clambering up increasingly narrow areas of colourful padded plastic. First green, then blue, difficult yellow, dangerous orange and finally rebellious red which was so high up, it looked like you could nearly touch the roof.

I got a bit scared somewhere between the yellow and orange and I froze for a while, but I forced myself to think about talking to the boy instead of falling from a terrific height. Eventually, I made it to the top.

"Your mum's calling you," were the first words I ever said to him as I gripped the red cushioned walls. I sounded like a proper goody-goody. "Can't you hear her?"

The boy stared at me.

"Are you deaf?" I asked, but not in a mean way. One of my best friends at school, a girl called Olive Abiola, had hearing differences. I knew it was just a part of life. I made sure I faced him when I let go of the sides and tried again, signing at the same time. I could speak British Sign Language pretty well, thanks to Olive teaching us in the playground. "Your mum is calling you."

He shook his head. "I heard you. But she's not my mum."

This was confusing, seeing as the woman was definitely shouting in our direction. Most of the other children were in a different part of the play area, queueing to shriek and slide into a huge ball pool.

"Is your name Max?"

"Yeah."

"So whoever she is, she's calling your name. So you'd better get down."

Max kept staring at me. "Why?"

"Because..." I didn't know. But when a grown-up told you to do something, you did it. The alternative was being told off, and nobody wanted that!

Max didn't seem to care, though. He was so brave!

"You can't make me." He wiped his nose on the back of his hand. "So I don't know why you've come up here. This is *my* red bit."

"It's *everyone's* red bit." My prim voice was back. "I have as much right to be here as you do." I'd heard my mum say this when she had a row over a supermarket parking space once. "Besides..." I played my trump card. "If you're Max Renzo, then I got your birthday card this year. It had boring dolphins on it. So it's like we know each other already."

This last part made no sense, I realised, but he was kind enough not to say so. Instead, he perked up. "My envelope said Ali Rashid." He shot a nervous glance at the woman who'd been shouting at him. She'd obviously given up on him, or maybe she was less worried now that I was with him. She'd settled at a table with a plastic cup in front of her. "Mum didn't let me open it because it had someone else's name on it. But it had a stamp on the outside that said 'happy birthday' and it was my birthday, so... Are you Ali, then?"

"My name's Ciara. It's from Ireland, like my mum, and you say it 'key', like in a lock, and then 'rah'."

"I know how to say it, because you just said it."

"Oh, OK." That seemed fair enough. But I realised something. I pointed downwards. "Wait a minute. You just looked at that lady and said 'Mum'."

Max nodded. "Yeah."

"So why did you say she wasn't your mum?"

Max shrugged. "I don't tell the truth to just anyone."

I had this big feeling then – like a wave of wanting that rushed all the way through me to my fingertips and toes. I wanted this strange, sad boy to decide that I, Ciara Ryan, could be the kind of girl he wouldn't lie to. A friend, even. I also wished I could cheer him up.

"Want to jump in the ball pool with me?" I offered.

"Nah."

I was disappointed. "Why not?"

He went quiet for ages, staring hard at the red flooring.

I almost gave up. I was on the brink of chirping 'suit yourself' and flouncing away when he looked up.

"If I tell you, will you promise not to laugh?"

Oh now, this was intriguing! "Why would I laugh?"

He stared at me. "Promise."

"OK."

"How can I believe you?"

It was an interesting question. I thought about it for a while. "If I laugh, you can make me send you a birthday card next year."

Max shook his head. "I don't think you care about birthday cards. You opened mine and you didn't even like the dolphins."

He had a point. I could see my offer wasn't good enough. "OK, then. If I laugh, you never have to speak to me again."

"I never have to speak to you again anyway." He sniffed.

I made my brain work as quickly as it could, before he lost interest. "My mum said she would buy me some sweets later if I brush my teeth properly and stop pestering her! If I laugh, you can have some of my sweets."

He considered it. "They have good sweets here. I like them. But anyway, promise you won't laugh."

"I promise."

"OK." He took a deep breath. "Going up was easy, but now I'm here, I can't get down. My head goes all spinny if I think about it. So I'm stuck. And I'm scared."

That didn't seem like anything to laugh about. "OK. I know what to do."

"Really?"

"Yeah, it's easy peasy."

He frowned.

"You just have to stop thinking. Or think about something else. I'll help you."

His expression cleared into the biggest smile I'd ever seen.

We climbed down slowly together, his face scrunched up from concentrating so hard.

I didn't laugh once.

And later, back on safe ground, I shared my sweets with him anyway.

∞∞∞

CHAPS: Seven Plus – part 2, 1997

Our mums hated each other at first sight. I didn't really notice at the time, and neither did Max. At the age of seven, our mums were our world, but they were also part of the furniture of our lives. We didn't really think of them as human beings with likes, dislikes and irrational prejudices. They were just... there.

My mum had survived the seventies as Sarah Kelly, a flower-powered teenager who grew up in Dublin and then moved to suburban London to embrace the eighties with vigour. She lived in a different time, as she always told me, and life was a struggle at first. She described herself as a bit of a hippie even though she followed a conventional path, and there's no way she thought of herself as any kind of snob. But despite that, she said things I found confusing. Especially when it came to Max's mum.

It was puzzling that my mum sounded cross about Max's mum. I really liked Max's mum. She was fun and so relaxed. She'd come back from the buffet with hot dogs and chips for Max, and even let me share some with him while my mum was off talking to the kitchen staff about a nutritious and preferably vegetarian alternative.

One day in the lunch queue, I overheard Max's mum tell someone else's parent that my mum was 'stuck up'.

Max's mum was Carol White. Her surname was different from the one Max had, which seemed really modern and glamorous, especially when I heard Mum say that it was because she wasn't married to Max's dad. She worked as a mobile hairdresser, but I thought her job title was 'a single parent' seeing as that's how my mum referred to her when she talked to my dad about our CHAPS adventures. Sometimes Mum called her a 'teen mum' as well, with a tone of heavy disapproval. It was confusing because my two big sisters, Alannah and Brigid, were teenagers at the time, and they definitely seemed way younger than Max's mum. I eventually figured out that Mum must have meant that Max's mum had been a teenager when he was born, although she wasn't anymore because of all the years that had passed. I couldn't see what was wrong with it in any case. Teenagers were old, and so were mums. My parents sometimes went out and left Alannah or Brigid to babysit for me, which just proved how ancient and responsible they must be. Maybe my mum hadn't been saying it in a mean way after all – maybe it was just a fact.

I knew that 'stuck up' was definitely a bad thing for Max's mum to accuse my mum of, though. I got a bit worried after I overheard that, because I didn't want to have to stop being friends with Max.

After the time I helped him down from the tower, I looked out for Max whenever we had playtime. My mum was still hanging around with Amelia's mum every day, and Amelia got annoyed that I wanted to play with a boy. When I suggested that all three of us could play together, she told me I was stupid, though she did try it for a while before storming back to her mum to sit prettily at a table.

"Boys are not as grown-up as girls," she stated the next day at breakfast. "It's a fact. If you don't mind, that's your problem. Maybe you're just as babyish as he is."

I made a mean face at her when my mum wasn't looking, and as soon as I was allowed to leave the table, I found Max. He was sitting on the edge of the ball pool, throwing a yellow ball in the air and catching it.

"Where's Amelia?" he asked.

"I don't want to play with Amelia, I want to play with you," I said in one breath. "Is that OK?"

"I don't mind not playing with Amelia." He threw the yellow ball in the pool and jumped in after it.

I waited, not worried at all.

He surfaced, smiling. "I want to play with you, Key."

"Key?"

"Key, like in a lock. Rah!" He threw two plastic balls at me at the exact same time. I caught them both.

It was that simple.

We ran across the room and climbed up and down the tower for the rest of playtime. Neither of us was scared anymore, even after we invented hazards like dragons and monsters that we had to defeat with coloured balls on the way down.

Whenever Amelia saw us, she stuck her tongue out at me.

Max and I became inseparable. This sometimes meant forcing our mums to spend time together too, which was awkward, but by the end of the week I'd stopped noticing it. I didn't know if Amelia was right about boys, but she must have been right about girls, because even though I was only seven years old, I knew I shouldn't mention to my mum that I'd heard Max's mum call her 'stuck up'. And I knew not to say anything to Max's mum about the 'single parent' and 'teen mum' comments I overheard from my mum, either.

When CHAPS was over and we all had to go home, I begged my mum to get Max's mum's address so that I could send Max a birthday card next year.

"He probably won't send you one back, you know," Mum warned me.

"I don't mind."

"And his address might change. Carol said they're having trouble with their council house."

I didn't know what that was, but I thought quickly. "We won't move, though, will we?"

Mum laughed. "The state of our house! Nobody would buy it. Your dad would have to finish doing it up first."

We were safe, then – we would never, ever move. "So you can give Max's mum our address, and then she can tell you if Max goes somewhere else!"

Mum sighed and shook her head at me kindly. "You'll see him again in seven years, you know," she said. "I think they'll stay in the programme. Carol said they need the free holiday."

I couldn't even imagine waiting that long to see Max again. Who would wait seven years to see their best friend? I knew he qualified as my best friend because he was more fun than any of my school friends, and I never needed to explain my games to him. Seven years was forever! I added it up. "I'll be fourteen! That's so old! Please get me his address now! Please!"

Mum laughed and smoothed my hair. "All right, Ciara. You've talked me round."

Later, I supervised carefully from a distance as Carol handed my mum one of her hairdressing business cards and my mum extracted a page from her mini Filofax diary with our address written on it for Carol.

"What are they doing?" Max asked me.

"Giving each other their addresses." I puffed proudly. "It was my idea."

He looked puzzled for a second before he beamed a huge smile at me. "Does that mean I can go and visit you? Can I go to your house in the outside of London?"

I hadn't even thought of that until Max said it. I couldn't believe myself.

It was an absolutely brilliant idea!

"Of course!" I promised. "Now, do you want to fight some fire-breathing dragons?"

He did, so we did.

∞∞∞

CHAPS: Seven Plus – part 3, 1997+

I didn't start Operation Invite Max immediately after we left the holiday park where CHAPS had been taking place.

I waited until we'd passed the third Little Chef – Mum hated motorways, so we always took a long way round on winding, sick-making roads – before I mentioned it at all. I was really proud of myself, because actually I'd thought of nothing else since the moment I said goodbye to Max and got in our car. But that day, for a length of time that spanned several Little Chefs, I'd managed to keep my mouth shut, which my big sisters said I was rubbish at. If only they could see me now!

Mum was waffling on about Alannah's school report, or maybe Brigid's. Something boring and teenage-related, anyway. And then she said something that was such a perfect opportunity, it would have been a crime to waste it.

"It will be good when she starts sixth form college," Mum said. So then I knew it was Alannah she was talking about – Brigid still hadn't done all her horrible big exams, the ones that made Mum and Alannah argue and shout a lot. "She can make some new friends at last – people who are more on her wavelength."

I realised that Max wasn't the first of her daughters' friends that Mum had been sniffy about. Alannah mostly hung around with three girls who hadn't even taken many big exams. They were getting themselves jobs instead of staying at school, which sounded like the coolest thing in the world, if you asked me. But Mum was always saying things like, "Don't limit yourself, Alannah!" and "I got to where I am because I had a proper education!" I assumed that Mum meant moving to a different country and having an important job at the doctor's surgery, and not the fact that she lived in a house where the water pipes made scary noises and you had to do a special pump-pump-pump thing to make the toilet flush.

"Max is on my wavelength!" I announced to Mum. "More than Olive and Sophie and everyone in my class. Can he come and visit me?"

Mum laughed, which seemed like a good sign. But then she said, "I can't wait to tell Alannah and Brigid about your little crush."

My little... what? Wasn't a crush to do with love and kissing and icky things? Yuck! Max was my friend! Grown-ups were weird, though — always saying things like that whenever boys and girls made friends with each other. I didn't get it, but never mind.

"So can he visit?"

Mum gave me a quick glance without really taking her eyes off the road. "I don't think so, Ciara. They live in Lancashire. We live in London."

"The outside of London," I reminded Mum, as that was technically correct and it was what I'd told Max. We lived in a place called Northwood, which made Alannah and Brigid complain a lot. They said it was boring and that all the fun happened too far away to get home at a time that our parents didn't mind.

Mum laughed again. "Ciara, it's really sweet that you got on so well with that little boy," she said.

I got a bad feeling then, but I waited just in case.

"But he can't visit us."

"But... MUM!"

"Ciara, come on. You'll forget all about him in a few hours."

"I won't. I won't, I won't, I won't. He's the best friend I've ever had! He is the best player of Slayer and Monster I have ever, ever met! Sophie won't even play because she says monsters are for boys!"

Mum pulled into the next Little Chef, the fourth one on our route, and the biggest.

"Are you hungry?" she asked.

I was always hungry, but that wasn't the point. She was trying to distract me and I knew it. "Can I have chips?" I tried.

Incredibly, she agreed. I was suspicious.

I ate my chips but I didn't enjoy them as much as I thought I would. Mum had offered me chips instead of Max. I wanted both.

I stopped my campaign for that day, because it was easier that way, but I kept it going on and off over the coming days, weeks and months. Every time, the answer was no.

And then a horrible, horrible thing happened.

My friend Sophie got hit by a car when she was out on her bike, right near her house.

It was the day after Christmas, too – a time when bad things shouldn't happen. It made everybody, all the mums and dads especially, extra upset. The car hadn't been travelling very fast, and Sophie had been wearing her Pocahontas helmet, which Dad said was lucky, because 'it could have been a lot worse'.

But Sophie's bike was ruined, even though it had been one of her Christmas presents so it was brand new and had multi-coloured streamers hanging from the handlebars. And much worse than that was that my friend was in hospital with a broken collarbone and bruises and she was really, really sad. I wasn't allowed to visit her yet, and I was scared. I told my mum I never wanted to ride a bicycle ever again. I wasn't really sure I wanted to do anything. It seemed much safer to stay in my room. Forever.

Christmas was always just over a week before my birthday, and two weeks after Olive's. Olive and I got presents practically every week! For two weeks, anyway. My mum had booked a leisure centre party for my big day, but I was worried about going there without Sophie. Olive came over to play and she was too upset to talk to me. Eventually she used sign language to tell me she didn't want to go to my party because Sophie couldn't go and it would be too sad. Then she cried and her mum came to pick her up. It was the worst after-Christmas, pre-birthday time ever. I was jealous of Olive. At least Sophie had been at *her* birthday party.

After Olive went home, Mum came into my room and gave me a big cuddle.

I snuggled into her shoulder.

"Oh, Ciara," she said. "Please don't worry. Everything will be OK. Sophie's dad is looking after her. Sophie will get better."

This had the opposite effect to the one Mum intended. I let out a sob.

"Ciara, Ciara," Mum soothed. She sounded desperate. "Listen, why don't we invite your little friend from CHAPS to the party? The boy?"

"Max?" I pulled back, my tears drying instantly, and stared at Mum. Did she really mean it?

She did.

"It's his birthday too," I wailed as the tears returned. "There's no way he'll be able to come!"

"Well, I'll try asking, OK?"

Mum called Max's mum. And, unbelievably, he could make it. My party was two days after our birthday, just before school started again. Max's dad was supposed to have him to stay during that time, so that Max could have a birthday celebration with his dad after he'd had one with his mum. But something had happened and Max's dad wasn't around after all, for some reason. I heard Carol shouting down the phone at Mum, something rude ending with, "Men!" So Max was free, and we'd be doing Max's mum a huge favour if he could come and stay, and it all got arranged. Dad went to pick him up in our car because he could combine it with some business thing, and before I could even get too excited, Max was in my house, in a sleeping bag on the floor in my room, making me feel brave again.

And Olive changed her mind and came to my party after all.

Max came to my birthday parties for the next three years, even though Sophie was totally better by then and she and Olive thought Max was annoying.

They were wrong, though. Max and I didn't see each other much, but we were still the best friends ever.

In the year we turned twelve, Max had a football match the day after our birthday so he couldn't make it to London. The following year, I wasn't really having a party anyway – I'd planned a trip to the shops with Sophie, Olive and our new friend Hannah. It probably wasn't Max's scene. I hadn't seen Max for two years, but it was OK. By that time, we had the internet at home – Max had his mum's computer and I used Alannah's old one – and we sent each other messages on MSN whenever we could. He was MassimoTheMonsterSlayer, I was the unimaginative Ciara90. We talked about school, television, gaming and how annoying our mums could be. We met online nearly every day. Sometimes we chatted for hours, until our mums switched off our modems, complaining that we were tying up the phone line and not doing enough homework.

By the time I saw Max again, at CHAPS at the age of fourteen, we had talked more online than we had in all the days we'd spent together in person.

I had also had developed a massive, massive crush on Max.

∞∞∞

NOW: The Grand Gesture

The morning after Flatmate Friday dawns in Croydon. I wake up much later than I intend to, and even then it's only because there's a strange sound outside my window. A crunching, grinding sound.

There's a construction site across from our flat so noise is not completely unusual, but I don't get why the builders are clanking away on a Saturday morning. There's obviously an urgent need for more luxury apartments across from our falling-apart ones. Sometimes I think they're just trying to use us as a contrast for potential buyers in the new developments. *"Choose the new-build to avoid that scruffy mess. Look at those losers on the other side of the street and be thankful!"*

I thought I might spend my day brainstorming ways to talk to Chester at work on Monday, complete with written proposals that I can impress him with. I don't usually like thinking about work on my days off, but my thoughts are so frantic right now that I might as well put them to good use.

Besides, it's not only work I'm planning to think about. I allow myself a fantasy or two about Chester looking deep into my eyes and breathing something like, *"Why Ciara, I never realised you possessed beauty as well as intelligence!"* Chester has weirdly gone a bit eighteenth century in this daydream, just stopping short of wearing a white shirt with ruffles.

The cacophony outside my window grows louder, to the point where I can't focus on my own stupid imagination. What are they doing out there, and why does it sound like they're actually inside my flat?

I walk towards the noise to get a closer look, but a huge crash makes me jump back into bed. It really sounded like something was about to smash through my window. What is going on?

My door bursts open and Louis appears in my bedroom – without knocking, which I have told him a million times is an outrageous thing to do. If my earlier fantasy scenario had gone on any longer...

"Fuck, what was that?" he says. "I heard it in my room, but it's even louder in here!"

"Why can't you knock?"

"Fuck knocking!"

Our swear jar is going to get nice and full this week, anyway. I'm looking forward to next Friday already.

"Swear jar," I remind Louis.

"Fuck the fucking swear jar!" Louis replies. "Fuck!"

There's an unearthly thud at the window and my whole room shakes.

I'm properly scared now. "Is someone trying to break in?" I whisper. "Through my bedroom window?"

"I don't know!" Louis whispers back, his eyes darting with terror. "Should I get Tilly? She'll know what to do."

Just then, Tilly appears in the doorway – because Louis also left my door wide open, but I'm not going to complain about that now.

"Tilly!" I'm so happy to see her.

She's rubbing her eyes and exuding a scent that can only be described as 'eau de hangover'.

"Whass going on, guys? Isss Saturday. Why all the crashing and banging?"

"I don't know!" Louis and I whimper, almost at the same time.

"Someone's at the window," I add.

Tilly looks sceptical. "Of our second-floor flat?"

"That's what it sounds like."

"Haven't you looked?"

My curtains are still closed. It's Saturday morning/lunch-time, after all. But Tilly the Brave, despite being clearly still half asleep, shuffles over to the source of the noise. And it's getting louder again, too.

"Tilly, no!"

Louis gasps. "What if it's an intruder? What if he crashes into our room with an axe and..."

"Don't do it! You'll be killed! Tilly... oh!"

Tilly sweeps the curtains open.

Louis speaks for all of us when he says, "What. The. Fuck."

We all stare at the sight through the window.

The builders are involved all right. But not in the way I expected when I first woke up.

And there are no intruders. Not exactly.

Instead, there's a builder's forklift truck thing, one of the ones with a carriage that fits a person inside and cranks up and down.

And there's a person inside, cranked up to the height of my window, and he doesn't appear to be wearing much clothing.

Or, in fact, any clothing.

Apart from a bright yellow hard-hat.

We should be shocked by this – the most peculiar flasher in the whole of South London – except that we all recognise the naked person instantly.

He has the face – and the body – of a model who is used to showing off his six-pack and posing in unusual places. Like inside a builder's truck thing.

It's Tomas.

And he's holding a sign that says, in badly scrawled lettering: "I LUV U LOUIS! COME TO PARIS WIV ME!"

We all stare.

"Aw, would you look at that?" Tilly sighs after a few seconds. "So romantic."

"It's a grand gesture," I realise. Exactly what Louis asked for.

We look at Louis.

He opens my window and shouts, "Wrong room, you twat!" But there are tears running down his cheeks.

A group of builders wearing hard-hats (plus all their other usual high-vis clothing) smile and wave at Louis from the ground.

Tomas's expression is full of sincerity as he brandishes his sign.

"So-oooo romantic," Tilly breathes.

"Romantic, my arse," Louis says, but there are hearts in his eyes as he takes out his phone and snaps pictures of the moving scene outside my window.

☼

NOW: Tomas 4 Louis 4 eva

My flatmates and I spend the rest of Saturday and most of Sunday in the aftermath of Tomas's grand gesture, which is a lot more time-consuming than any of us might have expected.

First there's the small matter of our downstairs neighbours, an elderly couple who put up with a lot and never complain about our loud Friday nights, but obviously draw the line at a naked man appearing by their window on a Saturday morning. They are threatening to call the police and it takes a lot of persuasion by both Louis and Tomas before they back down.

Tomas soon proves to all concerned that he was not in fact fully naked. He was wearing some nude-coloured long-johns from a pack that Louis had brought home from work. He'd taken them from a discarded pile of unwanted, unsold or 'soiled returns' stock. The 'scrap heap', as it's known, is something all staff at Something For Everyone are allowed to help themselves to, but we mostly ignore it because the clothes in it are so dire. Louis had given the long-johns underwear pack to Tomas as a joke present. ("We had an argument because he wouldn't wear them when I asked him to!" Louis tells us in a totally TMI moment.)

Anyway, Mr and Mrs Hassan didn't know about the nude underwear, so it didn't detract from their overall shock.

A few of our other neighbours join in with the commotion. My bedroom and the Hassans' front room were apparently not the only stops in Tomas's quest to win Louis's heart. It turns out that Tomas is no expert at operating construction machinery. "It's harder than it looks," Tomas explains in our kitchen, hugging one of Louis's expensive plush robes around himself. "Respect to the workmen I bribed! They were all laughing at me. Apart from the foreman, who was away when they agreed to it. He's scared he'll lose his job. But he'll be fine. Nobody ever needs to know."

"How did you persuade the workmen to let you do that?" Tilly asks in wonder.

"Cash. Plus I told them I'd used the machinery in the past for work, which wasn't a lie. Only I'd sat in it for a fashion shoot, which was much easier."

Tomas gives Tilly some money and she rushes out to get apology gifts for the Hassans and other neighbours, doughnuts for the cackling construction workers with extra sprinkles for the foreman, and posh pastries for us.

Throughout all of this, Louis goes into a dreamlike state where he alternately swears a lot, stares at Tomas a lot and drifts around the kitchen beaming and checking his phone. I suspect he is gazing at the photos he took of his potentially naked boyfriend declaring his feelings from a piece of industrial machinery.

At one point, when Tomas is out of earshot and otherwise engaged explaining himself yet again to a different duo of shocked neighbours who have turned up late to the fun, Louis whispers loudly to Tilly, "Do you think he really loves me?"

"Of course he does, you banana," she replies. "He was prepared to freeze his balls off for you! That's the very definition of love."

From a distance, Tomas smiles at Louis.

Louis gives a weak wave and turns back to us. "He didn't risk frostbite. He was wearing long-johns. They're a crime against fashion, but a thermal one."

"I bet it was still cold."

Louis looks doubtful. "Ciara?"

"Definitely still cold. Nothing on his top half. Think of the nipples!" I shiver in sympathy.

This doesn't distract Louis at all. "No, I mean, does he love me? You're a cynic, what do you think?"

"I'm not cynical!" That's why I'm planning to make everyone including Chester love me, I don't add. I decide to keep that stuff to myself from now onwards. In the cold light of day, and faced with the fallout from Tomas's antics, I realise my ravings from last night sound a bit ridiculous.

"If you say so. Do you agree with Tilly, then? Do you think Tomas means it?"

I roll my eyes. Louis can be so needy! "Definitely! You're accepting his offer, aren't you?"

Louis grasps his coffee with passion. "But how? How will I get the time off work? I'm not freelance. I don't live the model high-life, like some of us!" He glances at Tomas, who's managing to strike a gorgeous pose even though he's in a fluffy robe talking to angry neighbours. "I can't just take off for months! I have minus-half days of holiday left."

Tilly taps the side of her nose. "Leave it with me. Monique isn't as hard as she acts, you know." Monique is Tilly's boss, and the head of Human Resources. "We can probably get a temp in to cover for you. There might be special unpaid leave for young love, if I can phrase it right."

"Unpaid?" Louis wails. "I've got savings, but probably not enough for Paris!" He's hard to please, our flatmate.

"Wouldn't you be staying with Tomas? Isn't that the whole point?"

"I bet I can't! Tomas will be in some kind of top headquarters for the talent, a five-star hotel or something. You know what the world of advertising is like!"

Our advertising team at Something For Everyone are always complaining about 'crazy money' out in the real, non-catalogue fashion world.

"They're more spendy than Ciara's sociological research team," Louis elaborates.

"I keep telling you the places we stay are not luxurious." With the possible exception of the last hotel, the one we stayed in when we were twenty-one. But I try not to think about that. "They're researchers. It's practical – it's not about luxury."

"But advertising definitely is!" he cries. "Tomas might be able to smuggle me in sometimes, but I'm sure I can't stay with him for three whole months!"

Tilly shrugs. "Rent an AirBnB or something?"

"Brilliant idea, Tils!" I say. "Then he can go to you when he has spare time. The rest of the time, you can swan around Paris." I have a little daydream, imagining it's me and not Louis living this glamorous lifestyle.

"I suppose so. But I can't afford that and the rent here too!"

"That's easy. We just find someone else for your room!" Tilly munches thoughtfully on a croissant. "You know the landlord doesn't care as long as he gets his money."

She's right. Our landlord is surprisingly laid-back and we only pay month-on-month, a total amount to cover all three of us. In fact, it's supposed to be a two-bedroom flat, but Tilly uses the lounge as her bedroom and the landlord doesn't mind as long as he gets his required total. We also get a discount because he's friends with Tilly's boss.

"There are always people at work looking for places to stay," Tilly continues. "They keep asking me, like I'm some kind of accommodation expert just because I work in HR."

"People!" I join in, though a distant thought is niggling at me now and I'm distracted.

Max is looking for a place to stay. For three months, he said.

Louis is desperate for someone to cover his rent for the exact same period of time.

It could never work, not in a million years.

I push the thought out of my mind.

☼

NOW: Operation Happiness Begins

Monday arrives way too quickly, and I still haven't had a chance to sort out what my first step will be on Operation Make Chester Love Me.

I mean – Operation Happiness, or Operation Make *Everyone* Love Me. And obviously Chester would be included in that. But seeing as right now he's the main person at work who shows total indifference to me, he is my prime target.

I catch the bus to work. Tilly always leaves earlier than me and Louis leaves later, so despite working and living together, we don't see each other very much during the working week. It's probably just as well, as it makes our Friday night catch-ups more fun. Though I wonder what will happen to those after Louis leaves for Paris. It will be just me and Tilly... and whoever we get in to cover the rent.

As usual, my bus gets stuck in busy traffic so I get plenty of pondering time. I spend most of it on my big plan and only a small fraction of it thinking about Max and how he needs a place to stay, and if Louis goes away for three months, that's exactly the kind of temporary accommodation Max was talking about... But Louis might not go, and inviting Max would never work anyway. I try to focus on other things.

The bus idles at a red light right next to a building site, and I watch the people in hard hats and hi-vis jackets, constructing away. I think about Tomas pretending to be naked in a crane for romantic effect, and how he wasn't really wearing nothing, thanks to some discarded stock that Louis brought home. There was no commercial demand for nude thermal underwear, and yet it ultimately brought two people great happiness. It has to be a metaphor for... something.

I rack my brains as the bus crawls along the high street, past hundreds of hurrying, miserable-looking people. Everyone seems so unhappy all the time. Or maybe it's not unhappiness exactly? They're switched off, uncaring. Focused on their journeys to work, indifferent to their surroundings.

The perfect idea for impressing Chester pops into my head.

By the time I swipe my entry card and stride into Something For Everyone catalogue HQ, I'm dying to put it in motion right away.

There's a strange buzz in the air and I can tell instantly that something weird is going on. The cubicles in my section are empty, except for Steve, my next-desk colleague, who's bashing furiously at his keyboard. As far as I know, he's still on Housewares. He finds it deadly dull and has asked a million times to swap his 'hip moulded plastic-slatted laundry baskets' with my 'hip-hugging corrective control briefs', but I've rebuffed him and clung on to my underwear with defensive zeal. There's no way his frantic typing has anything to do with work. What's going on here?

As I walk towards him, Scary Cathy appears behind me. I swear she magics herself out of thin air. I've suggested several times to Tilly and Louis that she's actually a vampire, and they haven't completely rejected this idea.

"Staff meeting!" Scary Cathy announces.

"Today?" I dare to mumble. The next all-staff meeting isn't supposed to be for ages. I was going to talk to Chester alone first. I'm not ready to raise my big idea in front of everyone. I wanted to gather enough confidence beforehand, from the enthusiasm Chester displays... in my daydreams.

Scary Cathy gives me the hard stare that led to her nickname. "Staff. Meeting. Ciara. And hurry. You're already late."

"Sure, fine, of course. I'll just put my bag down and check my –"

"Now."

Seriously?

"You too, Steven," Cathy barks. "Didn't I already tell you two minutes ago?"

Steve jumps and immediately closes every single window on his computer, one by one. As if that doesn't make him look totally guilty.

I narrow my eyes at him.

He gives me a wide-eyed look of innocence in return, but I'm not buying it.

"Now?" Cathy reminds us.

Steve hits a button to blank out his screen, stands up and shuffles over to me.

Cathy must be satisfied that we're actually obeying her orders after all because she says, "Good. That's the copywriters rounded up at last. I've already got the admin and support staff." So

Tilly must be in the meeting room already. "Now for the design team. I'm wondering whether to wait for them or just put them at a massive disadvantage by holding this meeting without them."

She looks at me. She knows I share a flat with a prominent member of the design team.

"I can, er, text Louis?" I suggest. "I'm sure he's on his way."

"No need," says Cathy. "This is probably a good way of sorting the wheat from the chaff, so to speak."

What? Firstly: 'wheat from the chaff'? Who 'so-to-speaks' like that? But most importantly: is she referring to job losses? The way she's talking, and this air of gloom in the place... I've been there before in previous jobs, and it usually means there are going to be redundancies. Printed catalogues are dying, and although there's a huge online side to the Something For Everyone business, I wouldn't be surprised if that wasn't going brilliantly either. Shit. I know Louis is thinking of jetting off for three months, but I doubt he'll be happy to lose his job altogether.

I'm desperate to text Louis a warning now. Even if he's still asleep, my flatmate will always stir himself if he hears his text alert. I put my hand in my pocket and touch my phone, but Scary Cathy is glaring at me and there's no way I'll manage a sneaky text.

"The meeting room is that way." Scary Cathy points, her index finger shooting out rays of sarcasm.

"Yeah. OK. That's where we're going," I mutter, and Steve joins in with a generic mumble.

As soon as The Scary One is out of earshot I turn to Steve. "What the hell?"

"Don't worry, I emailed them all," Steve replies. "Including Louis. We're in this together."

I shoot him a look of pure gratitude. "You're a hero, Steve."

He blushes.

Right now, I love Steve a little bit. And he's never been completely indifferent to me, either. No, there's only one person in this company who has no opinion on me either way, and that's Chester.

Chester, who I was all set to impress with my Big Idea.

Chester, who is standing at the front of the meeting room with a very ominous look on his face.

An uncomfortable thought pops into my head. Chester hasn't been here very long, and he never chats to anyone. Could he actually be one of those 'business auditor' people?

Was he hired to fire us?

"Ah, nice of you to join us..." Chester says. "Sorry, I've forgotten your names."

Oh, great. "Ciara," I say. "And Steve."

"Yes," Chester acknowledges blankly. "Please take a seat, Steve and... the rest of the copywriting team."

I stifle a sigh. The other copywriters are already here. He means me, and he can't even remember my name for ten seconds.

"I think we can make a start now. Anyone who isn't here –"

A voice interrupts him, shouting out, "The design team are on their way!"

It was my voice. Oops. Steve stares at me with a mix of horror and awe. In the distance, I can see Tilly grinning at me from among the grim-faced HR team. She catches my eye and glances around her before she mouths, "Sorry." Her expression tells me this is as much a surprise to her as it is to me.

Chester blinks. "OK, thank you, er..."

"Ciara."

He doesn't seem to hear me. What is it with this man? Am I actually invisible to him? What do I need to do to get his attention? Dress in nude underwear and appear outside his room dangling off the end of a crane?

"So yes, it's time to make a start. And anyone who isn't here can catch up from their colleagues, but perhaps said colleagues can make them aware that there are going to be changes around here. And it's in everyone's interests to adhere to the expected timekeeping norms..." Blah, blah, blah.

Oh crap. My latest hunch about Chester?

I think I'm right.

"As you all know, these are difficult times in retail, and especially for catalogues with a print element..." Blah, blah, blah.

My heart sinks. Here we go. The last time I was made redundant, back in my small magazine days, our manager chirped on about how he would save us all, how he'd be the first to take the hit. We believed him, and to this day I don't think he was lying. But it didn't stop us all losing our jobs within months of each other, sinking one by one like we were on some business version of Titanic, with the manager clinging onto a door as a 'consultant' after we'd all gone. Until, rumour has it, he went under, too. In my short working life, I've gone through this whole sad process twice, and I don't particularly want to live it again.

"Now, I've been here watching you for about a month," Chester's saying, "and getting a good idea of how this place ticks. But for the next while, I'll need you to report to me so that we can work together –"

An obnoxious voice interrupts, "I've got an idea!"

There's a squeaky silence, like someone has run their nails down a blackboard.

The voice was me. Again.

"Er... yes, you. Member of the design team. Is something wrong?"

"Ciara. Copywriter." In Croydon.

"Member of the copywriting team, sorry. It's good to see enthusiasm, but this isn't really the time."

Oh, crap. If there's one thing I remember from the early days when a workplace announces future redundancies, it's that you're not supposed to draw attention to yourself. If they notice you, especially for a negative reason like making a nuisance of yourself, they sack you. Simple as that.

And yet, I can't stop myself. "I've had a brilliant idea. It could save us all."

Chester looks right at me, possibly for the first time ever.

"See me later," he says. I bet he still can't remember my name. "For now, I want you all to know that the management team are doing everything they can..."

He continues with a speech that's so similar to ones I've heard before that it's hard not to lose heart on the spot.

As his speech drones on, Louis and various other members of the actual design team start arriving, flustered and scruffy-looking, clutching coffees and frowning. It's still early for them so they must have been summoned by Steve's heroic mass email.

Chester pauses only to give them glances that say 'you're late, and I've noticed'. He doesn't show disapproval, though, of course. He's as expressionless as ever.

I cling on to the fact that he's agreed to see me.

It's not just about me anymore. My colleagues' jobs now depend on my brilliant idea.

☼

NOW: Chester

"So you're saying you want to monetise the scrap heap?"

I suppose that's what I'm saying, if Chester wants to put it so crudely. It took me about ten minutes to explain it to him in a much more lively, attractive way. But trust Chester to put an indifferent spin on it all.

And yet, despite everything, he's still quite good-looking, standing there looking corporate and serious. I should try to make him smile.

I shake that thought out of my head.

"No? Have I got that wrong?"

"Yes. I mean, no. You're right." I take a deep breath and try again. "It's just that I think it's wrong to abandon all that stuff completely. There are obviously things there that will be worth something to someone. I mean, you never know."

"One man's meat is another man's poison?"

"Er... exactly." I can't believe he used the exact phrase Louis was sniggering at in the kitchen on Friday! I remember the Granny Newman equivalent and repeat it to Chester. "One man's trash is another man's treasure." Why are these phrases all about men? Maybe women are supposed to make the best of what they have and shut up about it. "So, yes, I was thinking of a catalogue supplement to sell the unwanted goods."

Chester nods approvingly. I silently thank Granny Newman.

"Blue-sky thinking. I like it," he says.

In the eleven minutes I've spent in Chester's company, I've noticed that he talks like one of those business books with a punchy title like: "Who's The Boss? You're The Boss! Be The Boss in 10 Days or Less!" Extracting real human emotion from him is going to be a bigger challenge than I'd feared.

He frowns. "But haven't the items already had a chance? I know Catherine, and she's no fool."

Who? Oh, Scary Cathy.

"Catherine will have tried to sell the shit – pardon my French – out of those items," he continues. "And failed."

Ooh, his French is a bit unprofessional. Am I breaking him already? "Er, yes but –"

"And so we have the scrap heap – as I know you all call the contents of that particular storeroom – and I believe this is seen as a staff perk?"

"A... perk?" I thought perks were supposed to be things like company cars and money off things you actually wanted.

"Yes, as you've just been telling me. Your colleague obtained an item from the scrap heap that held a value he didn't expect..."

I didn't mention Louis's name, just in case. I told the story in very general terms. If Chester has put some kind of notional black mark against the entire design team, I don't want to draw attention to one member's successful use of unwanted nude long-johns.

"...which would make it a staff perk, no? At no cost to the management." He laughs. "The best sort."

Hmm. I'm starting to wonder about him. And yet I'd still like him to like me. It's a sickness.

I can't keep the sarcasm out of my voice, though. "If you say so."

There's a pause, during which Chester looks at me. I start to get fidgety. It's like he's noticing me properly for the first time. It's making me uncomfortable, even though it's exactly what I wanted.

Eventually, he laughs. "I like your spirit!"

OK, well, that's an improvement on not even knowing who I am, at least.

"And you know what? I'll give this some thought. Perhaps if you can find a way to increase profits, I could recommend you for promotion before I go."

Ugh. Who is this guy? "It's OK, there's no need for that. I just want to keep my job. And those of my team. And the design team. And HR..."

"HR are fairly safe. It's the creatives we could do with trimming. High salaries, low returns."

High salaries? He could have fooled me! Also, what's all this 'low returns' nonsense? "Typical," I blurt.

He does a double-take. "I'm sorry?"

Oh crap. I'm doing an extremely bad job of making Chester fall madly in love with me, that's for sure.

"It's, um, typical that everyone thinks the creative teams are worth less," I mumble to start with. I warm to my theme. "Like we're not important, just because we have arty degrees and we're not usually too good with money and numbers and all those things you lot worship. Like we're just incidental to the success of you business types." Did I just call him a 'business type'? Good one, Ciara! I tell myself to stop talking. "But we're not, you know. You lot would be nothing without us. You wouldn't even have your pen-pushing jobs!" Why oh why can't I listen to myself?

Chester is so stunned that he spins slowly in his chair. Twice.

Oh crap, oh crap.

"Well. That was refreshingly... forthright," he says at last.

"Um, yeah," I say eloquently.

"And utterly incorrect," he adds. "There is a surprising amount of creativity in numbers, you know."

"Yeah. Sure. Sorry."

"Yes," he says.

There's another pause while he seems to be thinking hard.

Eventually, I say, "So I'll go... back to work?"

"You do that. And I'll see you in due course." He looks me up and down. "Karen, was it?"

Oh, sweet Jesus. "Ciara."

"Ciara, right. Ciara, Ciara." It's like he's trying to memorise it. "Listen, Ciara, you should know that I disapprove of special relationships in the workplace."

What? Where did that come from? "Er... OK?" *Special relationships*? Does he mean what ordinary people call plain old 'relationships'?

"They're fraught with complications and generally a bad idea."

"Sure. I get that." Tilly has mentioned the headaches caused in HR by on/off couples in our building. She once said she'd back a total ban on workplace relationships.

"But I'm a temporary member of staff here. I think you know that, don't you?"

"Yes."

"Yes, so... I'll be leaving in a few months." He gives me a long look.

"Right." He seems to expect something more from me so I add. "I'll be sorry to see you go."

He smiles. It suits him. I consider telling him he should smile more often, but it seems a bit inappropriate. Mind you, so is what he says next, especially when I think about it later.

"I'll be sorry to leave. But perhaps we can keep in touch?"

"What... you and me?" I check.

"You and me. Perhaps we could meet up after I'm no longer employed here. Something to think about, maybe?"

"Oh, right. Yes, perhaps. Maybe."

He sighs. "You should know that this will not have any bearing on your employment status either way," he says.

I frown. "Er, OK." What won't?

"But all I'm saying is that I'm glad we had this conversation, Ciara."

"Oh, yeah. Me too." Though I'm mostly just glad he remembers my name at last.

"And I hope you'll consider what I'm saying."

Wait a minute! Could he be saying what I think he's saying? Is he sort of asking me out?

Seriously? Did I really get from zero to bumbling suggestion of a possible future date in one meeting? Just by speaking my mind and offending management types? I think I've underestimated myself. I can't wait to tell Tilly.

"Oh, right. Maybe," I say.

"Maybe," he repeats as I leave his office.

☼

NOW: Fluffy Flatmate Friday

Another Flatmate Friday, another stash of booze in our shared kitchen. We managed to buy more than usual this week due to the increased swearing which began with Tomas's grand gesture and continued when I told my flatmates about my progress with Chester.

We're gathered together now to share the 'gory details', as Louis puts it.

"You fox!" he says, delighted, when I give exact quotes from our conversation.

"You really think the creative departments are more important than the support departments?" Tilly pouts.

"No, of course not, Tils."

Louis laughs. "Yeah, right."

Tilly glares at him. "Excuse me. Who helped you get three months of unpaid leave? Want me to tell Monique you've changed your mind?"

Louis backtracks immediately. He points at me. "Yeah, what you said is outrageous, Ciara! How very dare you!" He shoots Tilly a huge smile. "Please don't stop me going to visit my boyfriend in Paris, oh valuable member of a central department without which we would fall apart."

Tilly huffs a bit but then she laughs. "It's good to know what you lot think of me, anyway. And I'll have you know we all think you're a bunch of fluffy hipsters with no useful life skills."

"Fluffy?" Louis looks horrified. "The rest of it I accept."

"Nah, I'm fluffy with no life skills," I say. "But do hipsters still exist?"

Tilly glares at me, but she can't stop herself from laughing. "Post-hipsters. Whatever. Oh, forget it! Let's just have a drink and celebrate the fact that Ciara is one step closer to making Chester love her."

"I certainly am!" I say proudly, clinking Tilly's glass.

"And that I have managed to get Louis three months off!" Tilly clinks my glass again.

Louis joins in, but he sighs instead of drinking. "I still need to figure out what to do about covering the rent here. I can't afford the time off as it is!"

"Oh yeah, I meant to tell you. I asked everyone at the coffee machine this week," Tilly says.

"And?"

"And nothing. But I asked. Like the less-worthy support staff person I am."

"Tilly! Stop it!"

We all laugh.

I'm not sure what gets into me then. Something about the atmosphere, and desperately wanting to make my flatmates happy, leads me to add, "I know someone who might want your room, Louis."

"Really? Who, who?"

I'm already regretting it. Louis's far too eager, and I'd hate to let him down. Plus there's the small detail that it could never work.

"Um, well. Remember last week when I got that text?" They won't remember, I'm sure of it. I'm just easing in slowly here before I run a mile away from the whole crazy suggestion.

"The text from Max?"

"Sexy Max who plays the sax?"

They both giggle like tiny children.

"Yes, I do mean my acquaintance Max, who I'm in a social study with." And nothing more, is the untruthful implication there. I hope they catch it. "He said he was in London and needed somewhere to stay for a couple of months."

"Seriously, Ciara?"

"Why didn't you say so?" Louis booms. "I mean, right away?"

"I... I wasn't sure if you'd be interested."

"What? It's perfect! The sax machine can definitely have my room!"

"Louis, you haven't even met him!"

"What's to meet? He's perfect!"

Tilly clears her throat. "Well, I'd like to go back to Louis's first question. Why didn't you say earlier? Is there something I should know?" she asks, ever practical. "Because, don't listen to Louis. He wouldn't even be here. It's me and you who would have to live with him, Ciara."

She's right. What am I doing?

"Well, yeah, there are some issues. Like, he might not be able to afford it – he's been staying in hostels in the middle of London since he got here..."

"In central London? Are you kidding me? The rent here will be a huge saving for him!"

"Hostels, Louis. Not luxury hotels."

"Ha! You're an outer-Londoner, Ciara, you have no idea. You haven't had to travel from some faraway city to make your way in the Big Smoke like me and Tilly. If he can afford central London hostels, he can afford one-third of our special-mates-rates two-bedroom flat in Croydon. Trust me."

"OK," I concede. "But there's more..."

"It's not important!" says Louis.

"Yes?" says Tilly.

"He's probably unreliable. Musicians often disappear."

"Isn't that magicians?"

"No, I mean, on tour and stuff."

"If he pays the rent, he can disappear into the Upside Down for all I care," says Louis, who re-watched the entire back catalogue of Stranger Things with Tomas recently.

"Yeah, Ciara, I'm not sure that's really an issue," Tilly adds. "I mean, an absent flatmate might be easier, in a way."

"But if he's *not* absent, though, then... you know."

"No," says Louis.

"No," Tilly echoes.

"You know. He could be, like, messy." I think back. Was he? I think I might have been messier. I press on anyway. "Really untidy."

"You're messy and untidy," Tilly says.

I frown. "Well, exactly. You don't want another one like me, do you?"

"Ciara, is there some real reason you don't want Max to stay here?" Louis asks. Then he takes it up a notch. "Is there some selfish reason you want to trample all over my happiness?"

Tilly joins in. "Yeah, Ciara? What's this about really?"

"Nothing," I say. "But he might say no."

"You won't know until you ask," Louis says. "Ask him!"

I look at Tilly. "Is that definitely OK with you?"

"Yeah," she replies. "To be honest, I'm intrigued now."

I groan. "There's nothing to be intrigued about."

"Ask him now!" Louis is bouncing on his stool. "Please Ciara. Please, before Tomas appears at your window again wearing nude pants. I'm not afraid to put in another request, you know."

I pick up my phone. "OK, now you've persuaded me!"

"Do it, do it!"

I jump off my stool, my heart in my mouth. "OK, I'll just..."

"Can't you ask him in front of us?" Tilly asks.

"Yeah, what's all this secrecy? We don't have secrets from each other!"

In this case, we do. "Says the man who didn't even tell us about Tomas until he turned up in this very kitchen one Sunday morning wearing only a pair of designer boxer shorts."

"Those were the days," says Louis.

"Seems to be a theme with Tomas," Tilly muses. "An underwear theme." She looks at me. "And you say I'm not creative!"

"I didn't say that, I said –"

"Listen, I don't care how you do it, Ciara," Louis interrupts. "Just do it! Ask Max to take my room and pay my share of the rent so that I can go to Paris with my sexy model boyfriend!"

So I do. I leave the room and select his number from my recently dialled list, my heart racing as it rings. Maybe he won't answer.

But he does, and when I explain, he doesn't hesitate.

He says yes.

***

Our last Friday with Louis rolls around far too quickly. He's flying to Paris in the morning and I'm not ready to see him go! Max is moving in a week later, on a Saturday morning. I'm also not ready to see Max again, but I push that thought out of my head.

I offer to make Louis a coffee while he packs.

He accepts, flitting in and out of his bedroom in a proper tizzy, shaking shirts and jackets at me and asking, "This one?" every two minutes.

"They're all gorgeous, Louis," I say truthfully. Apart from the nude long-johns, Louis has an eye for style and an impeccable taste in clothes. It's not a surprise that he got a job in fashion photography and attracted the attention of the stylish model of his dreams, no matter how much he likes to put himself down.

"I need a second opinion," Louis says. He dumps the latest jacket and takes the coffee I'm holding out to him, slumping onto one of our kitchen stools. "When will Tilly get back? She's always working late these days."

I check my phone. "No news. I think you're stuck with me. But that's OK, because I'm always right and you know it."

Louis makes a 'huh' sound. "I love you, Ciara, but 'always right' is not how I'd describe you."

"How would you describe me?" I ask out of curiosity.

"Fun. Loyal. Scared," Louis says. "Off the top of my head."

"You missed out awesome." I shake my head. "Wait a minute – scared? I'm not scared! Scared of what?"

"Doesn't matter. Maybe I was describing myself. We're all scared. It's only natural. Life's scary. I'm flying to Paris to hang around beautiful, successful people."

Honestly, there he goes again! "You're beautiful and successful too. Probably more so." I met some of Tomas's colleagues at a party once and I wasn't impressed. They did that rude thing where they looked you up and down and then glanced over your shoulder for someone cooler to talk to.

"Thanks, but... Do you really think I should take this jacket?" He holds it up again, shaking it in my direction.

"Yes. Louis?"

"Yes?"

"I'll miss you."

Louis gets up and gives me an enormous hug. "I'll miss you too. But I'll have Tomas, and you'll have sexy Max."

I stiffen. "It's not like that between me and Max."

"OK, OK," he laughs. "So you keep saying. You only have eyes for Chester, am I right?"

"You're absolutely right," I tell him.

We prepare for our Flatmate Friday evening in, getting the crisps and wine laid out ready for when Tilly comes home. It's the last night the three of us will be declaring our ridiculous 'flatmates together, in it forever', at least for a while. Soon, Max will be here in Louis's place. That's if he joins in with our wild Fridays.

Louis is absolutely right, I tell myself.

☼

CHAPS: Fourteen Plus – part 1, 2004

I could. Not. Wait. Could. NOT. WAIT!!! to see Max again.

I had built it into a massive thing in my mind. I'd read enough Meg Cabot and Louise Rennison books, watched enough Friends and Legally Blonde and listened to enough Snow Patrol to know that love could be fun, funny and hopelessly, swoon-worthily romantic. And I was hopelessly, swoon-worthily in love with Max, who made me laugh and made me think, and made me desperate to see him again.

Maybe we would kiss.

No, we would definitely kiss. And it would be fun and deep and amazing.

Max was my lobster.

I knew I was his, forever.

I daydreamed about him constantly.

At the previous CHAPS meeting we were so young we could have stayed anywhere with a few plastic balls and climbing frames and been happy, but seven years later we were much more sophisticated. Unfortunately, the CHAPS team researchers still thought we were children, which is why we were staying at a theme park with a sports and recreation ground. It was a large, brand new one in the countryside somewhere a long drive away from home. We were called in during the February half term, off season and before the park was completely ready to open to the public. The rides looked shiny and new, but also empty and sad, like there was no point to their existence until someone went on them. Obviously I felt way too old for this kind of thing, but also sort of excited about being one of the first to try out the rides – one of the theme park's willing guinea pigs.

We stayed in neat little purpose-built lodges on the outskirts of the theme park, with one assigned to each family. Mine and Mum's was next door to Max and his mum's, which I found out as soon as we got there and I scanned the guest list behind the reception desk while the receptionist collected our key. The mysterious Ali Rashid – rightful owner of Max's birthday card seven years ago and probably every year since, as I was still receiving Max's cards – was on the other side. They must have grouped all the 'R' surnames together. My best subject at school was English and I was excellent at reading, even when it involved a list of names that I could only see upside down.

As soon as Mum and I deposited our luggage in the lodge, I said, "I'm popping next door to see if Max has arrived. See you whenever!"

"Hang on!" Mum said. "You've got an assessment this afternoon."

I screeched to a halt, already halfway out of the door. "I've got a what?" It sounded like school.

"Have you forgotten why you're here?"

Of course I hadn't. It was a free holiday, wasn't it?

"It's not a free holiday, remember, Ciara? We've volunteered to take part in a research project."

Well, technically she had volunteered me, fourteen years ago, when I was a baby. Not that I was exactly complaining. It had been one of the best things in my boring, suburban life so far. It made me different from Olive, Sophie and Hannah, who didn't have anybody except teachers collating information about them. They hadn't contributed to any major longitudinal research at all, unless you counted school reports and parents' evenings.

Also, CHAPS had meant I'd met Max.

"Oh. My. God! So what do I have to do?" I shut the door and came back into the room.

Mum consulted a piece of paper. Strange – I hadn't noticed anything like that the last time we were at one of these places.

"You're allowed to opt out at any time. It says so right at the top. It's your right as a participant –"

Was she kidding? "I don't want to opt out."

"OK, well… we have a general meeting in the clubhouse at midday," Mum said. "And later there's an observation in the shooting gallery."

"A what in the where?" I could have sworn that the last time we'd met up, all I had done was play. Mostly with Max.

"I think the shooting gallery is one of the attractions here. And observation is just when the researchers watch you interact. It's all very unobtrusive – you're just supposed to do what you naturally do. They hang around and take notes and things. Sometimes they ask you questions. Don't you remember it at all?"

No. I had no memory of anyone ever asking me or Max questions when we slayed monsters in the ball pool as little kids. Sometimes the helpers in the play area had been a bit nosy, now I thought about it. We'd just answered them quickly and got back to our games.

"And you'll get some questionnaires to fill in. I did them for you last time, but this time they want both of us to contribute."

"Oh, OK." It didn't sound too bad. Max and I could probably sneak away somewhere when nobody was watching – find a quiet stairwell to be alone, or something, like high school characters in American TV dramas.

"So we've only got half an hour before we're expected in the clubhouse. Sorry, Ciara."

If Mum had expected me to put up a fight, she would have been pleasantly surprised.

I liked being part of this study. I wanted to do it.

Now that I'd stopped and given it a bit more thought, I was actually a bit nervous about seeing Max again. And an extra half hour to get ready and work on the makeup that I'd probably overdone earlier could be a good thing. Plus I might change my outfit a few more times.

When Max next saw me, he wouldn't know what had hit him.

∞∞∞

CHAPS: Fourteen Plus – part 2, 2004

The clubhouse was crowded with parents and teenagers when we got there. It was my fault, really – I changed my mind about the lipstick I'd applied just as we were about to leave, but no matter what I tried, it wouldn't come off. It was a 'mood stick' which was supposed to alter its colour depending on my body heat, or whatever. But what it actually did was go a far-too-bright icky pink colour and then refuse to remove itself, no matter how many tissues I scoured it with. I turned to wet wipes in desperation, but they were supposed to be for eye makeup removal. They tasted totally disgusting and they didn't even work.

By the time I'd given up, Mum was losing her uncharacteristic 'let's indulge Ciara' patience and goodwill. We were definitely going to be late.

I tugged my crop top down towards my jeans as we walked into the crowded room and tried to find an inch of space to stand in comfortably.

I scanned all the faces we passed but I didn't spot Max.

"Yoo hoo!" called a voice. "Sarah! It's me!"

Mum beamed. "Penelope! Hello! So wonderful to see you again," she gushed.

I groaned. I might have kept in touch with Max over the years, but Mum's best friend from CHAPS was Amelia's mum. They'd call each other every few months and have long, extremely boring conversations. I only listened in when they talked about their daughters, because those were the juicy bits. I gathered that Amelia was doing fantastically well at a private school and she rode horses in her spare time, when she wasn't busy winning medals for gymnastics and passing difficult exams. I heard my mum desperately trying to keep up by saying things like, "Well, my Ciara wrote the most beautiful poem a while back. It was printed in the end-of-term pamphlet, so it was." Pathetic. Though I had to admit I was still quite proud of that poem.

There was a woman standing next to Penelope. She had fabulous, iron-straight blonde hair in a trendy cut and she was wearing a stunning red dress that hugged her curves and made me wish my boobs would hurry up and grow to their full potential.

On closer inspection, the woman was Amelia herself.

"Oh, hello, Ciara," the vision of perfection said. How could she possibly be the same age as me? "You haven't changed a bit!"

"Um, yeah," I replied. How could I possibly still look seven years old? For a start, I was wearing lipstick that would never, ever come off! I remembered how little I'd liked Amelia.

"We must get together this week!" Penelope said to my mum, who was lapping the attention right up.

"Ciara and I would love that!" Mum enthused.

Before I could roll my eyes at Mum, we were interrupted by an amplified voice.

"Welcome, Cohort for Happiness!" It was the head researcher, or whatever his job title was, standing at the front of the room and ready to brief us on what we could expect in the coming week.

His explanation was basically the long version of what Mum had told me. He stressed we were there to enjoy ourselves and could opt out of any activity at any point. He said there would be a Valentine's disco at the end of the week, and that during our stay all the attractions were free to us. Though due to the low demand, with the park being open exclusively to a relatively small group, we needed to book in for rides and special events at the reception area. The opening times would be limited, especially for the water ride which took longer to get started and tested for safety.

Well, that sounded a bit crap. I looked at Amelia. She seemed attentive but unimpressed. She probably didn't want to get her perfect hair wet, or something.

Where was Max?

Maybe he'd be too scared to go on the rides. Maybe he was scared of heights, like he'd been on the first day I met him. Then I could help him again – and this time maybe I could hold his hand...

I missed the rest of the talk, lost in my Max daydream.

When the researcher stopped talking, I decided to make a break for it and see if Max had arrived. He and his mum had probably skipped this boring clubhouse bit. She'd always been a bit of a rebel. Or else she'd forgotten all about it. That was also Carol's style. Max's mum was so much cooler than my mum.

"See you back at the lodge!" I called to Mum.

Mum didn't seem to care. She gave me a little wave and carried on talking to Penelope, probably putting on her posh voice, if I knew her.

"Hey! Ciara!"

Oh, no. Amelia was following me!

Should I run?

"Ciara! Wait!"

Politeness made me stop. I'd give Amelia a minute and then lose her somehow. She was wearing red high-heeled shoes – no wonder I'd thought she was a grown-up – so she shouldn't be too difficult to outrun.

"Jee-sus," she said when she caught up with me. She wobbled towards me, grabbed my arm and held it tightly. I flinched before I realised she was steadying herself on me while slipping off her shoes, one by one.

She held the red heels in the air in one hand. "Phew!" she said triumphantly. "Thank fuck for that! These monstrosities are killing me."

"Um... you mean your shoes?" I asked.

She stared at me as if that was a stupid question.

"Well, why do you wear them, then?" I sounded defensive.

She rolled her eyes in the direction of our mothers, deep in conversation at the back of the emptying room. "The mothership! Anything for a quiet life." Amelia sighed. "I don't know what's more of a pain – these shoes or her!" She put on a high-pitched voice, "'Do this, wear that, be a *lady*.' A lady! It's like the millennium never happened in my mother's world." She shook her head. Then she flopped it forwards and swung her hair around frantically. When she raised her head again, her hair was all over the place. "That's better. Fuck that straight hair shit."

Well. This swearing, stocking-footed, wild-haired girl was nothing like the one I'd been hearing about through Mum's phone calls all these years.

"What?" she asked me. "Have I got a spot?" She patted at her nose.

I laughed. "No, you're fine." I decided to test her. "Do you want to sign up for some rides, or whatever?"

Amelia cackled. "Depends what you mean."

"I mean like the water ride..." Wait – did Amelia think I'd meant 'ride' in an innuendo kind of way? Like... sex?

I must have gone bright red because Amelia laughed even harder, but not in a mean way. "Don't worry, I know what you meant! And yeah, why not? I live for thrills. The scarier the better! Let's sign up for all of them." She laughed a bit more. "You're blushing. I said you hadn't changed! So sweet and innocent."

"I'm not..." I had a full-blown serious crush on a boy and everything.

It was like Amelia read my mind. "Hey, do you remember that boy you played with when we were seven?"

"Um..." Should I pretend I didn't?

"Max, wasn't it?"

I gave a small nod. I was probably even redder now. I could feel the heat burning my cheeks.

"Ha, I knew it! I reckon you had a massive crush on him even back then!"

"No, I didn't. No way!"

"Well, whatever. He worshipped you. I was so jealous!"

"What?" She'd been *jealous*?

"Not of you – or him – don't get me wrong." She cackled. "You're both very sweet, but neither of you are my type. You were just so *cute* together."

"You were the same age as us!" Honestly – this girl! "And it wasn't – isn't – like that. We're friends."

"Yeah, right. You can't hide it from me. I know everything there is to know about this stuff. You should see me in action – I'm a boy magnet." She laughed. "Stick with me, my darling. You and Prince Charming shall go to the ball! Or the end-of-week children's balloon party, or whatever delightful entertainment they'll put on for us."

"They said something about a Valentine's disco." Hadn't she been listening? I thought I'd been the one who was distracted, while she was paying perfect attention.

Amelia pulled a face. "Yuck. Still, we can work with that." She glanced around. "Where are you going now?"

"Nowhere..."

"You were in a tearing rush. I had to practically snap my feet off to keep up with you!"

"Um, I've got this observation in a shooting gallery, or something?"

"I've got the same one. It's in two hours." She raised her eyebrows in a 'tell me the truth' gesture.

So I did. What did I have to lose? "I wanted to see Max."

Her eyes lit up. "I told you. Young love!"

"You're the same age as me."

"You're hilarious!" She linked her arm through mine, so now we had shoes dangling between us. "Come on, then!"

We trudged round to Max's lodge. Amelia trod carefully, refusing to put her shoes back on. When we reached the path to Max's door, I nearly lost my nerve, but Amelia looked at me expectantly and I didn't want to let her down.

I knocked at his door and waited, my heart pounding.

There was no answer.

"Love can wait!" Amelia announced. "Let's check out the rides!"

∞∞∞

CHAPS: Fourteen Plus – part 3, 2004

The next day, Amelia and I were on our way to a rollercoaster when we finally spotted Max.

He was on a football pitch in the sports fields at the side of the complex. He was running around with a group of boys I didn't recognise, covered in mud and shouting animatedly.

Amelia nudged me. I called out, "Hello, Max!"

He turned round, frowning until a look of recognition dawned on his face.

He came jogging over. "Ciara. Hi."

"Hi."

"Hi." He smiled at me.

"Where have you been?" I blurted.

"We got here late yesterday. Mum had a bad morning."

"Oh. You missed the start."

"I know."

Amelia sniffed. "Hello, Maximillian."

"Hello," he replied. "Amelia, right? Hi. Um, it's Massimo. But I'm just Max."

"I know *that*," Amelia said with a contemptuous flick of her hair.

As if to underline it, his teammates called his name. "Oi!" I heard one of them shout. "Get back here – we need you!"

Max ignored them. He kept looking at me, smiling. "So Ciara..."

"You'd better go. They need you." I didn't think before I added, "And you're staying next door to me anyway, right?" Why had I said that? How uncool could I possibly be? "So..."

Max bit his lip. "So..."

Another of the football boys called out, "Stop chatting up birds and get over here!"

Max mumbled, "Sorry about them. I'd better..."

"Go," I finished for him.

He looked grateful. "See ya, Key."

He ran back onto the pitch and my heart sank. That hadn't really gone very well. Even though he'd smiled at me a lot, and he'd used his nickname for me.

"Birds? What the fuck!" Amelia said loudly. "Let's leave these Neanderthals to it!" She stalked away and I ran after her, trying to stop myself from glancing back at the crush of my life, who barely knew I existed.

And that was it for most of the week. I was sort of on edge to start with, thinking he might pop round, knowing we were in neighbouring lodges. But he didn't. Max played football. I hung around with Amelia.

I learnt something in those days at CHAPS, an important life lesson.

I might have been madly in love, but it meant nothing to Max. I would have needed to turn myself into a football or the back of a goal net for him to pay the slightest attention to me. In my human, female form, I had absolutely nothing he was remotely interested in.

This was part of my discovery. That just because you desperately want something – or someone – it didn't mean you'd get it. And there was nothing you could do about that.

Some people just weren't interested.

Amelia tried her best to cheer me up. That's what we were there for, after all. Happiness. It was the focus of our entire week. We had carefully worded interviews with researchers and we filled in questionnaires rating our feelings about every activity on a scale of 1 to 10, ranking how everything made us feel.

And I rated pretty highly on the happiness stakes overall. I was exhilarated on the rollercoaster with Amelia. I was snug and comfortable in my lodge with Mum, and with Mum, Penelope and Amelia most evenings, even though Amelia's mum really was awful. Now that I knew Amelia better, though, it was bearable. Amelia would catch my eye if her mum said something particularly cringeworthy and we'd get the giggles, which both our mums thought was adorable.

Mum was delighted that I was so happy to spend time with Amelia. "She's a lovely girl!" she enthused. I suspected she wished I could be more like her friend's daughter. Instead of upsetting me, it made me laugh. If only Mum knew the truth.

"My mum wishes I was you," I told Amelia as we queued for the water ride one day.

Amelia waggled her false eyelashes at some boys in front of us and they let us go ahead of them. She winked at one of them as she sashayed past. His eyes followed her.

"Of course she does," Amelia replied without a trace of irony. "I'm awesome-sauce. But so are you."

Another thing I learnt that week was that friendship didn't have to be built on being the same – or at least not completely. Amelia and I were definitely different, much more than me and Sophie or Olive or Hannah. But it didn't matter. There was never a dull moment with Amelia around.

And this was my biggest life lesson. That despite what you saw on telly and in films and all that everyone ever seemed to talk or sing about, the thing that mattered most wasn't being desperately in love with someone, whether they loved you back or not.

The most important thing was having a friend by your side – someone who made your sides ache when you laughed together.

The week sped by in a whirl of theme park rides and flirting with boys who weren't Max – though it was mostly Amelia who did that. I stood by and watched her in action, flicking her blonde hair and exuding a charisma that should have filled me with jealousy, but instead topped up my admiration for her. I wished I could be Amelia, even though it seemed utterly exhausting. Being near her was the best fun I'd ever had.

***

By the time the end-of-week Valentine's disco rolled around, I didn't even care anymore about Max. Or so I thought.

Amelia and I were dancing together in the middle of the dancefloor, the space that everyone else in the whole of CHAPS was avoiding because they didn't have the guts we had – the confidence Amelia had given me. I was sure everyone was staring at us, and some people were probably saying mean things, but I didn't care. Did. Not. Care. I threw everything I had into my dance shapes. Every throbbing beat of the DJ's mix was mine. I was having the time of my life.

Until I did a full spin on the dancefloor and as I turned, I saw him. Max, standing at the side of the room, watching me. He was wearing his football shirt, like most of the boys. The girls hadn't exactly dressed up either, except me and Amelia. We had gone to glam-town. She'd lent me a sparkling, body-hugging little black dress that didn't really fit me as I was at least two sizes bigger than her, albeit with smaller boobs. But I was wearing it anyway. I felt good in it and that was all that mattered.

The track finished and Max was still rooted to the spot, his eyes fixed on me.

Amelia noticed and nudged me. "Talk to him."

"I don't think –"

"Good. Don't think. Thinking brings everyone down. Don't think – just do! Talk to him. Do it, do it!"

"No..."

"Ciara, he can't take his eyes off you. He's got it bad," Amelia insisted. "Believe me."

"I don't care." I wasn't lying, either. All week, he'd known where to find me. He'd had his chance. I'd spent my week having fun with my friend, and I didn't intend to stop now.

She rolled her eyes. "Talk to him, or I'll talk to him for you." I wasn't exactly sure what she meant by that but it sounded like a threat. And maybe I did sort of want to talk to him, anyway.

I walked over.

"You're a really good dancer," Max said, not even pretending that he hadn't been watching me.

"Er, thanks."

He stared at his trainers and mumbled something.

"What?"

He looked up. His eyes locked with mine. "I said, do you want to dance? Um, with me?" He scuffed at one trainer with the other. "Although I don't know how to dance. But... I'll try."

He reached over and brushed the back of my hand with his, like he wanted to take my hand but he wasn't sure. It was the simplest touch – it was nothing, really. But my knees went weak. My heart raced and I felt dizzy. I instantly became a total cliché of a lovestruck teenager, because I was. In love. With him.

But it didn't change the fact that he'd largely ignored me all week. And I had been having a great time with my friend, a girl he'd never bothered to get to know.

Amelia, still dancing, laughed in our direction and shouted famous lines from Dirty

Dancing, the movie she and I had watched five times that week on her state-of-the-art portable DVD player. Amelia had the best gadgets.

The music changed and Max moved his hand again. This time he grabbed my hand and held it properly, and I let him. He intertwined his fingers with mine. We were still at the edge of the dancefloor but he took a couple of steps, tentatively, in time with the music. He moved close enough to me that I could feel his heart thudding, echoing the rapid pounding of mine. We shuffled together for a while and I could have let myself get lost in his closeness.

But I glanced at Amelia, dancing alone, spinning solo. She was throwing herself into the beat and she didn't seem to mind that that I'd abandoned her.

But I did. I cared a lot.

I pulled away, extracting my hand from his. Max's brown eyes searched mine. "Ciara?"

I mumbled, "I'm here with Amelia."

"OK, but..."

"No. Forget it."

I danced back to my friend and she threw her arms in the air and grinned like she hadn't noticed anything going on, like she'd been too busy dancing on cloud nine.

We danced together until the room spun and everyone else disappeared.

I didn't see Max again that night.

The next morning we all left CHAPS, and when I got home, I deleted MassimoTheMonsterSlayer from my MSN and blocked him on MySpace. If he couldn't be bothered to talk to me when we'd spent an entire week living next door to each other, what was the point?

Max and I shouldn't have met again for another seven years.

Maybe that would have been it between us. Years of friendship and one awkward hand-holding moment at a theme park disco.

It wasn't, of course.

∞∞∞

CHAPS: Fourteen Plus – part 4, 2008

It was more than four years before I saw Max again.

I wouldn't say my crush on him had died over time, but it all seemed distant and bittersweet. It had dimmed a bit in my mind. By then I was pretty experienced in kissing other boys. Sometimes it was a lot more than kissing, too.

I didn't get what all the fuss was about – it turned out that most of the romantic fiction I'd read was nothing like the real world. In reality, you enjoyed yourself and then got on with your life, which was full of exams, UCAS forms, student loan applications and worries about the future. There wasn't much room for wandering around obsessing about another person. Kissing, and whatever else I did, wasn't the entire meaning of life – it was just kissing and whatever else. But it felt good at the time, and it was something to gossip about with my friends for a while afterwards, so I joined in happily. We had casual hookups most weekends, working our way through a pool of available boys from school and then college, and also a couple of girls, especially in Sophie's case. In the end, she was the first of us to be in a long-term relationship, and we thought it was mega cool that it was with another girl. We were a bit grumpier about it when Sophie and Ingrid decided to go backpacking around Europe after A Levels and we barely saw our friend for over a year.

Hannah was the next to couple up. "He completes me," she swooned like some Hollywood heroine, referring to James who enjoyed completing cryptic crosswords and bleating on about how clever he was.

"He's completely boring," Olive laughed to me when Hannah wasn't around – which was most of the time now. It was usually just me and Olive, practising our Beyoncé dance like the single ladies we officially were. I didn't get the attraction of tying yourself to another person, someone who might make you listen to music you didn't like, watch boring films and invariably wouldn't understand your sense of humour. (This last one was a common theme for me – usually the boys I met didn't even realise I was joking half the time, which led to some pretty big and stupid arguments, including the one where some boy declared me 'too independent!' before he stormed out of the pub I was supposed to be grateful he'd taken me to. "He feels threatened," Olive explained when I related the incident to her. "He'd prefer it if you didn't have a brain.")

Turning eighteen was uneventful. Sophie was away visiting Ingrid, Hannah had dropped out of sixth form to get a 'proper job' that made her too sensible to party, and Olive and I were too busy stressing over uni applications. For this reason, Olive decided that we'd make a fuss over turning nineteen instead. Our birthdays were both in the Christmas holidays, which meant that even though we lived in different cities now, we could get together easily. I reminded Olive that my birthday was on a useless day, one where everybody was fully partied-out, so there was no point in inviting anyone for mine. Olive refused to let it lie, though, and instead she insisted on a compromise. She nagged and nagged until I agreed: we'd have a joint party in December, on Olive's birthday.

I suggested that Olive should keep the Beyoncé theme she'd been dreaming of, which was partly inspired by the boy at her uni who'd told Olive that she looked a bit like Ms Knowles herself. ("I'll take it," she said, "but it doesn't mean I'll sleep with him." I'd always admired Olive's principles.)

Olive suggested holding the party at her student house in Brighton, where she lived with six others. "Three of them can't get away from their parents," she said, "which means empty bedrooms! Plus the perfect party house, and not even that far from London."

It was really going to be more her party than mine, but I didn't mind.

One evening about two weeks before the big day, while we were putting the finishing touches on our party plans over several bottles of cheap white wine, Olive frowned at her scribbled guest list and announced, "Ciara, I need more men!"

"You need to lower your standards," I quipped. "I've had plenty."

She swatted me with the list. "I'm serious. Have you seen this? There are about three men on it, and that's including Hannah's James. It's never going to work."

"It'll be fine. It's not like there won't be any relationship drama." I glanced at the list. "I mean, you've got two of Ingrid's ex-girlfriends on there. They hate each other."

"That's not the point!" Olive wailed. "We can't have an all-female nineteenth. We just can't." She lowered her voice. "I want a chance of meeting someone."

I shook my head. "You've been asked out five hundred times in your first term of uni."

"I'm doing Physics, Ciara! It's a heavily male-dominated student body. They'd ask out a pot plant if they thought it was female."

"Well, then. Invite some of them! The guys. Or the pot plants."

"I said 'Physics', Ciara. I don't think you're listening. We do not want Physics students at our party."

"Apart from you."

Olive nodded like it was obvious. "I'm the exception that proves the rule. It's basic science."

I sighed. She was impossible.

"Can't you invite anyone from your course?" she pleaded. "You must have some Southerners, even all the way up there. Or people who are willing to travel." Olive thought Manchester was ridiculously far north.

"I'm studying English, Olive. English – have you heard of it? It's like Physics for women."

She smiled. "Point taken."

We both swigged more wine.

"What about friends of friends?" Olive asked, not letting it go. "That posh girl from your brain-shrinking project – the one with all the designer clothes? I bet she could bring some men!"

"You mean Amelia?" I had come back from my fourteen-year-old CHAPS meeting going on and on about my new friend, showing my old friends photos and driving them crazy. I only realised when Hannah snapped one day at school, "You have fun with us too, you know. Amelia's not the only friend in your life!" Then I felt guilty and made a big fuss of Hannah, Sophie and Olive until my guilt wore off and everything went back to normal. It wasn't like Amelia was still around, anyway. When we joined the latest social media sites, Amelia and I always friended each other. But if I sent her a direct message, she hardly ever replied. I moaned about it to Mum once and she said Penelope was the same. "Some people don't really like the technology," Mum explained. "It makes them nervous."

I eyed her suspiciously. That might apply to Penelope. "But Amelia's eighteen years old, Mum."

"Well, she's probably just busy." The last time Mum had tried to ring, Penelope had said she couldn't talk and would call back, but she hadn't. "People have lives, Ciara."

Yeah, yeah. Everything Mum said merited an eyeroll these days. It's a good thing I was mature enough now not to show my frustration, or at least to show it a tiny bit less.

"Ask Amelia!" Olive said.

"OK, I'll try, but she probably won't come." Our party wouldn't be anything like the glamorous, classy gatherings she was probably used to.

"Or – I know – that boy!" Olive continued. "The one who came to your birthday parties when we were little. He was annoying, but he was cute. I bet he's even cuter now. And you definitely lusted after him!"

"Oh my god, Olive. I did not 'lust after' Max!" I was such a liar. "And he wasn't annoying, anyway! I never understood why you and Sophie said that!"

"Max – that's it! Me and Soph thought he was such a *boy*." She laughed. "And I don't care what you say – you definitely liked him! And you probably still do – listen to yourself now, defending his honour!"

"I –"

"Can you ask him to the party? I bet he's got some fit Northern mates."

Seriously? "No, I can't. We lost touch." When I deleted our online connection. He could still have contacted me, though, couldn't he? I was on most social media. And his mum had my home address. How hard could it be?

Olive fired up the sleek white MacBook she'd got for her eighteenth. "What was his last name?"

"Renzo." I spelled it out for her before I added, "But don't look him up!" I'd managed to stop myself doing that for so long now. "Olive! Don't!"

"I can't hear you," Olive said as she typed. She often did this to me and Sophie – played on her hearing differences when she wanted to get her own way. If we complained, she'd say it was 'a legitimate perk of living with a so-called disability'.

"Fine," I said to my friend as she typed away. I mean, technically this wasn't me looking Max up, and I had to admit I was curious. "Oh, and I know you suddenly can't hear me at all, but in case it helps – he definitely used to be on MySpace."

It took her about ten seconds. "Found him," she said, scooting over so that I could see over her shoulder. "Max Renzo's MySpace."

I raised my eyebrows at Olive. "It's as if you heard me."

"I don't know what you're talking about," Olive said. "Anyway, it says he loves football and... well, mostly just football."

"Yeah, that'll be him." I peered closer. His profile picture was of a football shirt, which gave nothing away. The 'top friends' list was pretty empty – a few random boys and MySpace's Tom. It took me back. It was frozen in time from the days when I'd spend hours on MSN with MassimoTheMonsterSlayer. "It hasn't been updated for years. Look at the favourite bands bit! Do that lot even exist anymore?"

Olive was undaunted. "OK, but read the comments. His friends are talking about school."

"So it's definitely out of date!"

"But this one says the name of the school. And this friend has commented a lot. Wait..." Olive opened another window and clattered away like a hacker in a spy film. She'd always been so good at computers. "Here." She showed me the screen. It was a Friends Reunited page for Max's school, and the friend who'd commented a lot was listed.

"Maybe you can write to him?" she said.

"No way! Who even is he? And why do you have access to Friends Reunited? It's for old people who want to have affairs! We were still in sixth form until a year ago."

"I like all this stuff. I'm nosy. Maybe I've been waiting for a moment like this!" She opened more windows and clicked around. "OK! Here's that same guy on Facebook. I know he's got an ordinary name, but look at the school name. It's definitely him."

"Yeah, so?"

"So he knows Max." She sighed. "Who doesn't seem to be on Facebook at all. I'm going to invite this Jamie guy to the party. Maybe he can go with Max."

"Olive, no! Don't!"

Olive tapped meaningfully at her ear before she bashed away at her keyboard. "There! I've sent him a private message telling him to bring Max plus any other male friends he wants."

"Olive, what the hell? These people could be anyone!"

"Relax! It's not an open invitation, is it? Just Max and some of his friends. And Tyler will be at the party." Tyler was Olive's burliest housemate and he was paying for uni by working as a bouncer at various nightclubs.

"Why are you doing this?"

"I sense you have unfinished business with Max," she said. "I care about my friend's happiness. And I reckon he'll have interesting mates."

"He won't come, you know. He won't even get the message."

"So?" She shrugged. "It was just an idea. I don't really care whether Max comes or not."

I was shocked to discover that I did. I cared. Oh shit.

"Now, what other boys can we invite? Maybe some of those Physics guys will be OK after all…"

∞∞∞

CHAPS: Fourteen Plus – part 5, 2008

Amelia replied to say she couldn't make it because she'd be at some cousin's wedding. Olive didn't get a reply from Max's friend, as I expected.

I was so sure Olive's bid to contact Max through websites wouldn't work that I decided to search through Mum's stuff to find a business card, the one Carol White had given her all those years ago. I told myself I was doing it for Olive. If it worked out, I'd let her think her online sleuthing had been successful. She'd like that. It would be like an extra birthday present.

I waited until my parents were both at work. Mum's stuff was beautifully organised. She kept all her old notes in the cabinet by the phone in the hallway, and I didn't have to dig far to find the Filofax I remembered from when I was little. A bit more searching uncovered a tatty-edged card that read: "Carol White, mobile hairdresser. Professional styling – in your home!" The phone number was right underneath, in a zany font.

I stared at it. Could I?

There really wasn't much chance of Max answering. He would be probably be at work, or whatever he was doing now. I wondered if he'd stayed on for sixth form or gone to uni? Or maybe he was a professional footballer, playing in Brazil or something. I sometimes listened out during the sports news in case his name came up, but I never heard it.

I called the number. For Olive.

It rang and rang, but nobody answered. Eventually, a recording kicked in – a male voice, way too gruff and old-sounding to be Max's. The beep went and I swallowed hard. "Er, hi. It's Ciara. Ciara Ryan from CHAPS? Max, er... he came to some of my birthday parties in London? Um... can you tell him... ask him to contact his friend Jamie from school? Er, about a message..." Was that enough? "Um, Mum says hi," I lied for good measure.

I clattered the phone down. I immediately wanted to delete the message, but there was no way of doing that, of course. Had what I said made any sense? Did whoever's voice was on the answerphone even know Max? Max and his mum might have moved years ago. Some total stranger would be getting that message later. I tried to stop feeling embarrassed. At least I'd tried. For Olive.

The day of the party rolled around and I'd largely put the whole Max thing out of my mind. I only thought about it every five minutes or so as the guests started to arrive.

Sophie and Ingrid got there early. They'd already been travelling for a couple of months but they'd made a special detour back to England for this party, and to go to Sophie's dad's for Christmas. Olive and I were thrilled to see them and we dragged them into the kitchen to grill them about what they'd been getting up to. Time passed quickly as constant waves of people streamed in, allowed by Olive's housemate Tyler, who'd been unofficially employed as the designated doorman. We were so busy catching up with Sophie that we barely noticed the house filling up.

I was in the middle of an animated conversation about food in Greece, or something, when a sound distracted me. Low voices rumbled from the corridor. Another group of boys had arrived. In fact, a swift glance around told me that there were probably more boys than girls here after all. Olive would be pleased. She'd relented and invited nearly every Physics undergraduate and a couple of other science faculties too. This latest group was probably composed of yet more students. But something about one of the voices made me look twice through the open doorway.

I recognised him instantly.

It was Max.

Max was here. He'd come to my birthday party, just like old times.

Olive's plan – or my plan, or both – had actually worked. Unbelievable.

His friends were laughing, confident, not caring that they were at a total stranger's party. They must be used to this kind of thing – turning up in student houses in Brighton for no particular reason. They were scruffy and relaxed. Supercool.

Max looked more nervous. He was glancing around, searching.

He turned in my direction.

Our eyes connected and a thrill ran through me.

I groaned inwardly at myself. What was the matter with me? All this time had passed, and he still had this effect on me? He probably hadn't given me a second thought over the years. I had to stop being so pathetic. I had to forget -

"Ciara? Happy birthday. For, you know. Soon." Max was standing in front of me.

"You're here," I said, stupidly. I remembered to add, "Happy birthday to you, too. For soon."

We stared at each other.

He smiled. "I got your message."

"The phone one or the Facebook..."

"Both. Mum told me you wanted me to contact Jamie. It was tricky because me and Jamie lost touch ages ago. Sorry I didn't get back to you or anything but I didn't have your number. Also, I haven't got a computer and my phone's too old. Would you believe I had to go to the library to get online and find Jamie?" He gave me a shy smile. "Well, I did. I could only find a contact form for him at his work. Luckily he replied pretty quickly."

"You haven't got a computer?"

"No. Two of the lads had them but they got stolen... And the library computer kicked me off just after I got the details down. But if I ever see Jamie again, I'll thank him."

"He's not here?"

"No, he lives in the States now. I'm here with other mates. It was so lucky, this party was perfect timing. We all have to be at

Gatwick soon, so... you know, it's not far. I talked them into dropping in."

I barely registered what he was saying to me. I couldn't believe he was here. Standing in front of me. I couldn't take my eyes off him. And my main thought was that I'd been kidding myself all this time.

My whole body was screaming it at me.

I still had the most enormous crush on this boy.

I tried to stop staring and make polite conversation. "Are you a footballer now?"

He sighed and looked down. "No. I got injured. It was pretty serious. I kind of missed my chance."

"Oh no. Oh god. I'm sorry."

"It's probably what I deserve. You know, for ignoring you at CHAPS when we were fourteen. I'm really sorry, Ciara. I get why you were annoyed. I was kicking myself for ages afterwards. I wanted to see you, you know... but football was there and the other boys wanted me to play and it just seemed... easier."

Max was standing in front of me, apologising for something from years ago, when we were kids. Was I dreaming? Was this really happening?

Behind Max's back, Olive put her thumbs up at me. She leaned over and said something to Sophie.

Sophie raised her eyebrows and mouthed, "Max? No way!"

Olive put her glass down and signed at me. She'd taught me and Sophie sign language when we were little and, though we didn't use it much with her now, there were some phrases that had stuck with us from our early teens. Like the one she was signing right now. "He is fit. Fit!" she signed, emphasising the last word with an expression that couldn't leave me in any doubt what she meant.

I didn't want to continue my conversation with Max in front of an audience, no matter how well-meaning my friends might be.

Olive had assigned me a room to myself as co-host of the party. It belonged to one of her housemates whose parents were loaded and lived in a posh part of West Sussex, so this girl didn't really need a room in a student house, but she had one anyway, just for fun. Olive told me the girl barely stayed there, which was why she had the smallest room in the house and paid less rent than the others.

Tonight, the room was mine. And it was away from my friends' prying eyes.

Max ran a hand through his hair. He was so incredibly gorgeous. "Key? You OK?"

"Come with me," I commanded. I strode away and he followed me. We wound our way through throngs of people – Olive would be so happy at how our party was turning out. The Physics boys, knocking back shots, seemed a particularly lively bunch.

I led Max to Olive's housemate's room. My room.

I told myself I just needed a quiet space to have a chat with Max, away from my friends.

But I think I knew what I was really doing.

∞∞∞

CHAPS: Fourteen Plus – part 6, 2008

Olive's housemate's boxroom – my temporary bedroom – was tiny. There was only really space for a bed and a small desk. I contemplated whether to shut the door or not, as if I was at home, being policed by my parents. But I was technically an adult now – I'd been one for nearly a year – and I was allowed to close a door if I wanted to. Besides, there was still too much noise coming from the party outside, and I wanted to focus fully on talking to Max. And it's not like anything would happen, anyway. Too much time had passed. Hadn't it?

My heart raced anyway at the thought of Max and me, alone in a bedroom. I pushed the door shut.

I focused on what he'd told me before. "So, your leg! What happened to you?"

"Hi, Max, nice to see you," he joked.

I smiled. "OK, fine..." I put on a posh voice. "Nice to see you, Max. How are you?"

"I'm good. And it's nice to see you too, Ciara. It's refreshing when people don't immediately question me about my dodgy leg, and the fact that I'll never be a professional footballer, and how much I'm pretending not to care..."

I looked at him sharply. I knew I hadn't seen him for more than four years, but even so. This was un-Max-like conversation. "Are you drunk?"

"I've had a few. But I'm used to it now so... not really drunk, no. Just honest. Sorry." He sat down on the bed. "Should we start again?"

I settled next to him and turned to face him. "Tell me what's been going on," I said. "Tell me everything."

"Tell me about you first. How are you, Key?" He shifted on the bed until our sides almost touched.

I ignored the stupid thrill I felt at his closeness. I distracted myself by answering his question, boring on about my life. Getting into uni, moving up to Manchester, worrying about English essays, my middle sister getting married a bit too young (according to Mum, who'd got married even younger), becoming an auntie to adorable twins... I mean, I was practically putting myself to sleep, and yet I couldn't stop talking. Because Max was listening the whole time, hanging on to my every word, looking at me like I was the most fascinating person on earth.

Finally I managed to stop myself and gulp. "What about you?"

"Oh. Me." Max broke eye contact for the first time in ages. He stared at his leg, then up at the room's tiny window. Outside, snow was falling lightly, magically. It never usually snowed on Olive's birthday. "I told you already. I got this injury during an important game – when a scout was watching! It broke in three places and it's never going to be properly fixed. I have the worst luck."

"Oh, Max, I'm sorry."

"Yeah, well, and then Mum... well, she went through a bad patch. She has a lot to cope with. She hasn't been well at all for ages, so it's been hard." He brushes invisible lint off his leg. "And, er, her new boyfriend kicked me out..."

I wondered if he was the gruff voice on the answerphone. "Shit, Max, that's awful."

"No, no, it's fine. I'm an adult now, like he says. I can look after myself. Anyway, I moved in with some mates – someone's friend's friend with a spare sofa. You know how it goes."

I nodded as if I did. Even though my parents would take out a second mortgage before they let me or my sisters live on someone's friend's friend's sofa.

"And it led to something pretty great. They were all musicians, and they had a lot of spare time in the day, you know, between gigs. So then one of them taught me to play the saxophone. Which is really, really hard, but I got it in the end. You have to do this thing with your mouth..." He showed me. "And you kind of hiss, rather than blowing."

I died a bit. It should not have been sexy, really. But when Max did it, it was. Oh god. I had definitely never got over my crush. I'd pushed it away but it was still there, and now it was threatening to explode. I had to keep a lid on it. Had to, or else I would scare him off. I was scaring myself right now, my thoughts going haywire as he carried on talking.

"So I toured with them a bit, playing the sax."

"Wait –" I checked, as I'd been looking at his mouth instead of listening properly, "- so you played the saxophone in a band?"

"Yup," he said. "And other instruments, in other bands. Music has changed my life, Ciara – I was in a pretty dark place for a while there."

Our lives were so, so different. My darkest hour this term had been getting a B on my end-of-unit essay. But I'd worked so hard on it!

"That's great, then," I said. "About the music, I mean."

"Yeah." He smiled at me. "It really is."

My heart filled with feelings for him. They overwhelmed me. What was it about this boy? I'd been out with loads of people over the past few years – I was definitely in double figures by now. And we'd done stuff – kissing, touching, sex. And not one of them, with any of that, had made me feel anything like what I felt when Max just smiled at me.

"I'm in a new band now," he told me proudly. "A proper member this time, not just helping out. There's three of us, and I mostly play bass."

"That's great." I shifted nearer to him, closed the tiny gap between our almost-touching legs. I couldn't help myself. "Can I hear you play sometime? I mean, I'd love to..."

"Yeah." His voice was low. He lowered his eyes and murmured, "I'd love that."

I love you, I love you, I thought, which was crazy. But that was what was going through my head when he said softly, "Ciara?"

I forced my voice to sound normal. "Yeah?"

"Can I... Would you mind if I..."

I didn't let him finish. I reached for him and I found his mouth with mine. And I kissed him. Softly at first, as light as the snow drifting by at the window. But then, when he responded, an urgency flooded me and every one of my nerves tingled as I deepened the kiss. And he kissed me back with more passion than I'd imagined in my wildest fantasies.

His phone buzzed and we both ignored it. It buzzed again and again, becoming an annoying backdrop to our kissing. But soon I blanked it out, as all I could focus on was Max and his mouth, his tongue, his quiet sighs as we reached for each other over and over.

I lost all track of time. Minutes passed, or maybe hours, as we kissed. Or it could have been just seconds before I was climbing onto his lap, and he was groaning and holding me like he never wanted to let go. I pushed him backwards onto the bed and he laughed, such a sexy laugh, as I covered his body with mine. We kissed again in this new position, excitement fizzing out of our bodies, making the air crackle with our electricity. Or maybe it was the buzzing of Max's phone, which was still going. Out of the corner of my eye, I could see it lighting up on the desk. Eventually he noticed it too. I kissed him harder but he pulled away and mumbled into my neck, "Oh no, Ciara. We have to stop..."

"Why?" I asked into his mouth.

"Because I have to go," he managed to say in a gap between more kisses. "I'm sorry."

"You're not leaving," I told him, pinning him to the bed with my arms. *You're going nowhere*, I thought. *I've finally got you where I want you.* I don't think I said it out loud, though I might have done, in the heat of the moment.

If I did, it didn't make any difference. "I'm so sorry. I really have to go. Tonight. With the band. They booked a taxi from here and they're leaving in..." he broke away, stood up and reached for his phone at last. He pressed some buttons and gulped. "Five minutes ago. I mean, they're waiting for me outside right now, saying they won't go without me but... They've been texting me for the past two hours, checking I'm still here and reminding me when we have to leave." So it had been more than seconds after all. Hours of us kissing in this tiny room while the snow fell outside. How had we managed to make time go so weird? "I didn't even hear my text alerts. I... I can't let them miss that plane. We're on tour."

"Stay," I pleaded. I couldn't help myself. I replayed it in my head five thousand times afterwards, wishing I hadn't said it. "Stay with me."

"I can't. The flight's booked. We have to get to Gatwick. It might take longer with the weather." He glanced at the window. "We scrape travel money together and only make enough to travel to the next place. Oh god, Ciara. I never expected... I just thought it would be great to see you before I left and now..."

I shut my eyes. "Go."

"When can I... Can I see you again?"

"You see me at CHAPS, every seven years." For some reason, my voice came out all snippy. He had a good reason to leave. Why did I feel so rejected? It wasn't like I was fourteen again and he was off playing football and forgetting I existed.

His phone buzzed again. He groaned. "Can I see you before that?"

"Just go. Don't worry about it," I said, but to my relief I'd managed to take the snark out of my tone. "Be amazing! I mean it. Go."

He bent his head and kissed me again, full of longing. Or sorrow. Maybe both. Full-on, like everything Max did.

He left.

I didn't get his phone number. I realised it as soon as he'd gone. It was incredibly frustrating on our birthday, when I really wanted to send him a message. There was no point in trying to send it through his friend Jamie on Facebook. Max wasn't going to take time off his tour to find a public library, and Jamie was clearly unreliable as he never had replied to Olive. There was also no way I'd be ringing Carol White again. What if that horrible man answered?

Days later, I found Max on Facebook. Well, his band, as he still didn't seem to have a profile on his own. The band was called Four Part Cure and there were grainy out-of-focus pictures of its members, two similar-looking boys who could be twins, plus Max. I followed the page, desperately searching for updates and more information. They were in the Netherlands for ages, then in Germany, where they were a huge hit. There were crowds at their gigs, and some of them were sold out.

I didn't message Max through the band's page because I wasn't sure who would see it. Also, why couldn't he write to me first? Someone in his band must have had internet access or I wouldn't be seeing all these updates. And if Max had anything to do with the page, he'd see that Ciara Ryan was one of their followers.

He didn't write to me, but the reason was obvious. He was busy. I saw more photos of him onstage on the bass, and with an electric guitar. Then behind a microphone with a dark-haired girl who hadn't been in the pictures before. They had their arms around each other, singing together, laughing. They looked happy.

I stopped looking.

Who was Max to me, anyway? He'd been like some kind of fantasy figure in my life, someone I daydreamed about but only saw occasionally. When we met, when he had time for me, he was always about to leave. I'd built him up in my mind, making everyone else I went out with pale into insignificance by comparison. He was getting in the way of my happiness. I didn't need him. We barely knew each other, really.

I unfollowed the Facebook page and got a life.

∞∞∞

CHAPS: Fourteen Plus – part 7, 2009

I settled back at uni and threw myself into student life. I went out as much as possible, mostly to get away from my laptop. It was taking all my willpower not to trawl through the entire internet for pictures of Max, or information about where he was and who he was with. I refused to be that girl.

I was out on a date when I got a text from Max. It was just over three months after Olive's party. Olive was still seeing the Physics student she'd hooked up with that night – another exception that proved her rule, she insisted. Whereas Max had disappeared into thin air like a male Cinderella who couldn't even be bothered to leave a stupid shoe behind. Not that I cared.

Max's text said: *Why didn't we swap numbers, Key? Couldn't work out how to contact you. Think about you tons. Max.*

"Everything OK?" asked Dean, my date, who was a nice enough guy but had been boring my ears off by telling me all about the car his dad was going to buy him after he graduated, the maximum acceleration and torque it could achieve and how he'd be able to do 120 down the motorway. I'd made a mental note not to get in any car he was driving, should the occasion ever arise.

"Yeah, fine," I said. "Just a text from an old friend."

I typed a quick reply to Max. *How did you get my number?*

Olive, he replied within seconds. Then: *I tried through Jamie but he'd deleted Olive's party message. Still don't do Facebook! So I remembered where Olive's house was and went there. I'm in Brighton! Two nights only and then back to Bruges. Gigs tonight and tomorrow. Can you come?*

Oh, how tempting it was. How much I would have loved to see Max performing. I could stay at Olive's. I was sure she'd let me sleep on her floor, once I'd finished having a go at her for handing out my number to casual visitors. She'd be over the moon. She and Sophie, having seen Max again for about ten seconds last December, had decided he was perfect for me. I wouldn't be missing much in Manchester. The new term had only just started and my course could live without me for a couple of days.

But I couldn't. Why should I just drop everything and jump on a train? Max was nothing to me. All this fantasising had to stop.

Dean was looking at me strangely. "Old boyfriend?"

"What?" I asked sharply. What gave him that impression? This was only our second date. Was he going to get prematurely jealous as well as simultaneously terrify me and bore me to sleep?

"Definitely an old flame! I can see it on your face." Dean laughed smugly and reached for my phone. "Want me to sort him out?"

"No!" I yanked my phone away and stood up, my chair making a horrible scraping noise that made some of the other diners stare. "No," I repeated more quietly. "Listen, thanks for... tonight." I reached quickly into my bag and pulled some money out of my purse. "Here's my share. I have to go, I'm sorry."

Dean's face fell. "You're not really leaving, are you?"

I nodded, not meeting his eye.

"God. They said you were cold but I didn't believe them."

I should have been angrier, but I couldn't deal with this now. "What?"

"The lads, when I told them I'd asked you out." His mouth was set in a mean grimace. "They'd heard things about you. Apparently you're an ice queen. I told them it was probably just rumours. But now I see what they mean."

Ice queen? I was frozen to the spot, listening in horror. "Please stop talking."

He gave a smug laugh. "I still think they're wrong, though. You're not cold-hearted. You're in love with someone else." He nodded towards my phone. "The text 'friend'."

His words unfroze me. I turned and ran out of the restaurant, the entry bell rattling as I swung the door with massive force.

In the cold darkness of the city centre, I found a bench as far away from other people as I possibly could and sat down heavily, clutching my phone. I looked at it. Max had texted me again while Dean had been tearing into me.

Key? So can you come?

I breathed in and out. No, no, no. He couldn't keep doing this to me. He couldn't rule my whole life and only see me when he felt like it, when he had an opening in his otherwise hectic schedule. It wasn't fair!

I can't leave, I texted back. *Come to Manchester.*

It was a test.

I wish I could.

It was a badly set test. I wasn't sure whether he'd passed or failed.

On a whim, I asked him: *Don't you need to see your mum?* It was like I was watering down my request. But Max was from around here somewhere – I was ashamed to think it was part of the reason I'd applied in the first place. I wanted to see the places he'd grown up near, to walk down streets he'd walked down and drink in pubs he'd drunk in. When I first got here, I almost expected to bump into Carol White in Sainsbury's or something. I didn't, of course. And pretty soon Manchester became my city and nothing to do with Max, although I was sure I lived in a sanitised, student version of the place. I convinced myself my application had actually had nothing to do with Max. It was the best course for me, after all. The location was a coincidence.

Another text came through. Max had ignored my question about his mum. Instead, he'd typed: *I wish I could see you right now. I miss you.*

Oh, Jesus. I squeezed my eyes shut. How could he write things like that? Why was he always doing this to me?

I typed: *I miss you too,* but my finger hovered over the 'send' button. I didn't press it.

Seconds past. Minutes. I wondered what he was doing. Had he given up? Or gone out with his bandmates and not given me a second thought?

He texted again. *I'm glad I've got your number now. Can we text sometimes?*

I deleted my previous text. I typed: *OK.*

In the two-and-a-bit years until our next CHAPS meeting, we exchanged texts in bursts here and there, sometimes with months in between. He didn't say anything about the girl I'd seen in the pictures, the one he'd had his arm around. I didn't ask about her, or ask whether there were any other girls in his life. He didn't ask me about the boys I was seeing, although I mentioned one or two of them occasionally. Sometimes he told me again that he missed me. I still couldn't bring myself to say it back to him, but I thought about him all the time.

There were patches when we chatted for ages and it was like being twelve again, back on MSN, sharing random thoughts about life.

Other times, we sent quick messages, like the one where I reminded him when CHAPS was taking place, making sure he'd be there.

He wrote back, *Nooo, I thought it was the week after! Won't miss it but will have to get there a day late because of a gig. Can't wait to see you.*

I'd tried and tried, but when it came to not caring about Max, I'd failed miserably.

∞∞∞

NOW: The Boy Next Door

I spend hours preparing for his arrival. I realise even as I am doing it that it's all kinds of messed up. The thought doesn't deter me. This is going to be the biggest disaster in the world. In the future, academics will study this situation at important universities, debating the causes and after-effects, and whether it could have been prevented in the first place.

There is no stopping me as I carefully choose my favourite clothes, the ones that flatter me the most. I do my makeup in that way that looks like I'm not wearing any at all but just happen to have naturally big eyes, long lashes and blush lips. By the time I've finished, I shimmer with effort, barely-there perfection and excitement.

What am I doing?

Max is coming to live in my flat. He's going to be in the room next door to me, so close that Tomas mistook my window for the one that will now be Max's.

It's never going to work. Never in a million, trillion years.

I put my makeup brush down.

Why am I doing this?

Max said he'd get here around eleven. At ten-thirty I'm hovering in the kitchen, twirling with overflowing energy. Out of habit, I turn on the tap to wash up, but I quickly realise that there are no dirty plates by the sink. With Louis away, me hardly ever home and Tilly a bit of a secret neat-freak, our flat has become a haven for hygiene. I wonder how that will change with Max living here. I told Louis and Tilly that he might be messier than me, but the truth is I don't really know. All I remember is that my stuff was everywhere, the times we stayed together overnight... I am not going to think about that. I'm not.

At ten past eleven, he's still not here, and I force myself to stop washing the only two mugs I managed to gather up. They're the cleanest mugs in the world, and I'm a mug for cleaning them so thoroughly. And for thinking that Max would show up at the time he said he would. And for caring about Max in the first place. I know this is doomed and I wish I'd never suggested it to Tilly, and she'd never agreed, and -

The doorbell rings.

I freeze.

Tilly appears from her room. "Is that him?" She does an impression of Louis's wry-brow raise. "Aren't you going to answer it?"

I'm stuck to the spot. "I..."

"He's your friend, isn't he?"

"Um..."

Tilly gives me a sideways glance. "No problem, fine, I'll get it."

I give one of the mugs another wash. You never know what germs could be lurking. In fact, I should probably get a new cloth and...

"Hi, Ciara."

Max is standing in my kitchen.

At least, I think it's him. If you took the Max I used to know and cleaned him up a lot, shaved his stubble, cut his rock-star hair and put him in respectable clothes...

What is he wearing? Is this really Max?

The smart trousers and shirt might not look like anything he would ever wear, but he's carrying a guitar and a backpack. The guitar case has stickers on it that spell 'Max' and a torn, old-looking one that advertises Four Part Cure, the name of his band. It's definitely him.

"Max. Er, hi."

"Hi."

We stare at each other.

His eyes are as dark as I remember, with a depth I could lose myself in. And I have done, in the past. But not now. Too much has changed. I'm not the girl he's known since we were seven years old. He's not the same boy, either. It's obvious with one glance.

This doesn't mean I can take my eyes off him.

Tilly glances back and forth between me and Max. "So, I'll... leave you to settle in, Max." She gives me a quizzical look. "Ciara, I'll be in my room. Let me know if you need any help."

She leaves us alone. Together.

"So..."

"So –"

We speak at the same time. I'm the one who continues. "Max, can I say something?"

"Sure." He runs a hand through his oddly short hair. It suits him.

"I... It's great to see you. Honestly, it is."

"It's great to see you too, Ciara." Those eyes. It's like he's drinking me in.

I shut mine for a second. I don't know how to behave. Should I apologise to him for what happened when we broke up? But the time for that has long passed, surely, and we have technically seen each other since and spoken on the phone without mentioning it. He's acting like everything's fine, anyway. So I'll go with that.

I take a deep breath. "It's just... thank you for taking the room. You're really helping out my flatmate. Louis – he's great. Maybe you'll meet him one day."

"Er, yeah. No problem. Thank *you*, really. This is going to be a big help for me."

"Great. But I'm really busy with work right now. It's... they sprang these possible redundancies on us and I'm trying to impress someone to save my job..." And for other reasons I decide not to mention. "So sorry if I don't see you much, or anything. While you're living here, I mean."

Max blinks. "Oh, OK. I understand."

"Well, so... I'll be in my room. If you need any help." I realise I'm echoing Tilly's words. I wish she hadn't left me with Max. I feel defenceless.

I try to slink away but I don't think I've ever felt more self-conscious in my life. I turn my back on him but can still feel his eyes on me, and it's like I've forgotten how to walk.

"Ciara?"

I stop and turn round. "Yes?"

"You, er... You haven't shown me where my room is? I mean, Louis's room?"

Oh right. "Sorry! Of course! It's this way." I point down the hallway. "The one next to mine."

"Which one is yours?" He picks up his backpack and slings his guitar strap onto his shoulder. "And I might need to know where the bathroom is at some point too? Maybe you could show me round a bit? Just quickly?"

Yes, that's what you're supposed to do when new people move in, isn't it? Tilly would have remembered. "Yeah, sure. Come with me."

In a few short strides he's by my side, and that's fine. He's a new flatmate who needs to be given a tour. It's not difficult. He could be a stranger. He's just anyone.

The flat's small and the tour doesn't take long. I point to the closed doors of my room and Tilly's room and then I briefly show him the bathroom before flinging open the final door. "And this is your room." I step inside and Max follows me.

I've never seen Louis's room look so tidy. He must have taken a massive suitcase with him to Paris. Everything he's left behind is tidied into neat piles and tucked into the two corners either side of the window, covered by see-through plastic sheets.

"Nice." Max puts his guitar case down, slings his backpack onto the bare mattress and looks around.

"I can, er, lend you bedding if you need it? I mean, you've been staying in hotels and stuff..."

"It's all right, I've got my whole life in there." He nods at the backpack. "I've been in a hostel, not a hotel. I had to take my own sheets. And sleep with my valuables chained to my arm."

I give a nervous laugh. "Well, I can't guarantee it, but you'll probably be safe here."

He smiles. "Thanks."

There's a silence.

This is so awkward. We've been friends since we were seven. How did things get so complicated?

☼

NOW: Tilly in Love

Having Max in the house makes me utterly twitchy. I'm worried about leaving my room in case it means having to talk to him. I decide on an early night, but I have trouble getting to sleep. Every time I get close to drifting off, I hear the low rumble of Max's voice in the kitchen, followed by Tilly's loud laughter. She's keeping me awake. I'll have to have words with her in the morning.

I remind myself that it's Saturday night. What am I turning into? The grumpy flatmate who complains about some chatting and enjoyment when we don't even have to be up early the next day?

In fact, why don't I just go and join in with them? If it was Louis and Tilly laughing it up in the kitchen, I'd want to know why, at least.

But I'm in my pyjamas and I feel uncomfortable just thinking about it. I could change, but what would I wear?

I'm being ridiculous and I know it.

I get up, find my ear buds, plug into my playlists and shut out the sound of my flatmates.

My plans for Sunday are pretty hermit-like as usual – catching up on sleep, sorting out my clothes for the week, getting a head start on some work stuff, which right now feels more important than ever. I usually wander around the flat freely while all this is going on, but today I'm holed up in my room, only leaving when I absolutely have to, and then scooting back as quickly as I can.

I'm dying to make myself a coffee, though. I listen out but I can't hear anyone in the kitchen. Max and Tilly are probably still sound asleep after being up all night talking. I remind myself it's good that they're getting on. It would be awful if they hated each other and had blazing rows or something, and Max had to move out. Louis would probably have to come home early and he'd never forgive us for not making things work out.

I creep furtively to the kitchen and turn on the tap to rinse out the coffee maker. The water spurts a bit and comes out brown, which happens sometimes in our street, probably because the builders across the way keep switching off the water supply. I leave the tap running to clear it and I start assembling the other equipment I need for my coffee.

I'm so absorbed in my thoughts and the sound of streaming water that I don't notice Tilly come in until she's standing right next to me.

"Argh!" I say, dropping the new pack of filters I was taking out of the cupboard. "Don't sneak up on me!"

She laughs. "As if. I'm hardly a tiny wispy thing. You can't exactly miss me!"

Tilly used to make these remarks about her size a lot, especially right after Dougal left her, but Louis and I worked hard to compliment them out of her. We weren't lying, either – who cares what size anyone is? And Tilly's gorgeous. I'm slightly disturbed to hear the return of these comments. Maybe Dougal has been in touch and stirred up old worries? I really hope not. Or maybe she's met someone new and it's making her self-conscious? If so, he'd better not turn out to be as awful as Dougal.

"Tilly, you're perfect and you know it," I remind her.

She smiles and yawns. "Perfection can only be achieved with a cup of coffee," she hints.

I laugh and pull out another mug. "At your service, Madame Tilly."

I locate the ground coffee and give it a shake. I love the smell so I usually waft the open pack around a bit before I use it.

Tilly stands there, looking like she wants to say something.

Eventually she clears her throat. "So... you and Max?" she says casually.

I don't look at her. "Huh?" I mean, how else can I answer that? It's not exactly a question.

"It's just... I sensed something between you yesterday. I know me and Louis were joking around before, but you always said he was nothing to you. I should have guessed, really, by the number of times you said it."

Oh no. I don't like this line of questioning.

"So is he an ex?" Tilly asks.

Why does everyone always ask me that?

"No." I feel instantly awful for lying to Tilly. I backtrack. "Well, kind of. We did sort of get together a long time ago. A really, really long time ago. But we've both moved on."

"OK," says Tilly. "Sorry to be nosy. I just wondered. I asked him, too, to be honest."

I struggle to keep my voice casual. "What did he say?"

She laughs. "Pretty much the same as you, complete with almost denying it at first."

Oh. My heart sinks.

"It must be weird to have an ex living in the room next door to you. I'm not sure I could do it," Tilly remarks.

I focus on the coffee making. "It's fine," I say. "It's over between us. It seriously was ages ago – we were kids, really."

Tilly hovers near me like she wants to ask something else.

"What's up?" I ask.

"It's just... are you really sure? That it's over, I mean?"

I force myself to look at her. "Yes," I say. Then I wonder if Tilly's questions are going beyond simple nosiness or concern for her flatmate. "Why?"

"Well, promise you won't say anything, but..." She lowers her voice and glances around, although if she's worried about Max overhearing, it's already a bit late. "We stayed up chatting last night..."

I know, I think.

Uh-oh, I think. A feeling floods through me. I recognise it but I don't want to label it. Because I'm pretty sure it's called 'dread', and I shouldn't be feeling it.

"And, well... I think he's lovely. Gorgeous, and such a good listener. Don't you think? I mean..." She giggles. "Obviously you can't answer that. Not if you had a bad breakup, or whatever." She puts her head in her hands. "I'm sorry. I'm being tactless."

"Did he say that?" I'm certain I didn't. "Did he say we had a bad breakup?"

"Not exactly. He said it was complicated. Isn't it always, though?" She thinks a bit. "Except in my most recent case, which was a simple best-friend-betrayal straight out of the Worst Boyfriend manual!"

"Dougal made a huge mistake," I say on cue, and it's the most honest thing I've said during this whole conversation so far.

"Yeah," Tilly agrees. "But I mean it when I say I'm more upset about Jess, long term. So, you know... I don't want to tread on your toes." She frowns. "You're my friend. I wouldn't want a man to get between us."

The coffee's ready. I pour it carefully into the two mugs I've prepared.

"So..." Tilly says.

I hand her the coffee and squeeze some brightness into my voice. "It's definitely over between me and Max. You should go for it, Tils."

She smiles. "Well, I don't know... I don't even know if he likes me!"

"Of course he likes you! You're fabulous," I say, relieved to say another thing I'm a hundred percent sure is the truth.

"Yeah, but he probably won't like me in *that* way. I mean, I doubt anything will ever happen. But I still would never be able to forgive myself if there was any chance I was doing a Jess, or even thinking about it. So I had to ask you."

I'm at the sink with my back to Tilly, so I can get away with screwing my eyes shut for a second.

This is a turn of events I hadn't even thought about. Could Max and Tilly get together... under my roof?

Of course they could. Why wouldn't they? It's their roof too. And it's like the situation with me and Chester – the usual rules about not dating someone from work, or someone you share a flat with, don't apply. Chester's leaving soon, and so is Max. They're both temporary. They both present opportunities to get together with someone, with less of the risk.

I'm glad I've reminded myself about Chester, who's the man I really have my heart set on right now. And I'm getting somewhere with him at last. He has even remembered my name several times! And as for Max and Tilly, well. I can deal with it. Why not? Of course I can.

I fight that feeling I don't want to call 'dread' because it's threatening to take me over. I turn back to Tilly with a sunny smile on my face.

"Honestly, please don't worry about it."

"Thanks, Ciara. So, I was thinking of suggesting a pub lunch today or something. What do you think? Maybe for all three of us?"

Despite everything I've just thought and said, I don't think I can continue this conversation right now – the 'should I, shouldn't I' of the start of a relationship. Maybe another time.

"Yeah, sounds great, but I can't make it. Sorry, I've got some really urgent stuff to do. Have a brilliant day!" I grip my coffee and rush back to my room.

☼

NOW: The Horror Project

I'm relieved to go to work on Monday, away from the tension of sharing a flat with Max. I've been avoiding him – and Tilly too, now – as much as possible. I've spent my weekend listening at the door of my room and darting out when I think they're not around. It's been a real pain.

I'm already counting the days until Louis comes back. I send him a quick text on the way to work just to see how he is, and he replies with: *All fine here. Tomas is busy but we'll always have Paris. How's the saxy one getting on in my room?*

I don't feel like replying to that, so I save it for later. I pull my entry card out of my pocket and blip my way into the Something For Everyone building, wondering how I'm going to survive for nearly three whole months. I pass the comfy looking sofa in the coffee room. Maybe I could sleep there instead? I could live at work and impress Chester with my ability to get into work before everyone else, including him. Though he probably gets in at six in the morning and I'd still be asleep on the sofa, which might not give out the right kind of signals.

I settle at my desk and wake my screen up with a sigh. The first thing I see is a message from Chester asking to see me, which has to be a good start to the week.

"Ah, Ciara," he says when I appear at his office door.

I shift from foot to foot. Why am I feeling so nervous? "I got your email. What can I do for you?"

A lot of men would be tempted to come out with some inappropriate banter at that point, but not Chester. He beckons me towards a seat and remains utterly professional as he explains that he's taking me off the main catalogue to give me time to focus on selling the entire contents of the scrap heap.

"We're thinking of a supplement which promotes the unwanted items."

Hmm, I think, who's *we*? Isn't that what I suggested all by myself? I let him continue anyway.

"It can be exclusive, for selected regulars who are known to snap up deals from our catalogues. Call it Scrap Heap Bargains or... something better than that."

"I'll think of something," I say. I'm not calling it Scrap Heap Bargains, that's for sure. There's clearly a reason this company employs copywriters. I nearly say that to Chester, to remind him not to include any of my team in his dreaded 'audit', but now is probably not the time. I'll just have to prove it to him.

"I have faith in you, Ciara," he says. His eyes linger on me a bit too long, but nothing I could complain to HR about. Which is probably just as well, seeing as I'm avoiding Tilly, and also she knows I'm secretly after Chester anyway.

"I have an interview this morning," Chester tells me. "Monique's team have finally found a suitable applicant for the role of my assistant. But I should be finished before lunch, so do stop by if I can help with anything. Or maybe..." He stares at his desk. "...grab a bite to eat with me, if you find yourself at a loose end? Purely in a professional capacity, of course," he adds in a rush. "There are business matters I'd like a chance to discuss with you."

Ooh! Excellent. I can safely say that Project Get Chester to Love Me is going swimmingly. I want to tell Louis and Tilly right now! Well, Louis, anyway.

"I'll bear that in mind," I say to him, cool as anything.

Back at my desk, once I've stopped congratulating myself, I make some notes about what I'm planning to do.

Steve eyes me from his desk. "They've given me your underwear," he says after a while. "To work on, I mean. Now you're officially on that new project."

"Oh. Sorry."

"No, it's fine. I've always wanted to try your knickers. You make them look like fun. But now that I've started, I'm less sure." He frowns. "I think I might prefer to avoid underwear altogether, to be honest."

I give him a look, but he doesn't hear himself. "For ventilation?" I can't resist asking.

"Huh? No, I mean I'm struggling with knickers. They're so fiddly – all those multipacks. But good for you. It's like a promotion, isn't it?"

"Not really," I say. "No extra money, or anything. I'm just trying something new to show Chester that he needs us. All of us."

Steve nods. "I hope it goes well."

"Thanks, Steve," I say. He's a sweetheart, really. I hope he'll be OK with covering my pants.

Once I've scribbled out my plan, I go to the store cupboard where the scrap heap is kept. The door only opens a tiny bit and I have to shove it as hard as I can and then ease myself through the tiny gap that's available. I have no idea how Louis managed this when he helped himself to the nude long-johns.

I feel about on the dark wall until I locate a switch. I flip it on and it flickers several times, lighting up the room in bursts.

The first thing I notice is that there's a strange-looking bra wedged under the door, which would explain why I couldn't get it open. I force it out and dangle it in front of me in the still-blinking light. It's a horror bra, made from twisted strands of metallic material that points dangerously outwards. It reminds me of the photos I've seen of eighties Madonna, a popstar who Mum used to complain to my sisters about because she was 'too mainstream', in Mum's world. I check on my phone. Apparently, Madonna first wore a bra like this in the year I was born and started an odd trend that never fully went away. Well, fair play to her. It looks painful. I chuck it onto the scrap heap before I kneel down to survey the scene, now that the light has finally stopped flickering.

It's a disaster zone. A lot of the clothes are still in their clear wallets, which at least will have kept them clean, under layers of plastic and dust. But the cards in the packaging show illustrations of really odd pieces of clothing – a grey cardigan with built-in fingerless gloves, a crop top that's more like a belt, a knitted bikini in rainbow colours. Then there are the clothes which have been tried on and sent back. They're also in their packaging but in a total mess – all scrunched up and partly hanging out like they're trying to escape.

And then there are the loose clothes, like the vintage Madonna bra. These are tangled together in a spooky mass of limbs and torsos. You can't even tell where one item ends and another begins.

What have I let myself in for?

I sink to a sitting position beside the mess of clothes and sigh.

Never mind my internal joke about sleeping at the office. I actually might have to do that if I want to get this to work within the timeframe I've set myself. The one that Chester's expecting from me.

Well, it's my wild mission to save my job and my entire department, one scrappy piece of clothing at a time.

I set my phone beside me and begin sorting, isolating items, taking pictures and making notes under the images. I will crack this task.

☼

NOW: Welcome To Something For Everyone

When I next glance at the time display above my camera app, I'm shocked to realise that a couple of hours have zoomed by. It's lunch time and I'm exhausted. I'm also skint, so there's no hope of a trip to one of Croydon's finest eateries for an overpriced sandwich.

I remember Chester's offer of lunch. Should I take him up on it? What would people in the office, people like Steve, think if they saw us eating together, even if I tell them it's strictly business? Is it too soon for me to do something so date-like anyway? I'm supposed to use this time to befriend him and wait until he's left for anything else. It's the professional way. I wish I could ask Tilly for advice, but that feels a bit hypocritical. I didn't give her any help at all the other day in the kitchen when she was asking me about Max.

I shove the pile of clothes out of the way – I'm starting to hate it already – and get to my feet. I'm wearing the unofficial copywriter uniform of black jeans, so I have to dust my knees off for ages. I wonder whether anyone ever cleans in this room, and whether the unpackaged items in the scrap heap need a wash before I attempt to sell them.

I head for my desk as I know my drawer contains several emergency cereal bars. That will have to do for today's lunch.

At the last minute and without really thinking about it, I swerve away from the area where Steve is sitting, working away, and instead head back to Chester's office. The best way to make decisions, I've decided, is not to think about them at all.

Unlike this morning, Chester's door is closed. I knock and turn the door knob without waiting for an answer. I've seen Scary Cathy do the same hundreds of times, so I don't see why I shouldn't.

I peer into the room and get the shock of my life. Max is there.

He's sitting opposite Chester, wearing a suit and giving off that weirdly neat, efficient vibe that he never used to have. He hasn't even turned round or seen me enter the room – he's so focused. This is grown-up Max. It's unnerving.

"Oh, hello," Chester says over Max's shoulder. "Just give me a minute – we've nearly finished the interview. And I think we've found our perfect candidate..." He smiles at Max. "But I mustn't get ahead of myself."

"Have I got the job?" Max asks, sounding self-deprecating, cheeky and charming all at once.

Chester laughs. "We'll be in touch! I have to put this officially through our Human Resources department." He lowers his voice to a conspiratorial whisper that I can hear clearly. "But between you, me and the gatepost –"

Wow, Chester does love his slightly odd stock phrases.

"The job is yours if you want it. Welcome to Something For Everyone, er..."

"Max," I say.

Max turns then and looks at me.

"Hey," he says.

"This is Ciara," Chester introduces me, apparently not having noticed the fact that I knew Max's name. "Ciara, this is... I'm so sorry." He leafs through the papers in front of him.

"Max," I repeat.

Max gives me a raised eyebrow look of humour and I reply similarly with my eyes. It's like an entire conversation. Something like: *"Is this guy for real?" "Yeah, you should try working here." "I think I'm going to. Help!" "I'm not helping you – you're on your own."*

We finish off this exchange by smiling at each other.

There's a reason we've always got on so well, me and Max. That connection we've always had – it's still there. Oh, shit.

Chester still doesn't seem to have heard me, or noticed my unspoken conversation with Max. He's busy sorting through his paperwork. "This is Max," he announces finally. "He comes highly recommended by one of Monique's assistants."

Tilly? She's got him a job? Seriously? I resist the urge to roll my eyes. What's Chester going to say when he finds out he's hired someone into a 'workplace relationship', when Tilly and Max get together?

"And if you'd like to find your way back to reception, er..." he says to Max, "a member of staff there will see you out."

Max stands and shakes Chester's hand before heading for the door.

"And now, Ciara," Chester says. "I'm afraid I can't do lunch today after all, but could we try tomorrow?"

Max turns back very briefly but I can't read the look on his face this time.

I can't believe Tilly has done this.

Now there's no escape. I'll have to avoid Max at work as well as at home.

☼

NOW: Stupid Scrap Heap

Within days, Max starts working for Chester, and a couple of weeks after that, I start to get over the awkwardness.

By this time, I've perfected my ability to avoid him at home and I've extended this skill to the workplace. I barely see him at Something For Everyone, apart from a few times when I go and see Chester for this elusive lunch he keeps inviting me to and never actually managing. Max is sometimes in Chester's office, or at his desk nearby. We say hello to each other when I see him, but nothing more. It's strictly business.

I'm firmly in the new habit of skipping the Flatmate Friday drinks nights, and it isn't that difficult. The first time I had a streaming cold, so it was an easy excuse and Tilly didn't even question me too much about it. She doesn't like germs at the best of times.

The second Friday, Tilly was a bit more insistent, but I pleaded tiredness and she let me get on with it. From the third Friday onwards, she doesn't even ask. I'm not planning on going back to Flatmate Friday chats until Louis comes back from Paris. I tell myself I'm doing Tilly a favour, anyway. She gets to have lots of alone time with Max. They deserve to be happy together. I'm happy for them.

Even though I've been hiding myself away from my flatmates, I've been keeping an ear out for Max and Tilly, and I haven't heard any evidence that anything has happened between them yet. The evenings are quiet, with Tilly and Max disappearing to their own rooms. But it's probably just a matter of time. I can't help remembering the first time Max and I got together properly, and it was definitely me who made the first move. Maybe I should warn Tilly – tell her to be a bit more forward with him. Max can be quite shy, but mostly I think it's because he's respectful. He wants to be sure. But once he is...

My mind drifts and it takes me ages to pull myself back to the job I'm supposed to doing. I've been working really hard but I'm still knee deep in the scrap heap, literally. I'm on the floor in the storeroom, surrounded by a mess of clothing.

It's taken me ages to get this far, partly because I keep getting pulled off the project to go back to my usual duties, which Steve doesn't seem to be coping with particularly well. "Nobody's as good with underwear as you are," Steve tells me when I drag myself back to my desk to help out. "You're a true knicker expert, Ciara."

I'm as flattered as I am frustrated. Maybe I should stop worrying about losing my job. I could be in high demand, always having a bright future in the description of intimate apparel.

Back on the scrap heap storeroom floor, I'm at least a week behind where I wanted to be and I'm seriously starting to regret starting this project. I work late every night, which is partly because I'm in no rush to go home, but mostly because there's so much to do.

I sort systematically through another tangled mass of clothes. I pull out three identical black dresses. They're pretty normal when viewed from the back and I wonder how they got here, until I notice that the plunge on the neckline at the front reaches almost to the hemline. Still, it's nothing some glamorous actress wouldn't wear at the Oscars, probably. That can be my angle in the description. I take a picture and make a note, folding the dresses into my sorted pile.

The next top I select is sleeveless and covered in sharp-edged sequins which actually attack me when I pick it up. A drop of blood forms on my finger followed by a twinge of pain.

"Shit!" I call out. All the sensible staff have gone home now, anyway. I can be as loud as I like. Stupid scrap heap!

There's a knock at the storeroom door. "Ciara?"

I must be overtired because my imagination's playing tricks on me. It sounds like Max.

The door opens tentatively.

It's him. It's Max, looking at me with concern.

"I was just leaving," he says. "I heard you on my way past, so..."

Trust him to be walking by at my time of pain. And to recognise it was me swearing.

"I hurt my finger," I explain. I hold up the wound for him to see. "My work is killing me slowly. Death by a thousand sequins."

The worry in his eyes quickly turns to laughter as he looks around. "Oh, I get it. Is this some kind of re-enactment of an old fairy tale? You have to spin this stuff into gold? And if you prick your finger, you'll sleep for a hundred years? Until a knight saves you?"

"Something like that." I laugh. God, I remember our games when we were seven. They often had similar plotlines, and I was the knight in the scenario as often as Max was, if not more. "But no knight can save me now," I state in a solemn voice. "I have to save myself. It is the way of the modern, realistic princess." I look at the pile of terrible clothes. "And I can. I will do this."

Max kneels down beside me. "Well, I wouldn't dream of trying to save you," he says. "Even if I could. But would you let me help?"

"No!" I watch as he picks up a pair of metallic purple shorts. "You've already done a day of work! You have a home to go to."

"Yeah," Max says, "and so do you. Same home." He smiles at me. "And if I help, we'll both get there quicker, won't we? So tell me what to do."

I sigh and get ready to insist that he goes, but I relent when I see how quickly he's mirroring what I'm doing before I've even had a chance to explain.

"It's just... sorting," I say. "Looking for treasure, or gold, like you said. I have to think of ways to sell this stuff, however unlikely it seems. The first step is making it look a bit less like... the scrap it is. But also I have to spin stories out of it for the sales pitch. Like this..." I pick up a woolly jumper with a sinister-looking bear on it. The artist obviously chose realism over cuteness, but possibly went a bit too far. The bear's jaws are terrifying. "Soft and warm as a teddy bear, but with added growl and bite!"

Max laughs and picks up a pair of bright tangerine-coloured slipper socks. "Nothing rhymes with orange slipper socks!"

"No, not like that!" I laugh. I put my head to one side thoughtfully. "Although, actually... That's quite good. I can almost see that on the page..." I take a pic on my phone and make a note. "OK, you can definitely stay."

Max looks pleased with himself.

Oh, help.

Why can't I shake this man out of my life?

I distract myself by waffling on at him for a while, explaining my ideas and plans for this project. He listens, following my instructions.

We fall into a comfortable silence, working away on the floor.

☼

CHAPS: Twenty-one Plus – part 1, 2011

Two obvious additions at the next CHAPS meeting were alcohol and proper adulthood.

The first one we'd been practising for a few years already, whenever possible. The second was a weird state we were supposed to understand, even though we felt like little kids half the time, and worldly-wise know-it-alls the other half.

Well, I did, anyway.

Amelia, who'd already behaved like a grown-up at the age of seven, didn't understand when I told her what I thought of being an adult.

"I don't know what you're talking about. I'm so-ooo glad our mothers don't have to come with us to these weeks away anymore." She took a long drag from a cigarette. She'd persuaded me to accompany her to the smoking area outside the stately home we were staying in – we'd graduated from holiday camps and theme parks to boring old houses with history before you could say 'key of the door'. Apparently we were in a hotel and management training centre used for conferences, so there would be paintballing and team-building exercises, which made me wish we could still go on rollercoasters after all. We'd escaped one of the exercises a few minutes earlier, and now we were sitting on a bench outside the hotel bar, drinking and smoking.

Well, Amelia was, anyway. I didn't understand the point of smoking but had a begrudging respect for people who could do it without coughing up a lung and wishing they'd bought chocolate cake as a treat instead.

Amelia puffed away and looked like she'd never consider chocolate cake in a million years. Obviously I hadn't seen her for a very long time, but I didn't think she'd been this thin at fourteen. She looked drawn and tired, her hair scraped back and her eyelids heavy. Or maybe her appearance was just a side-effect of being sophisticated and mature. Either way, I wasn't going to mention that I'd been a bit shocked when I first saw her again.

I took a large gulp from my wine glass. Now, drinking I understood. I'd just graduated from university and it was a skill I'd perfected during my time there.

"Hmm," I agreed with Amelia's comment about mothers. I'd moved back home a month ago and my parents were already treating me like a baby and driving me crazy.

"There is literally nothing I miss about being a child," Amelia said. "Come on, name one thing."

I could probably list hundreds. "Sweets?" I tried weakly.

"I never much liked them anyway, but still, if that's your poison, Cutie Ciara, all sweet and innocent..." She patted my arm.

I swatted her away. "As if!"

She laughed. "As I was saying, if that's what you want, then that's fine. You're a grown-up now. You can eat all the Haribo you want and no-one can stop you. Nobody can stop you doing anything... anything legal. And even illegal, sometimes..." She lapsed into a daydream as she puffed. I doubted she was fantasising about eating sweets.

"So how's life, anyway?" I summoned her back. "Any hot lovers?"

"I don't have much time for earthly pleasures," she drawled jokingly. "I might tell you about it later, if you're good." Her laugh was dry. "But you go first. Have you finally got over Max, your childhood sweetheart?" She smiled. "Remember at that disco when he held your hand? Never mind Haribo – that was sweetness overload. I developed five cavities just watching you!"

Oh, honestly, I was twenty-one years old. Why couldn't I control my blushing?

Amelia sat up straighter. "Ooh, I sense a development here! Tell me everything!"

My cheeks were on fire. "There's nothing much to tell. We only met once after the last CHAPS..."

"Go on, go on! This is better than any DVD box-set."

"It was at my friend's nineteenth in Brighton. Well, it was my nineteenth too. A house party. We invited you, too. Remember? I think you had some family wedding thing that day."

"Oh. Yes," she said distractedly. "Don't change the subject!"

"Well, it wasn't easy, but somehow we managed to invite Max too. And he turned up."

"Yes? Yes? What happened?"

"We kissed." My friend was looking so eager that I added, "A lot."

She faked a swoon. "Finally! Wait, is that all? No..." She waggled her eyebrows suggestively.

"Yeah, none of whatever you're implying with your funny face. Just kissing." I thought about that night a lot, even though I tried not to.

"Oh, well. It's a start. Was it amazing? Did he sweep you off your feet?"

Did he? I wouldn't put it like that. But just thinking about it...

"You don't need to answer that! Your face says it all. So what went wrong? Why no...?" She let her eyebrows do the talking.

I sighed. "No reason. We ran out of time, I suppose. He was leaving – going on tour. He's in a band. And I haven't seen him since. We've had a few text chats but... That's it, really."

Amelia didn't say anything. I studied her face in the dimming light of the sunset but I couldn't tell what she was thinking. All of a sudden, I really needed her opinion on this. She was a woman of the world – she'd know whether I was being ridiculous with the way I was clinging to the idea of me and Max. He was a boy – a man, now – who'd been touring faraway countries filled with adoring fans. And there must have been wild after-parties, women throwing themselves at him, all of that. How could he possibly still care about me?

And yet, I was sure he did. I was sure we had a connection, something special. Something nobody and nothing could tear apart.

I was a lovestruck fool.

I waited for a verdict from my worldly friend. It didn't take her long.

"Hang on to him," she said. "He makes you happy. You've no idea how much that's worth."

∞∞∞

CHAPS: Twenty-one Plus – part 2, 2011

Now that I was a mature twenty-something, I hadn't tried to read the guest list upside down or figure out where exactly Max would be staying. I felt cool and calm, like I could deal with anything life threw at me.

Of course, I also knew Max wouldn't be there on the first day. This meant a worry-free evening of many drinks with my old friend in the hotel bar, gently easing into the CHAPS week.

By the end of the first night, Amelia still hadn't got around to telling me much about her life and what she'd been up to for the past seven years, but in many ways we'd picked up right where we left off at the age of fourteen. We laughed hard together, and I admired her quips and the way she made everything fun. Some of the other CHAPS participants recognised her from last time and one or two of the men tried to flirt with her, but she gave them the brush-off in such a witty, polite way that nobody seemed to mind. Maybe she had a bit less energy than I remembered, but she oozed as much easy charisma.

It was pretty late when Amelia and I said good night went our separate ways, as we were staying on different floors. My room was gorgeously luxurious and contained a four-poster double bed with a white canopy floating above it and a selection of luxury cosmetics arranged by the gilded taps of the sink in the ensuite bathroom. This was the life. I silently thanked my mum for signing up to this project twenty-one years ago.

It should have been the best night's sleep of my life, in such comfortable surroundings, but instead I found I could barely sleep. My stomach fluttered with excitement at the thought of seeing Max again. So much for my new-found maturity – I might as well have been fourteen again.

The next day began with a wad of self-assessment questionnaires, delivered together with the room service continental breakfast I'd ordered the night before from the card in my room. I sat in bed with the papers, sipping fresh orange juice as I read through what was expected of me and trying to make a start on some answers.

The questions seemed harder this year. Was it because I was older? Did having graduated from uni mean that I was overthinking everything? Previously easy ratings – like "On a scale of 1 to 10, how optimistic do you feel about the future" – took me absolutely ages to answer. What did they mean by 'future'? Ten years' time, or tomorrow? What did they mean by 'optimistic'? Did I think I'd get a job and earn enough to pay back my student loan? Was that even the kind of thing I was supposed to aspire to with my 'optimism'? Or was it more day-to-day stuff? I wasn't sure. Everything felt a hundred times more complicated.

Everything including Amelia. She was in a strange mood when I saw her later, after I finally hauled myself out of bed to attend the team-building exercise that had been set up for us in the great hall. She stood at the back and withdrew into herself, refusing to participate as members of our group took it in turns to be blindfolded and follow instructions from the group that led them to 'treasure', or a box filled with chocolates. Whenever one of the confused CHAPS delegates made it anywhere near the chocolates, cheers and laughter erupted around the room. It was like an elaborate game of pin-the-tail-on-the-donkey and it was pretty silly, really. But I suppose it was the nearest a self-respecting twenty-one-year-old could get to children's party games.

I tried to get Amelia's attention, intending to roll my eyes with her and send silent messages of ironic enjoyment. But she didn't look in my direction, and she certainly didn't seem to be seeing the funny side of what was going on as another CHAPS member stumbled towards the chocolates to a chorus of shouted instructions.

I watched Amelia shrinking on the sidelines and longed for the days when we flirted with boys in a rollercoaster queue before whizzing up and down, screaming at the top of our lungs. I made a mental note to find out what was going on with her at the earliest opportunity. Maybe it was something serious.

My name was called, interrupting my thoughts about my friend. It was my turn to be blindfolded and spun round three times before people shouted instructions at me. I was instantly disorientated, unsure who to listen to in the cacophony of voices drifting my way. My hands moved instinctively to the eye mask, wanting to tear it off and get back to normality. What exactly had I signed up for?

A distinctive voice reached me from among the others, ringing out loud and clear. And posh and female. It was Amelia, I was sure of it. She'd always stood out among others, larger than life.

"Forward! Step forward, Ciara!"

It had to be Amelia. Who else here knew my name? Well, maybe one or two people, and I'd had my name read out a few minutes ago, of course. But still, I was sure it was her. It was good to hear her joining in, especially after what I'd seen earlier. I took some steps forward. They were tentative but I felt more confident now that I knew I had Amelia watching out for me.

"And again! Straight ahead! Keep going!"

"Don't listen to her! That's not right!" shouted another voice. I didn't recognise it.

Others joined in. "You're going the wrong way!" I didn't recognise them, either. Why should I listen to them over my close friend?

"That's it, Ciara. Two more steps. Keep moving," said the Amelia voice.

"No, no!"

"Yes, keep moving. Listen to me, Ciara. Straight forward!"

"No! Why would she say that?"

"Forward!"

"Why is she only listening to her? Listen to us! Stop, you're heading straight for –"

"Get out of the way!"

I crashed into something. A shock went through me. What was happening? I pulled at my blindfold and blinked as the light streamed back in.

I'd walked into a person, not a thing.

I'd walked right into Max.

He held his arms out, steadying me. "Hi, Key," he said.

"Where did you come from?" I was dazed.

"I just got here. They told me to join the activity."

"Why did she make you crash right into another person?" someone asked me, pointing at Amelia.

"Why didn't you get out of the way?" someone asked Max.

Out of the corner of my eye, I noticed Amelia slipping out of the room. I swear I saw her smile. I'd be having such a go at her about this later.

Max followed my eyes. "Amelia directed you to walk right into me?" he asked.

I shrugged. I suppose she had. "Mr Loud-Voice over there has a point, though. You didn't move out of the way."

He shifted closer. "You were walking towards me. Why would I stop you?"

He stared at me.

I stared back.

The people around us lost interest in me and my inability to follow instructions and reach chocolate treasure. A new name was announced, the blindfold was taken out of my hand and soon another CHAPS member was being shouted at.

Max and I shrunk back towards the door and didn't join in. He cast shy glances at me, which I knew because I was casting them at him. Our eyes kept connecting.

Eventually he whispered, "Should we sneak out?"

"We can leave any time we want to," I said in a normal voice. "It's the rules."

"You're right. Come on, then!"

He held his hand out to me and I took it.

As soon as we were outside the room, Max pulled me to the nearest wall. We collapsed against it, crashing together. He bent his head and I craned towards him until our lips met in a crushing, breath-taking kiss.

When we came up for air he stroked my face and whispered, "I've been dying to do that again. For so, so long."

I shut my eyes. "Me too," I mumbled.

We kissed again.

We only broke apart when the activity in the hall finished and people started streaming past us, some of them giving us eyebrow-raised second glances.

"I'd better unpack," Max said after a while. "I went straight to the activity before. I couldn't wait to... Can I see you later?"

"I'm out with Amelia tonight," I remembered. I'd made plans yesterday, when I still couldn't quite believe I'd ever see Max again. Or that maybe I'd see him and something would go wrong. But nothing had.

"I wouldn't dream of getting in your way," Max said, smiling.

I had a fleeting moment of wishing he would – of wanting to spend my evening, night, following morning, everything with him. But I told myself off. I'd made plans. Amelia came first.

Max brushed the side of my mouth with his thumb. He looked deep into my eyes. I wanted to push him back against the wall and kiss him senseless.

"I'll see you tomorrow, then?" he asked.

Tomorrow seemed so far away. "Sounds good," I replied.

I congratulated myself on having played it cool, even though I couldn't stop thinking about him for the rest of the day, evening, night...

∞∞∞

CHAPS: Twenty-one Plus – part 3, 2011

I wasn't sure how much to worry about Amelia. Once again, during our big night out, she carefully avoided any of my questions about her life. I knew there had to be a reason and I suspected it was something to do with a man – maybe some James Bond-type government employee, or someone posh and suit-wearing who worked in hedge fund management in Canary Wharf. I imagined that this man had stolen her heart with his charm and self-deprecating wit but then turned out to be a cad and a bounder, like most good-looking British actors in Hollywood rom-coms.

I was sure she'd tell me all about it sometime soon. We'd have a laugh and drink Martinis – shaken, but not stirred – before we made a plan for how she'd move on and never think about him again. I was already thinking of love-life advice to dispense to her: don't get too involved until you've see what he's like with your friends, judge him by how he treats you when you're pre-menstrual... That sort of thing. I'd talked about stuff like this a lot with Olive and Sophie, who were already on their second (Olive) or third (Sophie) serious life partner, so I had some good ideas for what to say to Amelia about her romantic life. I was almost looking forward to it.

The truth about Amelia took me completely by surprise.

She turned up at my door the following morning looking washed-out and sad, even though she was wearing a gorgeous black top that was probably by some big designer and looked amazing on her. Its sequins reflected the sun streaming through my window. But when the light danced on her face, it only made her look more grey.

Amelia's expression was stone. "Ciara, I have to tell you something."

I knew it was serious. I didn't smile like I normally would at the sight of Amelia. "Come in. Sit down. Please."

She perched on the padded seat by my dresser mirror, a grand, elaborate ornament that looked out of place in the twenty-first century.

"Tell me," I prompted. "Tell me everything."

She took a deep breath and stared at the ground. "I haven't been honest with you. I'm really sorry."

I wanted to put my arms around her, but I wasn't sure if she'd want that. She wasn't giving off 'please hug me' vibes. "It's OK. It doesn't matter. Tell me now."

She shut her eyes. "I've… There's a reason I haven't replied to your messages over the past few years."

I couldn't resist a quip. "You hate Facebook? You think social media is the spawn of the devil?"

She had actually said both these things a couple of days earlier, when I'd told her in detail about Olive and the way we'd contacted Max, so I didn't think it was a totally tasteless joke. But Amelia didn't laugh.

"Well, yes, it started off like that, so you're not wrong." She sighed. "After a while, I couldn't reply, though. I've been... ill."

"Ill?" My stomach dropped. I think I understood right away that she wasn't talking about catching flu or a stomach bug. "What's wrong? What happened?"

"I wish I knew." She gave a dry laugh. "It's ironic, really. I'm on this project all about happiness. And I always loved life – I did!" She swallowed hard. "But then I woke up one morning and... wished I hadn't woken up at all. I don't know how else to say it."

"Amelia..."

"I don't know if it was as sudden as I'm making it sound. I suppose before that I had ups and downs, like anyone. And I can be a bit of a drama queen, as you know." She tried to smile at me.

I tried to smile back.

"But this was bigger. I was fifteen and I felt like my life had just drained away. It was like a cloud hanging over my head... God, sorry about all the clichés. I don't know how else to describe it." She sniffed. "I can see how those phrases all got so popular, though."

"Black dog?" I mumble.

She nodded.

"God, Amelia. I'm so sorry."

She squeezed her eyes shut. "I'm sorry I didn't write to you. I wanted to. But I've been in and out of hospital, thanks to my parents' health insurance. So I missed a lot of the things you sent me, or got them really late. And the others... I couldn't reply to. When you're in the thick of it, it's hard to concentrate on anything. Anything except... darkness." She swallowed hard. "It's exhausting."

"What can I do?" I asked. I didn't know if it was right to ask, but I so desperately wanted to. "How can I help?"

"There's nothing you can do. I've just come to say goodbye."

"What?"

"I have to go." Her voice was flat. "They've suggested I should leave. The researchers."

"They've – what?" I was outraged. I started ranting. "They can't do that! Can they? I'm sure they can't! We should protest this. I'll walk out! We should all walk out. I'm not having this – they will not push my friend around!"

Amelia's expression didn't change. She was blank. "Ciara."

"Don't try to stop me! I mean it – I won't stand for it!"

"Ciara, I'm really touched. I am. Honestly." She didn't sound it, though. Her voice was devoid of emotion. "I love the way you care. But I don't. I don't care. At all. So it's OK. Do you see?"

"No. No!" I was still on the rampage.

"The thing is, they haven't kicked me out. They made the suggestion, and I decided to go. This is a project studying happiness. I've had depression for years now. I can't take part anymore."

I still didn't understand. "So they need to study you, don't they? They need to work out how to make you happy!"

"It doesn't work that way. It's not what their project is about. I belong in a different study, maybe. I need professional help, not a week pretending to enjoy being blind-folded and led to chocolate treasure." She sighed. "Don't you see? CHAPS isn't for me. The opposite of happiness is sadness, isn't it? It's temporary. You might be down but you wake up the next morning a bit chirpier. You cheer yourself up with music and laughter and friends. The opposite of happiness is not... nothingness. I feel nothing. I'm clinically unsuited to this study."

I still didn't get it. I refused to. "You're my friend," I said. I didn't care how soppy it sounded. I wanted her there. So of course she should be there. It felt that simple.

"You're such a sweetie, Ciara."

I groaned with frustration. "You keep saying things like that. Like you think I'm just being nice, or polite, or something. But I care. I genuinely care about you. Doesn't that help?"

There was a long silence.

I shut my eyes.

She didn't want to say 'no'. She didn't want to hurt my feelings.

But she was thinking it.

Instead of answering my question, Amelia asked, "You know what would make me happy?"

"What?" My heart was sinking further and further. She wasn't the girl I remembered from our teen years after all. If I was totally honest, she was making me nervous. Why couldn't she just... stop? Just go back to those fun, carefree days?

"It would make me happy if you and Max got together. Properly together. If you stayed together. It might restore my faith in humans." She laughed, but there was no humour in the sound. I didn't know whether she was joking or not.

"Who knows what will happen with me and Max?" I asked, trying to lighten the mood. This conversation wasn't fun at all. "We're hopeless, aren't we?"

"Hopelessly in love with each other. It's so obvious. And I want this for you, but also for me. I want to believe it's possible. Happiness." Amelia sighed. "We've been unnaturally focused on it, don't you think? I wonder how it has affected us. I wonder what it has done to us?"

"What do you mean?" I asked. She was talking quickly, darting from one sentence to another.

"This project. From a really early age, I was filling in questionnaires with my mum about everything I did. I was a child, rating the soft play facilities out of ten for the way they made me feel."

It was weird how I didn't remember these details at all. Was it because of a difference in our parenting? Had my mum hidden the questions from me, protected me, while

Amelia's mum had put pressure on her to answer? To give a 'right' answer, if I knew Penelope. Or was I being unfair? I knew I was. Depression was an illness. It wasn't caused by an overly pressuring parent who seemed to want you to be someone you weren't.

I bet Penelope hadn't helped, though.

"Mum did everything she could for me," Amelia said, as if she'd been following my thoughts. "She only wanted what was best for me. She did tell me there were no right and wrong answers – she read it off the instructions. But I knew she was lying. She used to suggest that I rated certain things a bit higher than my first instinct told me. Sometimes I thought she saw it as a test I had to pass, a bit like all those exams at school, where anything lower than an A* wasn't good enough." Amelia had sped up so much now that it was hard to keep up with her. "But she was only trying to help. She's paid for so much therapy for me, and private hospitals and treatments I should probably appreciate more. I know I should. I'm a crap daughter as well as a fuck-up in every other way."

I didn't know if it was the right thing to say but I couldn't stop myself. "You're not! Stop talking about yourself like that! You've always been amazing. I've admired you for years!"

"You really are the sweetest, Ciara. That's been the best thing about coming here – seeing you again. So I'm not sorry we lied."

"You lied?"

"Mum lied on the forms. You know the interim questionnaires we get, checking up on our situation and throwing in little disclaimers and quick happiness tests?"

"Yes." We did hear from CHAPS every now and then, with the emphasis that filling in the forms was optional. I always sent them back, though. They weren't exactly time-consuming.

"Well, Mum was filling them in for me, pretending I was the lightest, breeziest teenager in the world, even if I hadn't got out of bed for three weeks."

"She lied on the forms?"

"She lied everywhere. She hid what was going on from everyone."

"She didn't return my mum's calls," I said, the memory dawning on me.

"She avoided people whenever she could. If she couldn't, she lied. Even Dad thought I'd just been getting flu a lot, or whatever, any time he reappeared from Dubai for a day or two and found me lying in bed. It went on for ages. I mean, he knows now, of course. She had to tell him in the end, when they needed to pay for my therapy and all the other stuff."

Wow. "She lied to your dad about you?"

"They barely see each other. I think he has another woman in Dubai. They're not exactly happily married. But I'm telling you, Ciara. She lies to everyone. The worst thing is..." Amelia gulped. "The worst thing is that she lies to herself!"

The pain was written all over her face. I desperately wished I could help her.

"She's ashamed of me. She can't stand me."

Bloody Penelope. "She can't stand your illness, maybe. Not you."

Amelia's eyes filled with tears. "I don't know. I don't know what's real anymore, Ciara. I was on all this medication for ages, and it made me feel calmer, I suppose. But I hated taking it. I didn't feel like myself anymore, you know? So I stopped, and now I don't know what to do. But I know I have to go." She looked at my suitcase on the floor, all messy with my scruffy clothes pouring out of it like some kind of art installation. I wondered if hers was neatly packed on the bed. "I have to go."

Oh no, I was going to cry too. I struggled to swallow back my tears in case it made things worse for her. "Listen, you know where I am online, yeah? You've been getting at least some of my messages?"

"Yes."

"Well, please write to me. Tell me everything. It doesn't matter what it is. You don't have to pretend you're OK. Just anything." I thought quickly. "Can I borrow your phone?"

She fished it out of her bag and handed it to me. It was the latest iPhone, the kind I've always wished I owned. "I've always wanted one of these," I said.

"Keep it," she replied.

I laughed, pleased that she was joking with me, at least. "Yeah, right! Don't worry, I've got a degree now and I'm super-employable," I joked back. "I'll get my own in about... twenty years." I'd fiddled with the demo model often enough in Carphone Warehouse to know what to do, so I did it and handed the phone back to her. "There. Now I'm a favourite in your contacts. Phone me or text me anytime. I mean it. I expect to receive texts from you and I don't care what they say. Just please, please get in touch."

"Ciara..." Her tears had dried up and her voice was flat again. "I don't deserve you."

"Bollocks. You do. I'm awesome-sauce, but so are you."

She gave me the tiniest smile. "So will you do anything for me?"

"Anything," I promised. Then I read the expression on her face. She'd gone from flat to mischievous in ten seconds. "Whoa! Wait a minute. Are you going to ask me to do specific lewd things with Max?"

"Lewd! Yes, definitely. I love that word," she said. "You know me so well." But she added, "Just do whatever makes you happy. Then I can be happy for you."

∞∞∞

CHAPS: Twenty-one Plus – part 4, 2011

Amelia left and I was summoned to see the hotel manager, both in the same afternoon.

I was already used to visiting researchers in their rented conference rooms for CHAPS-related interviews that week, but seeing the hotel manager was new. I wasn't sure whether to be nervous – maybe they'd want me to apologise for the mess in my room, or something? I'd stayed in a few Premier Inns with my family and been equally messy without any problem, but who knew with a five-star hotel? I half wished my mum was with me after all. She'd protect me from the scary manager.

The man leafed through some paperwork. I couldn't see what was scrawled across the top, but I imagined it was something like: 'Messiest guest: Ciara Ryan'.

He lowered his glasses and looked at me. "You're a friend of Amelia Montague-Brown, is that right?"

"Um... yes?" I hoped I was supposed to admit it. What did the state of my room have to do with Amelia?

"I have a message to pass to you from Ms Montague-Brown."

"A message? But I spoke to her a few hours ago." I glanced at my phone but there was nothing from Amelia.

"I see. All the same, she has asked me to pass a message on to you." His smile got nowhere near his eyes, but at least he tried. He cleared his throat. "Ms Montague-Brown would like me to inform you that she has booked a room for you here, for the week following your conference."

"She's... done what?"

"Reserved a room. For you and..." He ran his finger down the paper. "Mr Massimo Renzo."

"Max? No way! What?" I babbled. "Amelia has got a room for me and Max? She's crazy!" I realised what I'd said and backtracked immediately. "I mean, please could you repeat that? Are you joking?"

"No, Ms Ryan. The room is booked." He regarded me coolly. "You don't have to take it, of course. But it's been paid in full and there's no, ahem, refund available. We did make that clear to Ms Montague-Brown, but she insisted she wanted to proceed."

I pictured myself calling Amelia, telling her off. Laughing at what she'd done. She had more money than sense, that girl! It was Amelia all over. When we were fourteen, she'd told me so many stories of sneaking out of her private school grounds and visiting the local shops to buy treats for all her friends.

I told myself it was a good sign. Amelia might be struggling, but she still had her naughty side. She'd be laughing about this, her obvious attempt to throw Max and me together.

"No, it's OK," I said to the man. "I'll take it. I could do with an extra week away from home." I nearly added something about my parents being annoying and how hard it was to live at home again after uni, but I sensed the snooty manager wouldn't understand or care.

I wondered what Max would say.

***

Max couldn't believe it either. "She's done what?"

"Booked us a room. Together. For a week after CHAPS is finished. I'm not sure she'd want me to tell you much more but... Basically, she's happy for us. She wants us to be together."

Max looked sceptical. "She's never even liked me."

"She likes *us*! Me and you together," I tried to explain, though it was difficult when I didn't fully understand it myself. "She wants us to be happy."

He frowned. "It's weird, Key."

"I know." He was right. "We don't have to take it. I'm sure you have somewhere to be, anyway. After this is over, I mean." Max always had somewhere to be.

He looked into the distance. "I'm supposed to visit Carol."

"Well, then. Say hello to your mum from me. Don't worry about it."

"I'd rather stay here with you."

He kissed me for so long that I forgot what we'd even been talking about.

CHAPS finished and all the other cohort members left. Max and I stayed. For most of the past week, we'd been spending every possible minute together during the days and evenings, but still going back to our own rooms at night. I didn't know why but it was always his idea. We'd walk around the grounds, stopping to kiss in quiet corners, but whenever I contemplated inviting him back to my room he'd say he was tired and we'd end up going our separate ways. It seemed like he wanted to take things slowly for some reason.

But now we were supposed to be sharing a room and he'd have nowhere to go. Butterflies danced in my stomach at the thought of it.

We moved to another part of the hotel, into the room Amelia had booked for us. It turned out to be some kind of luxury suite with a lounge area containing a sofa. I hoped Max wouldn't announce he was sleeping there.

Max's small backpack and my messy suitcase were swamped by the vast, empty space. Even when I made my usual half-hearted attempt to unpack, my mess barely registered in the immaculate tidiness of the room. There was a minibar but we were scared to touch the little bottles in it in case we couldn't afford to pay for them later. We went downstairs instead. I bought Max a drink and he bought me one back. We chatted, his arm slung around me in the hotel bar.

With the structure of CHAPS gone, we didn't know what to do with ourselves.

So we went to our new room, sat on the bed, like we'd done in Olive's boxroom, and kissed. A lot. So much that, before long, I was reaching under Max's t-shirt and pulling him closer, pushing against his hard body.

He mirrored my actions, his hand caressing my sides under my top, toying with the edges of my bra strap until I moaned, "Don't stop."

He froze as if he'd only just realised where this was going.

He moved away.

I managed not to groan in frustration.

"What's wrong?" I asked him. I was out of breath and my voice was thick with longing.

Max ran a hand through his hair.

"Is it about Amelia getting us this room?" I still wasn't too sure how I felt about it, to be honest. I'd sent her texts to thank her, I'd offered to pay her back in instalments and I'd also told her to ask for her money back, despite what the manager had said, because there was something iffy about what she'd done. I hadn't heard back from her yet.

"No," Max replied. "Though I still think it's weird. But I'm glad. Because it's amazing, being with you, with no interruptions. And…" He kissed me deeply. "This."

I had to agree. "So why can't we…? Don't you want to…?"

Max hesitated. "It's just that… Um, I haven't exactly done this all that much…"

Was he saying what I thought he was saying? It seemed unlikely. "But you were on tour! In a band!"

"On tour I was so tired that if I went to bed, I went straight to sleep. I mean, not always. But mostly I didn't have much time for..."

I waited, not quite believing what I was hearing.

"It's just that I think you probably have a lot more, um... experience than me. And I want to get this right."

So he did mean what I thought he meant. I sat up straighter. "Oh my god, Max, how sexist is that?"

"What?"

"Are you saying... Just because I've had sex with other men..."

Max looked horrified. "No! No, all I mean is... You're all... expert and stuff. And I'm... less so."

"I wouldn't say I was that much of an expert," I admitted. "Though there wouldn't be anything wrong with it if I was."

"Of course not! I didn't mean that!" He put his head in his hands and sunk heavily back onto the bed. "This is going all wrong. I give up!"

I lay down next to him. "No, it's not." I whispered into his ear. "Please don't give up."

He looked at me. "I'm sorry. I'm just feeling the pressure. It's... it's huge."

"Oh, huge, is it?" I couldn't help teasing him. I put on a silly voice. "You worried I can't handle it?"

He smiled. "Ciara, please shut up. You know what I mean."

"Not really. Because there's nothing to worry about. No pressure. You don't have to do anything you don't want to."

"Oh..." His voice caught in his throat, low and sexy. "I *want* to."

My stomach flipped. "OK, good." I reached for his hand. "So then you just need to take your mind off the worry. Think about something else. Like when we were seven and you needed to climb down in the play centre. Remember?"

He lowered his eyelids. "Course I remember."

"So do that."

He shook his head. "It won't work."

"Why not?"

He didn't answer.

I prompted him. "What did you think about that day to take your mind off your fear?"

"You really want to know?"

"Yes," I encouraged him.

"OK, then. I'll tell you." His eyes met mine. "I thought about *you*." He touched my hair, ran his fingers through the ends. "I thought you were the bravest, most intriguing person I'd ever met. And also really pretty."

"Pretty?"

"And brave and intriguing. But yeah – pretty. Give me a break, I was seven. Now I know you're beautiful." He shrugged like it was just a fact. "And ever since, whenever I lose my nerve, I think of you. So, you see, I'm stuck. What do I think about now?"

Oh, wow. "You still think about me." I stroked my hands up his body, lifting his t-shirt, touching his skin, holding him close. "Think about *us*. We're in this together. We won't fall."

He kissed me again, stirring over me with a passion that nearly killed me. I'd been waiting for this for so long. Nothing got in our way this time. No buzzing phones, no waiting taxis, no doubts. Just me and Max, together at last.

And maybe I was wrong to promise, because it did feel like falling. We tumbled, both of us, for the longest time. Freefall from a great height, spinning and floating. Dizzying. And it felt amazing.

For the rest of that magical week, we did it again whenever we could, finding new ways to lift each other to terrific peaks. There were days when we barely left the room. We switched off our phones. We forgot about the rest of the world. If I'd had questionnaires to fill in they would have been the easiest ever, because my happiness rating was off the scale. Tens all round. Hundreds, even, if that was an option.

I was in a bubble with Max, floating and dancing on the air.

I should have known, really.

Bubbles aren't exactly famous for their non-bursting qualities.

∞∞∞

CHAPS: Twenty-one Plus – part 5, 2011

The news reached Max first. He woke up before me and, as he described later, tripped over my trailing charger cable on the way to the bathroom, nearly knocking my phone off the shelf where I'd propped it up. The hotel rooms must have been designed in times when not everyone needed a plug point by their beds, and my phone was anchored badly to the nearest one I could find. I'd switched my phone on the night before, after I'd found it lying on the floor, out of charge and dead. I didn't really want to let the world back in, but it was nearly the end of the week and it had to happen sometime, I supposed. I plugged my phone in, propped it up, turned it on, turned to Max and forgot about it.

Max told me later that he hadn't meant to read the message. He was just moving my phone back to safety, to stop it crashing to the ground, even though it was carpeted. He knew how attached I was to my new smartphone. It wasn't as state-of-the-art as Amelia's but I loved it and I'd customised it and everything.

But when Max picked up my phone, he accidentally touched a button that displayed my latest message at the top of the screen. It was already mid-morning but we'd been sleeping so soundly that neither of us had heard any alerts. He glanced at it, did a double-take and looked again in disbelief. He wanted to let me sleep but he agonised over it and decided I needed to know what he'd seen. He unplugged my now-charged phone and clung on to it as he got back into bed and gently touched my shoulder.

"Ciara." His voice broke into my sleep. I'd been on some kind of outdoor activity weekend with Max, launching ourselves down a zipwire into a ball pool and... My dream was already fading.

I turned to snuggle against him. "Hmm," I said, warm and happy about waking up next to Max. It would never get old. It was the stuff that dreams were made of.

I realised he wasn't lying next to me. Instead he was leaning over me, holding my phone and looking at me with concern.

"Ciara, you have to see this." His voice sounded weird. "I'm so sorry."

I sat up so suddenly that I hit my head on the fancy headboard. I barely registered the pain. A cold wave of fear washed over me. "What? What's happened? What's wrong?" At the back of my mind, I thought, *are you leaving?* Because that was still my fear with Max, even if I didn't admit it to myself. We'd been having the most amazing time but a small part of me couldn't help wondering when it would be over, when he'd walk out of my life again.

"Your phone – I saw your message, I didn't mean to but..." He explained about the tripping over and everything. I barely took in his words. "Here." He handed me the phone and shifted away from me as I looked, trying to give me space.

The text said: *Hello, I am Amelia Montague-Brown's father and I'm afraid I have some bad news. I'm sorry to say that Amelia has passed away after a battle with serious illness. She is now at peace. She provided a list of numbers to contact and you are among them. Please contact me for funeral arrangements should you wish. Regards, Hugh Montague-Brown.*

I threw the phone away from me as hard as I could. It landed unsatisfyingly on the soft duvet at the end of the bed. I nudged it to the floor with my foot. It could smash for all I cared.

"Ciara..." Max went to put his arms around me.

"No," I said, shrugging him off. "No, it's OK. It's a joke. A stupid joke. I don't believe it."

"It's kind of... a really odd joke, don't you think?" he said gently.

"Who writes 'regards' in a text?"

Max didn't reply.

"It's Amelia messing around," I stated firmly. "That's all it is. She's so annoying. I'll call her."

"Ciara, I'm not sure."

"Get my phone!" I barked at him. "I need my phone!"

He walked silently around the bed, retrieved it from the floor and handed it back to me.

The message was from an unknown number, but that was probably part of the prank. Amelia had organised it somehow. Maybe I'd laugh about this with her one day. Right now I was furious with her. Did she seriously think that message was funny? Was her dad even called Hugh or had she just picked that as the kind of name I'd believe her dad would have? Penelope and Hugh Montague-Brown. Even that sounded like a bad joke.

I scrolled through my texts. Before this joke one, there were two from Amelia's number, from a few days ago. So I was right! One said: *Are you there?* The other, sent about an hour later, said: *Don't worry, be happy, love you.*

My next message was the fake one, the one Max had just shown me.

I found Amelia in my contacts and pressed the call button angrily. It rang forever. Max stood at the foot of the bed, his expression filled with annoying concern. I glowered at him.

I was about to give up and throw my phone across the room when the line crackled. A voice – a posh man – said, "Hugh Montague-Brown speaking."

What the hell? "Can I speak to Amelia please? Tell her it's her friend Ciara from CHAPS. Tell her it's not –" I wanted to say 'funny', but something about the pause at the other end of the line made me stop.

"Ciara?" The voice sounded officious yet dazed, like a sleepy high court judge. "Are you Ciara Ryan? Did you not receive a message from me?" Another pause. "This is dreadful. Utterly dreadful. I'm afraid have to tell you some tragic news."

"No," I said. "No."

It was as if he hadn't heard me. "Amelia passed away three days ago. It was... the result of her illness."

"What? How?"

"It was... I'm afraid... Well, it was a carefully calculated overdose."

What a strange choice of words, I thought. Almost like we should be admiring the care she'd taken and the calculation skills she'd displayed.

"I've been trying to contact Amelia's friends as she... requested. Amelia's note expressly asked that I should send you a text message, though I must say it feels barbaric to hear such news in this way. I have her phone here so I could obtain your number... which you know, of course, as I'm speaking to you on it now. I do... I do apologise. Were you close?"

I couldn't reply. If this was really her father on the line, why didn't he already know the answer to that? Had he ever even heard of me before? Did he know anything about his daughter's life? I wasn't just angry with him. I was incandescent. I wanted to rage at the entire Montague-Brown family. Would Penelope say we were close? Probably not. Were we 'close'? Amelia was my friend. Did it matter? She was my friend and I wanted to speak to her. If this man wouldn't let me, I needed a second opinion. "Can I speak to Penelope?"

"I'm afraid... It's not a good time. As I'm sure you'll appreciate. She's quite... devastated. As are we all. I flew straight back into Aldenham to help in any way I can." I remembered what Amelia had said about him living in Dubai and barely seeing her. "I can pass on your regards." Hugh's voice, relatively strong until this point, wavered. "It's a terrible business. Terrible. I can't... I'm awfully sorry. I'm afraid I can't continue this call at the present time." He hung up.

I stared at my phone. I didn't feel like throwing it anymore. Instead, I ran to the bathroom and threw up.

∞∞∞

CHAPS: Twenty-one Plus – part 6, 2011

When I came out of the bathroom, Max was waiting for me.

"Ciara?" He moved towards me. "Can I help?"

I let out an enormous wail that racked my whole body.

Max wrapped his arms around me and held me, and I let him. I sobbed into his shoulder and clung to him. He stroked my hair and whispered, "I'm sorry. I'm so sorry." A few minutes later he added to that with, "I didn't even realise she was ill."

"Depression," I stated flatly. "Suicide." The word made me tremble. Nobody had said it yet. Hugh Montague-Brown certainly hadn't mentioned it in his speech about careful calculations.

Max tightened his hold on me. "Oh my god," he whispered. "I had no idea."

It was stupid, the way nobody knew. It was pathetic, the way I'd only found out myself a few days ago. Why hadn't it been part of the updates that Penelope used to give my mum, the ones where Amelia passed every exam she took, rode horses and won medals, or whatever? It was beyond ridiculous that Amelia's father had used the language of terminal cancer in his text. *A battle with a serious illness*? What the fuck was that? Why hadn't Amelia been properly armed before she went into battle? If the illness was so serious, why had nobody even mentioned it?

It was stupid. It was all fucking stupid and I hated it.

And Max was there and trying to comfort me, but it was his fault too. It was his fault I'd been so distracted this week. We should never have accepted this hotel room from her in the first place. Even in the haze of my earliest grief, I knew I'd never forgive myself for that. When the manager told me about the room she'd booked, I should have rung Amelia immediately, instead of sending her a few idle thank-you texts. I should have kept ringing and ringing until she answered, and I should have demanded to see her. I should have said, "Why are you buying me this over-the-top present? You weren't joking about me keeping your phone, were you? I won't stop asking until you answer me, and then I'm telling everybody about this, and somebody is going to help you. And I'm not leaving you alone for a second until that happens."

But I didn't do any of that, and this happened. It was all my fault.

And Max's fault. I would never have taken my eye off Amelia if I hadn't wanted him so much, if I hadn't ached to make things work with him. It was his fault I'd let my phone die – after what had happened at Olive's house, with his phone buzzing every two seconds, I'd been happy to let our phones disappear from our lives. It was his fault I'd missed Amelia's texts. And while I'd been in seventh heaven with Max, Amelia had been going through hell.

I pulled away from Max. "I shouldn't have let her go."

His expression filled with understanding. He always understood me. At that moment, it was intensely irritating. "It's not your fault, Ciara."

I didn't believe him. He was lying. He was trying to make me feel better when I'd never, ever feel OK, ever again.

I didn't want him near me.

He tried to hug me again but I shoved him away.

He persisted with his understanding. "I'll go. I'll give you some space."

"Go. You're always going anyway. And never come back!"

"Ciara..."

"I mean it. Actually, no." The rage had hit me again. "Don't go. You stay."

A flicker of relief crossed his face.

I grabbed my suitcase and flung it violently onto the bed. Some clothes flew out. "You stay, and I'll go. This time, *I* will leave *you*!" I threw my clothes back into the case. Then I rampaged about picking up my toothbrush, cosmetics and anything else I'd left lying around, launching them at my suitcase. I marched into the bathroom with some of my clothes and emerged dressed, warrior-like.

Max stood by helplessly. "Ciara, please. I know it's hard. I do, honestly. But, listen –"

"No!" I snapped my suitcase shut. "I never want to see you again!"

"I'll call you in a few days…"

"Don't call! Don't text! Ever! I mean it!" I swung the door open and stormed out of the room, calling behind me. "And don't follow me!"

I managed to get myself together enough to ask the receptionist for a taxi. I waited outside the hotel for its arrival, half expecting Max to appear and try to talk me out of my rage, but he didn't. It wouldn't have worked anyway.

I'd let my friend down in the worst possible way and it was because of Max, and I would never forgive him. I would never forgive myself.

***

I attended Amelia's funeral with my mother, who couldn't believe what had happened. "She was so full of life," she kept saying to anyone and everyone. I knew that. I knew it more than my mum did. My mum barely knew her. *Her* mum barely knew her!

Penelope's face was pale and stricken. She'd turned completely grey and she didn't come close to smiling even once, even when people I didn't know tried to share happy memories of Amelia with her. When Mum and I said goodbye to her, she gave me a confused look, as if she couldn't quite place me.

"So young," she said. I think she was talking about Amelia, but she might have meant me. I felt ancient, though. I had aged a thousand years in the past few days. And now I would keep growing older than my friend would ever be. She'd miss the latest fashion trends and dance movies, and the world would keep turning, moving and changing in ways she'd never know.

Another wave of guilt washed over me. What was I doing here, hanging around with Amelia's parents without her? It didn't make any sense.

Mum took my arm as we walked back to the car. On the drive home, she said, "I love you, you know, Ciara." Mum rarely said things like that. If she did, we usually made a joke about it. But neither of us felt like joking that day. Mum had been so quiet around Penelope that I almost wished we were back at CHAPS at the age of fourteen, with me and Amelia rolling our eyes at our parents. I think Mum and I were both feeling it at that point: survivor's guilt. I read about it a lot in the years that followed.

Not long after I stormed out of the hotel, Max tried to call me, despite my instructions. I refused to answer. He tried again a few hundred times. I turned my ringer off. He texted me a lot, and then, over time, less frequently. His messages sounded patient, then frustrated, then heartbroken. At first I read the texts even though I never replied. Then I started deleting them without even glancing at them. Eventually, the phone calls and text messages dwindled. I still got the odd one, but deleting them had become a habit.

Months passed, then years. I thought a lot about everything that had happened. I read articles online, frantically trying to make sense of it, desperately trying to feel less guilty. Nothing worked. Olive and Sophie tried to help me, in their own ways, but I found it hard to talk about it, beyond the obvious, trite phrases. *It was a shame, a terrible waste, so sad, she was so young...* Even to my oldest friends, I couldn't bring myself to say anything more meaningful, more real. I squashed my feelings down and pretended everything was fine. I don't think my friends believed me but there was nothing they could say to change anything. After a while, they stopped trying. They treated me more gently for a long time, but eventually that wore off too. When I realised, I was relieved. I didn't deserve their kid gloves.

As time went on, I reached a point where I could think about Amelia without being overwhelmed by grief, sadness, anger and guilt, guilt, guilt. Or at least not all of those emotions, all of the time. But when I thought about Max, when I remembered how happy we'd been, it felt like looking at someone else's life. Some other version of me, someone I used to know. Someone I'd lost touch with. Like Hannah, our old friend, the one who'd prompted me to shut up about Amelia.

I realised I hadn't been fair to Max. I tried to put myself in his shoes. If things had been the other way around, I don't think I would have sent so many messages, been so patient. I hadn't given him a chance, but it was too late now. I supposed I'd treated him pretty badly. Max probably hated me. I understood. It was fair enough.

I knew I'd probably see him again, if we both went to the next CHAPS meeting. But I was sure I could safely ignore him and get through the week. Then that would be it for another seven years, by which time we'd have moved on even more. And that was fine.

When it came to Max, I felt nothing. I felt numb.

∞∞∞

CHAPS: Twenty-one Plus – part 7, 2015

Years later, I bumped into Max at St Pancras Station, of all places. He was with a petite blonde girl who was extremely pretty. They were laughing, carefree, with backpacks and guitar cases weighing them down as they studied the departure board. They looked scruffy and comfortable, like they'd been travelling for a long time.

I was with someone too. I'd been seeing a man called Henry, a friend of a friend from work, for a couple of months. We'd met and got together the old-fashioned way, at this friend's birthday night in a pub. Unlike Sophie and Olive's latest partners, who they'd met online or through dating apps.

On a whim, Henry had decided to whisk me to Brussels for the weekend for no particular reason. I didn't want to sound ungrateful, but I'd had a stressful week at work and I'd have probably preferred a quiet night in with a takeaway and an old movie. I also wasn't overly bothered about Henry in any case, and I was fairly sure we wouldn't be staying together much longer. I was a bit worried that the Brussels trip would make him think things were more serious than they actually were, but

I didn't want to hurt his feelings so I'd gone along with it.

When I noticed Max at the station, a jolt of recognition shook right through me. It felt like a bolt of lightning hitting my stomach. I stared, thinking it couldn't possibly be him.

Maybe he sensed my gaze, because he looked up and right into my eyes. I went hot and cold all over.

It was him. It was Max.

He approached me, the blonde girl following him with a puzzled smile on her face.

"Ciara," he said. "Oh, wow. How are you?"

"I'm…" I didn't know the answer so I went for the default. "I'm fine."

"Oh, good," he said. "That's great. This is… this is Manon. Manon – Ciara."

"Hi," said Manon with a warm smile.

"Hi." I felt dazed. I remembered Henry. "Er, and this is Henry."

"Hello," everyone said. Some of us repeated it more than once.

"How, er, are you?" Max asked again. "Wait, you already answered that. Do you live around here?"

I tried hard to stop staring at him. "I live in South London. You?"

"I tour around, mostly. With the band. I'm not sure I exactly live anywhere." He laughed and glanced at the girl with him. His girlfriend – it had to be. "Right now I'm showing Manon around. She's from Leuven in Belgium. She's been to England before, but never out of London."

"It's true," Manon admitted with a self-deprecating grimace. She seemed really sweet.

We all nodded and smiled at each other a bit more before mumbling things about catching trains and needing to get away. Max and Manon left first, disappearing into a crowd that had formed by a ticket barrier.

"Old boyfriend?" Henry asked, looking in the direction of the platform they'd headed for.

I set my expression to neutral. "What makes you think that?"

"The way he looked at you. And the way you looked at him." Henry didn't smile before he added, "You never look at me like that."

Oh, here we go again, I thought.

I resisted the urge to roll my eyes at Henry or storm away, or anything equally childish. "Aw, are you feeling neglected?" I joked instead. I kissed the sulky expression off his face and squashed down my irritation.

I did try, but Henry and I didn't make it through the weekend. We split up on the first night and I managed to get an early train home, leaving him to chat up Belgian girls in chic bars. I knew he'd be OK. I didn't really care about the breakup, but I was slightly worried about myself – again. I remembered that boy I'd gone out with at uni and how he'd said there were rumours about me being 'cold'. Henry had said something similar. He'd told me I was 'hard to get close to'. I wondered whether they were both right about me. I wondered whether I could – or should – do anything about it. Counselling, or something. Not that it had helped Amelia very much.

Max texted me the day after I got home. I had the same number after all these years – I'd transferred it every time I got a new phone. Max's number was different, but he'd thoughtfully signed his name for me.

His message said: *Hope this is still you. It was so great to see you again. Really hope life is good. Max x*

I replied, for the first time in years. I wasn't sure what had changed. I suppose I was tired and off-colour what with the breakup. I was determined to be a bit less closed-off in my life. Also, I didn't know why, but things felt different now that I'd seen Max in person.

I wrote and deleted about ten texts. First there was: *It was great to see you too.* Then: *Hope you and Manon had a good holiday! Where did you go?* Followed by: *What are you up to now?*, *How's life?* and *Are you happy?* There were several other attempts before I wrote: *I miss you.*

I didn't send that one either.

Instead, I wrote and sent: *See you at CHAPS.*

I might as well have typed: *Don't contact me again.*

And he didn't, until that Friday night nearly three years later, when I was chatting to Tilly and Louis. And for some reason, that night, I called him back.

And now I was face to face with Max again. He was living in the room next door to me. He was in my life again and I wasn't sure how I felt about him at all.

But 'numb' definitely didn't describe it. Not anymore.

∞∞∞

NOW: Past Breakups

For the next couple of weeks, I carry on with my new normal. I avoid my flatmates as much as possible both at home and during the working day, knowing it's just a matter of time before they get together. I spend my weekends in my room, only emerging if I absolutely have to. My weekdays are quiet, full of work.

After doing my normal job, as soon as I finish the underwear copy which Steve has entirely given up on, I go to the storeroom to work on the scrap heap. Usually just minutes after I've settled, Max appears and works beside me. We chat about work, colleagues, clothes and films. We laugh while we sort, and I can't describe how amazing it is to have him in my life again. It's the brightest part of my day, although I know I shouldn't think this. The minute we get home, I disappear into my room and avoid him again.

On one of these evenings, we're in the storeroom and he shakes a weirdly shaped stripy brown t-shirt at me. "Reconnect with the earth in this truly disgusting t-shirt?" he suggests.

I laugh.

He carries on sorting and I realise I can't take my eyes off him. I watch him for ages, admiring the concentration on his face, the way his muscles move as he reaches for another piece of clothing, the way he's meeting my eyes... oh crap.

"What?" He smiles at me.

"Nothing."

He goes back to what he was doing.

"So how are you getting on with Tilly?" I ask as casually as I can manage, after a while. It's been on my mind, and I can't resist asking. I force my eyes away from where they're ogling him and back to the clothes in front of me.

"Yeah, Tilly's great," he replies. "Thank you again for finding me a place to stay, Ciara. I can't tell you how good it is to be out of the hostels. It's such a relief."

"No problem," I say, wondering how to turn the conversation back to my original question.

He smiles. "And I can't believe she got me this fill-in job, too! It's like the full package – home, job, friendly people – way more than I could have hoped for."

And he's handed me the perfect opportunity to try again. "Yeah, so about Tilly... What do you think of her?" I realise I sound like a schoolgirl now, but I can't think how else to say it. And for some reason, I really want to ask.

He stops and gives me a puzzled look. "I already said." A look of realisation crosses his face. "Oh! Oh. You don't mean...?" He looks down. "Well, yeah. She's really lovely. But I'm not... I'm not looking for a..." He stops. "Wait, before I say anything else, do you mean what I think you mean?"

He looks so confused and adorable right this second that I could pounce on him right now and...

I couldn't, of course. I have to stop these thoughts. What we had died long, long ago. I should know – I killed it myself.

I register what he actually said. "You're not looking for a...? Were you going to say 'a relationship'?"

"Yeah, I suppose so. And I'm not." He shakes his head. "Sorry. I don't want to upset anyone. Tilly's great – she really is."

He said that already, I think. *He's not looking for a relationship*, I think. Fine. That's fine. Isn't it? Poor Tilly, but she'll adjust. She didn't seem completely set on the idea anyway, last time I spoke to her. Which was ages ago now, but still.

"I'll, um, make sure that's clear next time I speak to her, or something," he mumbles.

Ugh. That sounds awful. I wish I'd never brought it up now.

"Why aren't you looking for a relationship?" I blurt.

"I just... I can't."

"You can't? Why not?" Surely anybody can have a relationship if they want one, even if it's just a casual one! Can't they? I can even have my strange one with Chester, who keeps almost taking me to lunch. I don't say any of that.

"I don't know," Max mumbles. He looks down, coughs a bit and stares at the shirt he's folding. "Things have changed for me lately, I suppose. It's made me think about stuff more."

There's a long silence. I want him to keep talking about this but I can't think what to ask that isn't totally nosy. I go for it anyway. "Is this since you split up with the Australian girl?" The one who helped him achieve his unexpected dreams of becoming an accounts assistant?

"Oh. Yeah, no, that didn't end well. I... I never really got over a past breakup, I suppose. I've realised it hasn't been fair on other people I've gone out with."

My heart thuds. Is he talking about one of the millions of girls he must have been out with in the past few years? Maybe the one from his band, the one I saw in the photo years ago? Or the smiley girl I saw him with at St Pancras Station, the Belgian one with the interesting name – Manon? It could be anyone. I don't know much about Max's love life.

Or could he be talking about me?

"Oh," I say.

"Hmm," he murmurs.

I want to ask him to specify which breakup he's talking about.

I want him to say it's me, and that he's never got over me. But that's wrong of me, isn't it? I'm a terrible person.

Also, I want him to know how rapidly my heart is beating right now, just because he's next to me. But none of this is fair. To him or to me. He doesn't want a relationship. I'm trying to win over Chester, his boss. Sort of my boss too, in a way, though I don't report directly to him. I've got to stop thinking like this.

"What about... you?" Max doesn't look up from the clothes he's sorting. "Anyone, er, special in your life?"

Instantly my brain says '*you*', but thankfully it doesn't reach my mouth. "Not really. Well, maybe. I don't know."

"Henry?"

"Who?" I remember the time I bumped into Max at St Pancras. "Oh, no. That ended before it even began."

"OK." He thinks a bit. "I get the impression that Chester seems... interested. In you. He's rubbish at names but he always seems to know yours." He smiles.

"Yeah, um, Chester's... Well, part of my plan to..." I have no idea how to finish that sentence in a way that makes any sense and I wish I hadn't started it. I let it drift for so long that I hope he's forgotten I was speaking in the first place.

He doesn't say anything else. He keeps sorting the clothes, shaking things out and tidying them up. He smooths the edges of a peculiarly crumpled shirt he's just folded and I find myself watching his fingers, an ache forming inside me. A longing. *This has to stop*, I tell myself firmly. *Stop it now, Ciara*.

"Did you... Did you keep in touch with Amelia's family?" Max asks suddenly.

This startles me out of my daydream. It feels totally out of the blue. My thoughts about Amelia are private, squashed as far down inside me as they could possibly go. Even Sophie and Olive would think it was weird if I started mentioning her again now, when we have one of our increasingly rare get-togethers to sort out each other's lives. I remember how Hannah snapped at me about Amelia when we were kids. We all lost touch with Hannah years ago, apart from being Facebook friends, but her words still echo in my mind. *"Amelia's not the only friend in your life!"* I often think of Hannah's words when my sadness about Amelia threatens to take over. I remind myself to be grateful for the friends I still have. For years now, I've worked hard at thinking as little as possible about Amelia, to stop the pain overwhelming me, and to keep my friends from being upset. If I never, ever talk about her – which I don't – it's for my own sake as well as everyone else's.

But now Max says her name casually, like it's not sacred, and a wave of realisation washes over me. If I did want to talk about what happened, he's the only one who could possibly understand. More than my mum, who sees it from a parents' point of view, the tragedy of losing a daughter. Max shares a birthday with me and Amelia. We were all together at CHAPS at the age of seven, fourteen and twenty-one. Max was there when we got the awful news. He's part of the pain. I'm pretty sure I still blame him in some ways, however irrational I'm now sure that is. I know I definitely still blame myself.

But if there's anyone I can talk to about any of this, it has to be Max.

He looks at me. "Because I did," he says. "I kept in touch with them for a long time after... it happened. I still talk to Amelia's mum sometimes now."

☼

NOW: About Amelia

I can't believe what Max has just told me.
"You kept in touch with the Montague-Browns?" When I didn't? Every time I thought about contacting them, I was overcome with awkwardness, not knowing what to do or say, or how. I asked my mum and she suggested I should leave it. "It might be painful for them, hearing from her friends," Mum said. That was fine by me. Not getting in touch was way easier, after all. I swallowed my guilt and knew I was doing what was right. It was what Amelia would have wanted.

But Max, who hadn't even really been friends with Amelia, who hadn't gone to the funeral, had contacted them?

"Mostly her mum," Max explains. "Penelope. Hugh was less... communicative. I contacted them through CHAPS. The researchers sent us that thing, remember...?"

I didn't. That whole time was a blur in my mind.

"...telling us about Amelia. There was an address for donations, and I wrote to it. Penelope wrote back with her number, and I called her."

"But why?" I ask him, stunned into bluntness.

He concentrates on folding another strange shirt. This one has zebra stripes combined with leopard spots, like a bizarre animal medley.

"At first, I think I did it..." He hesitates, not looking at me. "I did it for you. To show you I cared, or something." He shrugs. "Maybe I thought you'd be impressed and... I don't know. Forgive me, or something. It was stupid, I know." He stares at the ground.

"Max..." I gulp. I can't bear to think how much I hurt him. "So what do you talk about? With Penelope?"

"Well, it wasn't easy, especially to start with," Max confesses. "I mean, there wasn't a lot to say, really, apart from how sorry I was, and how I had no idea. I didn't really know Amelia all that well. She was just my girlfriend's friend."

"Your...? Oh." He means me, of course. It's weird – I don't think I ever got as far as thinking of Max as a boyfriend. Not exactly.

"Yeah." He gives me a quick smile. "Sometimes I used to resent her a bit for taking you away from me. You know, back at CHAPS."

It feels so odd to hear him talking about me like this. It's like a parallel life I've featured in, in ways I don't even know about.

"I know how pathetic that sounds, don't worry," he says. "I grew up and got over it. And I knew it was wrong, even when I was a little kid. That day when we were seven, when you said you wanted to play with me and not her? Best day of my life." He laughs at himself. "I literally jumped for joy, right into a ball pool."

I don't know what to say. It hurts to think about him – and us – back then. I force myself to do it anyway. "I didn't notice," I mumble. I remember

Max at twenty-one, though, and he definitely hadn't seemed jealous or anything.

"Well, good. Amelia was famous at CHAPS. My football friends all had huge crushes on her when we were fourteen. They all knew her name."

"I remember her flirting with tons of boys!"

"Yeah, and lots of my mates flirted back, but really badly. She was the girl of everyone's dreams, except mine." He gives me a quick glance. "One of the lads got her number, you know, that year. We gave him stick about it for ages, but the others were secretly jealous."

"Did he call her?"

Max smiles knowingly. "He said he would. Apparently she'd agreed to have phone sex when they got home. But I think he was lying. The number he showed us didn't even look like it was for a mobile."

"Maybe he was planning to do it on the landline? I'm not sure whether Penelope would have approved of that."

We both grin at the thought.

Max's smile fades. "You know, I ran out of things to say to Penelope pretty quickly."

"But you kept in touch with her anyway?"

He nods.

"Why?"

"Well, mostly because she seemed so keen on it. She kept asking me to call again – said she hated the idea of losing contact with young people. Amelia was an only child, you know."

"Yeah, I know." I used to envy her for that and ask her what it was like to get all the Christmas presents and attention. And she envied me right back, asking about my big sisters all the time even though I told her it was like having two extra mums, with three people telling you how to live your life and three lots of nagging. "I always wished I could be an only child, like Amelia. And you."

"Yeah, no..." Max hesitates. "Never mind. The weird thing was that Penelope remembered me from CHAPS, far more than I remembered her. She surprised me with her knowledge of the CHAPS kids, you know. I bet she even knew who Ali Rashid was!"

"No way!" I had tried over the years, and so had Max, but so far neither of us had uncovered the identity of the mysterious Ali Rashid, rightful owner of Max's birthday cards. It had become a bit of an in-joke between us, which I'd almost forgotten. How much fun had I cut out of my life when I severed all contact with Max?

"But also, she made this suggestion after a while that seemed like a good idea. She wanted to start a charity to help young people with depression. They're pretty wealthy, you know, Amelia's parents..."

"They're loaded," I agree.

"And she wanted to put some of that money into helping others. For Amelia. So then she asked me if I could contribute. And I said yes. It's still around – it's called The Amelia Fund. They support the work of charities like Papyrus and YoungMinds, and they do their own stuff too. I was involved in it for a few years."

"But you were a touring musician!"

"Not all the time. We had a lot of downtime."

"So what did you do for The Amelia Fund?"

"Oh, fundraisers, admin, that sort of thing. Some charity gigs with my band. The aim was to raise awareness, more than money. There's still so much ignorance out there about mental health. Though it's getting better, I think."

"Wow. I had no idea about any of this."

He goes very quiet. "Yeah. I didn't think you did."

Wait. Why did he say it like that?

Oh... "Did you tell me about it? In your messages?" The ones I deleted so quickly, without even glancing at them.

"Um... yeah." He stares at the ground. "I didn't get why you wouldn't be interested, even a little bit. I thought maybe you couldn't cope with the thought yet, but it would be a matter of time. It took me ages to realise you weren't reading what I wrote. I couldn't believe myself."

"Oh..." Oh my god. Tears spring to my eyes, but I can't let them out. I'm horrible, and it's all my fault.

He looks at me. "I should have just told you I had intelligence on the identity of Ali Rashid. Then you would have paid attention."

I appreciate his stupid joke more than he can ever know, because I was about to cry and now I feel like hitting him instead. Although a sad part of me is thinking that he could have sent me that text and I still wouldn't have read it. I was so determined to avoid him forever.

"So do you know now?" I manage to joke back with minimum wobble in my voice. "Do you know the true identity of Ali Rashid? Can you show me at the next CHAPS?"

"No. I'd probably have to take Penelope with me and ask her to point him out."

I laugh a tiny bit. "I'd love to see that."

"I don't know..." Max says. He stares at the floor again. "Ciara, I have to tell you something."

My heart sinks in anticipation. When people say that, it's never good news. "What? What's wrong?"

"Nothing's wrong." He sighs. "I just... It's about the next CHAPS."

"What?" I'm filled with sudden panic. "You're going, aren't you? It's the whole reason you're here! Isn't it? You came back from Australia and needed a place to stay in London until CHAPS. That's what you said!" I try to steady my voice. I'm sounding a bit hysterical. "Sorry," I mumble.

"I was planning on going. It's just..."

"You have to be there! You have to!" So much for toning down the hysteria. But he can't not go! I need him there.

As soon as that thought crosses my mind, I know it's out of order. Max doesn't owe me anything. I shouldn't expect it of him.

But I realise that's exactly it. I *have* been expecting it. I know that going back to CHAPS without Amelia, even in a different location, will be one of the most difficult things in the world. And I know I've pushed Max away as hard as I possibly can, to the point where he'd stopped being in my life altogether. But I see now that on some level I've always thought he'd be there for me, no matter what I did. And I know that's wrong.

I shut my eyes. "Oh god, I'm sorry." I say. "Please forget I said that. Any of it. Really."

"Ciara..." Max moves over and puts his arm around me, comforting me. "I'll be there for you. I promise."

I'm so confused. I breathe in the warm, clean smell of his skin, his closeness stirring feelings I know I shouldn't be having. Why is he still being so nice to me, after everything?

"No," I mumble. "You do whatever you want."

As if he needs my permission. But he doesn't move.

We sit like that for a while, Max with his arm around me, me fighting the urge to snuggle into his shoulder. And to kiss him. And more.

He breaks away first. "Do you think we should get going? Have we done enough for today?"

Nowhere near enough, I think. *I want to kiss you. And more. And, oh yeah, do further work on the project too.* "Yeah, sure. Actually, you know what?" I look around. The storeroom has been transformed, with nearly all the weird discarded clothes in neat piles that almost make them look attractive. Even the floor looks cleaner, probably because we've slowly dusted it by sitting there every weekday. My phone memory is full of pictures and notes on how to sell the items. It's time to get the design team in and share my ideas with them.

"I think we've finished. I'll move to the next stage now. Thank you. I couldn't have done it without you."

He gets to his feet, dusting off his work trousers although they're not so bad today. "Let me know if I can help with the rest of it, too? I want to help if I can. I mean it, Ciara."

I smile at him. "Sure, why not?"

Why not, apart from the fact that I just went into a wild panic at the thought that he might not be with me at CHAPS.

And the fact that I need to stop spending time with him if I'm going to stop wishing I could jump on him and kiss him senseless.

☼

NOW: Feeling Good

I move to the next stage of my project, which starts with texting Louis for advice and hiring the second-best member of the design team – as Louis is obviously the best and told me so himself in his own unbiased opinion. After he writes all this, Louis adds: *What gives with you and Tilly?*

I thank him for the advice and conveniently neglect to answer the Tilly question. Louis texts back that he's rushing off now to do something glamorous and Parisian, and he doesn't ask me again.

I get permission from Chester to involve Louis's recommended member of staff, a woman called Amit. She has three little kids who she has to collect from after-school club every day, so I have to change things around to work with her during normal working hours, reversing my schedule to use the after-work time to catch up on the underwear that Steve can't handle.

Amit and I arrange a low-budget photo shoot for the end of the week and we choose the quirkiest looking character models we can afford on our tight budget, the ones that exude the most attitude in their lookbooks. Nobody involved in our shoot could be described as conventional in any way – there are no easy defaults at play here. It's not that kind of publication. It's also all being done a shoestring, and an extremely cheap one at that. Chester doesn't allow me any extra resources at all, so it's pretty much just me and Amit doing everything. She doubles up as photographer and art director and says it's the most fun she's had at work in ages.

I'm incredibly excited about the whole thing.

I'm also exhausted.

I'm at my desk one evening after Amit's gone home, listening to loud rock through my headphones to help me concentrate, and also because the Something For Everyone building gets a bit spooky when everyone else has gone and silence descends on the workstations. I'm busy working, describing some new super multi-way bras which are going to have a page to themselves in our next catalogue, when I sense someone standing next to my desk.

"Ciara?"

It's Max, looking sexily rumpled and five-o-clock shadowed after his day at work.

I pull my headphones off. My music throbs its muted beats into the still air around us.

"Hey," I say.

I've hardly spoken to him since our evenings in the storeroom, except the odd hello when I'm on my way in or out of Chester's office. My ability to avoid him at home could win me some kind of super-stealth award at MI6, if such a thing existed. I always listen out for the silence that means he and Tilly are in their rooms before I nip out of my bedroom for essentials.

"You're always here so late. How's it going?"

"Good." I smile at him. "Thank you again for all the help you gave me." I sound so formal. It's not how I feel. I wish I could drag him into the storeroom we used to meet in and roll on the dusty floor with him.

This is exactly the kind of disaster I was expecting when I invited him to live with me. I should never have let Tilly and Louis talk me into it.

"Have you nearly finished?"

What's with all the questions? "Not really." I point to my screen. "Bras. These ones can be worn in endless configurations, adapting to all occasions."

He considers it. "They sound great. Very useful."

"They really are. And a snip at only five times what any sensible person would pay for one. Want to order now?"

"Hmm, maybe not today." He taps his fingers on my desk. "Hey, I got too much shopping yesterday. How about I cook for us tonight at the house?"

"I won't be home for ages. I'm sure Tilly would love that, though."

"Tilly's at a party. It's Monique's birthday. They did invite me but I'm not in a party mood. I'm more in a cooking mood! I could prepare something and leave it for you for later?" he offers. I think I must look startled because he adds, "I'm worried about you. Do you get to have meals?"

I give him a stern look. "I'm fine, Mum."

He smiles. "You know what, just for that... Have you saved your work?"

Now what's he asking me? "It saves automatically every five seconds."

"Good. So you won't lose anything when I do this..." He reaches over my shoulder and presses the off switch on my Mac. The screen goes black.

I jump up in alarm. "What the fuck, Max! What are you doing? I have five more bras to finish before I can leave!"

"Bras can wait. I'm taking you out to eat."

"You're not. You can't! You can't afford it."

"Oh, well, that makes me feel great. Thanks, Ciara," he says, though he's still smiling. "First the mum comment, now this. You really know how to make me feel good about myself."

"I can't afford it either," I say. "So you're nothing special. I mean..." It's all coming out wrong. I just can't believe he switched off my computer!

"There you go again!" He's laughing now. "So now you've destroyed me completely, I'm taking the crushed shell of my former self home and making something to eat from the groceries I managed to buy yesterday. You're wrong, though, because I *can* afford to take you out. I've come into some money. I just choose to cook for you instead." He picks my coat off the back of my chair and holds it out to me. "And as the person who crushed me, you owe it to me to eat some of my food. So come on."

I take my coat from him and put it on. What else can I do?

We wait for the bus together and when it comes he sits next to me, so close that our knees touch and I never want to move. He chats to me about his day at work and laughs about people in the office, and it's all so easy and natural that I feel stupid for having avoided him so much.

We get home and he stays true to his word and cooks for me, a delicious pasta dish that I wolf down, realising I have actually been really hungry for ages.

When we've finished eating, he moves to wash the dishes and I say, "Leave it! I'll do it later."

Max shrugs. "If you're sure."

"Course. It's only fair." I yawn a bit, so comfortable with him. "I feel like sitting around watching rubbish telly, like in the olden days," I say. "Before we all just watched Netflix on our laptops." I imagine sitting on a sofa with him, side by side and cosy. We don't have a living room in this flat – or rather, not one that isn't used as Tilly's bedroom.

"We could watch my phone together?" Max says. "I've got a YouTube app."

"It's not quite the same."

He smiles. "I'm sure we could make it work."

I stand up and stretch and Max copies me. Before I've given it too much thought I'm at his side, throwing my arms around him.

"Thank you for tonight," I say, hugging him tightly. "You were right. I needed that."

He nods and hugs me back, natural as anything. I rest my head on his shoulder and he touches the back of my head, stroking my hair to its ends. I remember how much I used to love it when he did that.

"Mmm," I murmur.

We stay like that for a while.

"Ciara," he says eventually. "What are we doing?"

My voice sounds sleepy when I reply, "I don't know." I just want to keep doing it, whatever it is. It feels like the right thing to do.

He sighs. His voice is soft but his words are harsh. He moves his arms from around my waist. "Look, I know you don't want me in your life. You made it obvious before, when you ignored me for years. And you've made it obvious again since I've got here."

Suddenly I'm wide awake, shocked by his words. I thought I was doing exactly the opposite, at least right now. Is there no end to the misunderstandings between me and Max? Sometimes I think about our past and wonder how we've been so connected for so long, even if it has been on and off.

Other times, I wonder how we ever managed to stay apart. I swear when we're near each other there's some kind of magnetic force that pulls us together.

He takes a step away from me. "I know you've been avoiding me whenever you can. Even Tilly said something. And you've been avoiding her too. She's really worried about it. When she gets back, you should talk to her."

"Tilly fancies you." I sound like a little kid.

"You suggested that before, and it's flattering, but it's not what I get from her."

Oh. "Have you spoken to her about it?"

"I haven't had to. She doesn't seem to hate me or anything, but I'm not getting any other kind of vibes off her."

How good is Max at detecting vibes? I wonder. Right now, for example. Can he tell that I'm standing here wishing I could drag him to my bedroom and... I squirm on the spot and try to focus on what he's saying.

"Lately she's mostly asked me about you. She thinks you're annoyed with her."

"Oh right."

"You're not, are you?"

"No. Tilly's lovely."

"OK, then. You should talk to her."

"I will."

He looks at me. He's still near, still in hugging distance in the chilly kitchen.

I take a step forwards and close the gap between us again. I brush my mouth against the side of his face.

He sighs.

I kiss his cheek.

"Ciara..." He turns his head.

I kiss his mouth. Wow.

"Ciara..."

"Hmm?"

His voice cracks. "I can't do this."

"What, this?" I kiss him again, lingering on his lips.

"Yeah," he mumbles, shutting his eyes and kissing me back.

"Or this?" I ask, slowly untucking his shirt and reaching my hand up his chest, feeling his hard warmth against my fingers. I'd forgotten how amazing Max feels. I find his neck with my mouth and kiss there softly, tracing my mouth up towards the back of his ear as my hand moves across the top of his body, stroking, taking him in.

He groans but he doesn't move. He strains under my touch. "I can't, Ciara. I can't."

"Yes, you can." I sweep my tongue across his lips. "Why not?"

"Because I want to so much," he whispers. "Too much." He pulls away at last. His breathing is ragged, his voice low. "I'm sorry." He steps away from me. "It's just... I can't go through it again." He moves towards the door.

I watch him.

He stands in the doorway and looks at me. "When you left me at the hotel that day, all those years ago, it messed me up for ages! I spent years looking for you everywhere... Even when I was with someone else, I was looking for you. I looked for you in them. I only realised it afterwards. I think I hurt people – nice people who didn't deserve to be hurt. I hate myself for it. I just missed you..." He turns to leave the room.

"I missed you too," I mumble. I did. I told myself I didn't feel anything for him, but I was stupid. I was wrong. Everything he's said about himself could also apply to me. Nobody ever came close to Max in my world. I didn't let them. "I missed you so much."

His eyes darken. "Then why did you delete all my messages without even reading them?"

I have no good answer. He's right, isn't he? I can't keep doing this to him.

"Good night, Ciara."

He walks out, leaving me alone in the kitchen. The air feels freezing cold in the space where he was.

☼

NOW: Feeling Bad

I move to the sink. I wash up in a trance, thinking about Max the whole time.

Later, I'm sitting in my room with a book, trying not to be distracted by thoughts of Max in the room right next to me, when there's a knock at my door. I know Tilly's at that party and I haven't heard any signs of her coming home, so it has to be Max. I take a deep breath. "Yes?"

He opens the door and steps into my room. "Ciara?"

"Yes?"

He shuts the door behind him. "OK, so I've been thinking about it. About you. And..." He marches over where I'm sitting and pulls me up, wrapping his arms around me. Then he leans in and kisses me firmly on the lips.

I'm stunned.

His gaze is fierce. "Is that what you wanted? Earlier?"

"Yes." Though there was more.

"Or was it this?" He kisses me again, deeply, for longer.

I sigh against him and he tightens his hold on me.

"Yes to all of it," I say. I don't want to break the spell, but I can't help asking, "What happened? Why did you change your mind?"

"I didn't change my mind." He strokes the side of my face with an intensity that makes me shiver. "I've just given up fighting it. I can't resist you. I never could. Nothing has changed." He kisses me again. "This is what I've always wanted to do. And every time I've done it, I've wanted to do it again. Haven't you?"

"Yes."

I shouldn't be doing this, I think. *I can't go back there. I can't.*

The thought isn't enough to stop me. Right now, I don't think anything could. He wants me and I want him, and we're kissing and touching, reaching for each other. I never want to let him go.

I pull him onto my bed.

"Ciara... Oh god. I've dreamed about being with you again."

"Me too," I whisper. My fingers fumble with the buttons on his shirt, then reach lower. At the same time, he's frantically pulling at my clothes, touching under my top, inside my waistband and towards my inner thigh. We tangle, our half-discarded clothing getting in the way until finally we're there, naked against each other in the most delicious way.

"Key..."

"Yes?"

"You're so beautiful. Are you sure this is OK?"

"Yes." I'm more than sure. I want to feel our bodies move together, I want him inside me, I want him to rock his hard body against mine until we're both gasping with excitement, and nothing in the world can touch us except each other.

And all of these things happen, and it's like we haven't forgotten a single thing about each other, and it's even better than I remembered, like everything we've done before has been building to this moment. His hands and my hands and our mouths reaching, touching, bringing each other to the brink and then stopping before freefalling together again and again. Like old times. Better.

We lie together for a long time afterwards, skin to skin, getting our breath back.

I fight the panic that's threatening me from the depths of my mind. Memories of the morning after the last time we were together like this... I can't go back there. I can't let those feelings in. *It's fine, it's fine*, I tell myself. It's better than fine. It was amazing.

Max strokes my hair and I curl into him. "Ciara, I know I might regret asking you this, but... Where do we stand? Because I want this to work between us. So much. I don't want this to be the only time."

Oh no. The floodgates open in my head, panic rushes in. I wish he hadn't asked. I can't deal with it. "I don't know," I say quietly. I want to cry. "You're not looking for a relationship," I remind him. It calms me down.

"Yeah." Max sighs. "I said that, didn't I? It's just that..."

"What?"

"Never mind." He reconsiders. "But can I... could we just see how things go?"

No, no. I don't know. "Maybe."

There's a long silence.

"Max?"

"Yeah?"

"I'm sorry. I'm..." I can't explain, but I feel like I should try. My voice gets smaller, down to a whisper. "I think I'm... scared."

"Oh," he whispers back, like he understands. He caresses my face with his fingertips. "Can't you think about something else?"

Our old thing. Our first time, in that hotel room... Before, before. My heart thumps, remembering.

"I don't think so," I say. I shouldn't have let this happen. It hurts too much – remembering... "I just... I can't."

"OK." Another silence.

I shift away from him.

"Ciara? I could... go now if you want me to."

I don't know what to say.

"Do you want me to go?"

Yes, yes. No. I don't know how to answer. "I think so. I'm sorry."

"OK. You're amazing, Key. Good night." He gets up, gets dressed and leaves. I hear the door to his room click shut.

I shut my eyes and wish I knew how to live with this, with the sheer heart-stopping joy of it, without letting in all the bad stuff in.

I hear Tilly arrive from her party. She's crashing around the kitchen, which is always the sign of a good night out. I'm going to need to speak to her really soon.

Tomorrow, I promise myself. I have to tell her about Max, even if it doesn't last, as I'd hate it if she found out some other way.

It occurs to me that, despite what Max said, I might be 'doing a Jess' to her, and I can't stand that thought.

I'm so, so scared.

And also so happy.

☼

NOW: If You Can't Talk About It

The next day at work, I've lost all focus. My mind drifts, daydreaming about Max. I'll have to tell him we can't be together, for the sake of keeping my job, apart from everything else. I'll have to tell him that what happened between us is a disaster in more ways than one. It was fantastic, but it can't continue.

A memory of last night flashes into my head and I let it play out. Just once more.

Amit looks up from the page layouts we're supposed to be working on together. "Are you OK, Ciara?"

I startle back to earth. "Yeah, why?"

"I'm not sure I've ever seen you so... distracted. And you keep going all red." Amit smiles. "You're either coming down with flu or you're falling in love. The symptoms are similar."

"Neither," I say, fanning my face with a catalogue supplement. "It's this stupid building. Always too hot or too cold!"

"Right..." Amit says like she doesn't believe me at all.

I can't go on like this!

After everyone else has gone home, Max stops at my desk again.

"I can't!" I say, barely looking at him, shielding my computer's 'off' button with my hand. "Don't make me! I'll get miles behind. It's not just about me. Steve was nearly in tears at his keyboard today! Amit has kids!"

Max laughs and touches my shoulder. It's the softest touch but it still sends shivers through me. "I haven't even suggested anything," he says. "But OK, I get it. See you later back home?"

I meet his eyes. "Yeah, OK."

This exchange is enough to fire me up. For the rest of my working evening, I'm supercharged, filled with adrenaline and anticipation. What exactly have I agreed to?

I'm almost disappointed when I get home and the flat is silent. I shout a big hello from the kitchen but there's no reply. Max and Tilly must both be out. Or in their rooms. Maybe they're together? *Together* together?

I make myself a snack and take it to my room. I sit on my bed eating it, absently scrolling through YouTube recommendations on my phone and trying to settle on something to watch. I can't concentrate on anything.

Not much time passes before I hear the front door click shut and Tilly and Max talking and laughing. A while after that, there's a knock at my door and when I shout hello, Max pops his head round. "Can I come in?"

"Yeah." I take the last bite of my sandwich and brush crumbs off my lap as he enters the room. "Were you out with Tilly?"

"Yeah, we went food shopping. She was feeling rough after last night's party and she wanted some company. She's in her room now."

"Oh, OK." I remember that I have to speak to her very soon about what happened with me and Max. Whatever it was. Unless... "Did you tell her? About... us?"

"No. I wasn't sure if you'd want me to." He clears his throat. "Or if there's anything to say... you know."

I definitely know. I've been thinking about it all day, how I have to tell him I'm not ready for anything. Anything more. It has to stop. But now I'm faced with him, I'm not so sure.

"Yeah, no. I'll speak to Tilly soon. I think I should tell her. Even if..." Oh, this is ridiculous. I shouldn't be so tongue-tied at my age. Why can't I just talk to Max properly? Olive would say if I can't talk about it then I shouldn't be doing it – something her mum used to say to put her off having sex, as if it could ever work. Olive can always talk about anything, in more than one language.

"OK." Max looks at the bed. "Can I sit down?"

"Oh yeah. Course." I shift a bit to make room for him.

He settles as if it's perfectly normal for him to be sitting on my bed next to me. "I've been thinking, Key."

"Er, yeah?"

"About what you said last night... this morning. I don't want you to be scared," he says gently. "I want you to be sure. Of me. Of us. So..."

So? I look at him.

"So maybe we shouldn't..." He can't talk about it either. This thought oddly cheers me up. "We probably shouldn't..."

"Yeah, I don't think we should. It's a bad idea. And you said you can't have a relationship."

"I did say that."

"I know. And that's fine, of course."

"OK."

"Yep. So... I'm glad that's sorted."

"Yeah." He gives me a searching look.

"Yeah." I lean over and kiss him.

We fall back onto the bed, tearing at each other's clothes.

He leaves hours later, checking the corridor for signs of Tilly before sneaking back to his room.

☼

NOW: Sophie's Emergency

The following Friday, I get an urgent text from Olive. It says: *Emergency. Sophie needs us. Have arranged cheer-up mission at hers, 7pm Saturday. Bring shoulders to cry on.*

I write back: *What's going on?*

She heard from Ingrid, Olive replies. *Wedding invite. It shook her up. First loves are the worst.*

Tell me about it, I type. *I have Max living in my flat.*

I haven't told my friends what's going on between me and Max. I wouldn't know what to say, because it's nothing, really. And also everything.

Bring Max, Olive texts back. *It will distract her.*

This is a terrible idea. But there's also something attractive about the thought of taking Max away from the Croydon flat, away from Tilly, and back to a place he visited lots of times when we were little, when he stayed with me for my birthday and we'd pop over to Sophie's and Olive's together because we had to. Because wherever I went, Max had to follow.

He'll probably say no, I reason.

I ask him anyway.

"Sure," he says. "I haven't been to 'Outside of London', as you used to call Northwood, for years. And Olive makes me laugh."

"Sophie might want it to be girls-only," I warn him. "I'm not really sure why Olive said I should bring you."

"I'll definitely disappear if I'm not wanted," Max promises.

I tell Mum I'm coming home for the weekend for a party at Sophie's and she's over the moon. "It's about time. I've not seen you for ages, Ciara! I never see Alannah either. Mind you, I see Brigid and the twins a bit too much!"

I listen to her complain about her grandchildren and all I hear is that she loves them to pieces but won't admit it.

I explain to Mum that I'm bringing Max. I've mentioned that he's living with us temporarily and so far she's taken it at face value and not made any annoying comments about it. But now she's suspicious. "Why is Max coming with you?"

"He's friends with Olive and Sophie too, remember? Sophie wants to see him."

"*Sophie* wants to see him?" She sounds dubious, which is fair enough seeing as I made that up. "Will I make up Alannah's room for him? We can't have him in your room, can we? You're not children anymore..."

The hint is so heavy that she might as well have asked outright whether I'm sleeping with him. It's a good thing Mum can't see me go bright red. "Of course!" I chirp. "Max is a friend, Mum. And temporary flatmate."

"OK," she says. "Well, it will be good to see him again. And I'll be sure to send my regards to Carol."

Yes, because Mum and Carol have always been such good friends. Honestly, my mother!

Olive makes a massive fuss of Max when we arrive at Sophie's house for the emergency girls' night in. (Plus Max.)

Sophie seems pretty bouncy too and nothing like I expected from Olive's text. "I don't care about Ingrid," she says more than once. "I'm over it already. Good for her! But any excuse for a night with my best friends!" (Plus Max, none of us add.)

Max takes it all in his stride, his superior listening skills firmly on display.

Later, when he's out of earshot helping Sophie with drinks, Olive says, "You're having sex with Max, aren't you?"

Olive is so blunt.

"What? Why would you say that?"

"Because I swear I haven't seen you this happy since he turned up at our nineteenth birthday party and you snogged the face off him in the boxroom."

"It's not like that," I say. "He can't... doesn't want a relationship."

She looks as suspicious as my mum sounded earlier.

"And I'm planning on seeing someone else. This guy called Chester, at work."

"You're *planning* on it? Is this like a Five Year Plan for your love life?"

In a way, yes. "Olive, it's just not like that between me and Max, OK?"

We both look over at him. Max, who has been deep in conversation with Sophie at the other side of the room, catches my eye and beams a smile at me. It makes me shiver.

"Suit yourself, queen of denial," Olive huffs. "You two are crazy about each other, but I'll let you pretend all you want. S'your life."

When it's time to leave, Sophie hugs Max and says to me, "Your old boyfriend has the best advice. I wasn't feeling that bad before, honestly. But now I'm even more ready to face the world!"

I smile at my old boyfriend.

Sophie gives me a massive hug. "Thanks for coming, Ciara. You're the best."

I take Max's hand as we walk home – back to my parents' house – and I don't even worry about it. Who would see us out here in Northwood? Does it matter anyway?

He swings my arm and says, "That was fun. I like your friends."

"They like you. They always have."

Max laughs. "No, they haven't! They made me feel really unwelcome when I was little. They were scary. Olive once told me to my face that I was annoying."

"Max! Why didn't you tell me at the time?"

"Because I didn't care – not really. If it meant spending time with you..."

Oh, this man.

I make the most of the fact that we're attached to pull him into the darkness, under a tree in the park between Sophie's house and mine. We kiss for ages, like teenagers. It gets so late that I worry Mum might deadbolt the door – she's not used to her daughters staggering in at all hours anymore. I force myself to break away from Max and we hurry home. I'm so turned on and rumpled from all the kissing that I have to take huge gulps of air and straighten my clothes before I put my key in the lock. Luckily the door opens. We tiptoe in and I'm grateful for the silence that means my parents have gone to bed. I say goodnight to Max and the thought of my parents upstairs is enough to stop me pouncing on him.

Later, though, I find I can't sleep. I sneak into the spare room – the room that used to be my sister's and was the first to be converted to Full Mum Style when Alannah moved out. Max is awake too, lying in the bed reading something on his phone.

"Ciara?" he says, turning his screen off. "Should you be in here? Your mum and dad...?"

"They'll be sound asleep by now." I sit on the bed. "And we're adults."

"Yes, but..."

"I just wanted to talk to you."

"OK." He sits up a bit and holds his arm out. I scoot under it and snuggle against him in the bed. This could be so cosy.

"Talk?" he prompts me gently. His breath tickles my cheek.

I can't think of anything to say. "Thanks again. For..." I admire the outline of him through his thin cotton t-shirt. I breathe in his incredible Max smell.

"For what?"

For you, I think, but I can't bring myself to say it. "Just, you know."

His eyes drink me in.

Lust courses through me. The cosiness turns to desire.

Max feels it too, I can tell. His arms tighten around me. He shifts so that our thighs are fully touching. His eyes meet mine, asking a question.

"We'd better not. Not here," I answer in a whisper.

He nods, understanding.

I reach over and touch him anyway.

"Ciara..."

My fingers dance under his t-shirt, over his bare skin, inching downwards and into his shorts.

He sighs deeply as I close my hand around him. He's so hard. He moans at my touch. "Ciara... oh..." After a while, between tiny gasps, he says, "Let me... Can I...?"

"Yeah," I breathe.

He eases his hand into my pyjama trousers, pressing his palm against me before spreading out his fingers, stroking me softly. When my breath quickens he changes his touch, teasing me. It's exquisite. I shut my eyes and focus on him, on me, on both of us.

We grasp at each other until we tremble quietly together, filled with perfect bliss.

I so want to fall asleep entwined with him but I tear myself away and sneak back to my room. I lie in the strange familiarity of my childhood bed, thinking about Max. It's like a dream come true.

We can't go on like this.

☼

NOW: Intruder

A few weeks later, my project is going better than I ever could have hoped.

It has taken longer than I'd expected, but our new supplement is ready for the printer. I've called it 'Treasure'. Amit has used our most striking shot on the cover – a plus-size model in the cone bra and a leather mini-skirt, the expression on her face saying that she knows she's made unusual choices and she dares you to care. It's got serious attitude and I love it.

The finished proofs come back from the printer. Amit and I sort out a few issues and within days I'm standing in Chester's office with my freshly re-printed publication, biting my lip as I wait for his verdict.

"Well, it's certainly striking," he says. He looks up at me. "You have an unusual vision, Ciara. I'm not sure whether this will work..."

My heart races. Oh shit, oh shit. All those hours for nothing. Less than nothing – I'll probably lose my job, and Steve's, and who knows which members of the design team. What about poor Amit? I would never forgive myself if this reflected badly on her. What have I done?

"But we'll give it a go. Get in touch with Distribution." He hands me the copy he's been looking at. "Well done, Ciara. We really should go for that lunch I've been promising. Are you free today?"

Oh no. Somewhere along the line, I seem to have lost any desire to make Chester love me, except in a professional capacity. The steamy times I'm sharing with Max on a pretty regular basis aren't helping this at all. We still haven't labelled whatever is going on between us, which is fine by me. We visit each other's rooms at night when we're sure Tilly can't hear us. We always make sure we're in our own rooms by morning. I still haven't managed to speak to Tilly about what's going on, whatever it might be. But I fully intend to, very soon.

Chester is waiting for a reply. He reminds me of the question. "Lunch?"

I realise this tricky situation is entirely my fault. Why do I always do this to myself?

I decide to leave the awkward conversation with Chester for another time. Maybe the problem will go away by itself, the way problems famously never do.

"Yeah, we really should do that sometime," I mumble.

I leave Chester's office. Max looks up from his desk and gives me an enquiring look. I wave the supplement in the air and put my thumbs up, mouthing 'thank you' at him.

He beams, then ducks his head and pretends to concentrate on his computer as Chester marches out of his office on the way to some meeting with Scary Cathy.

By the end of the next day, the Treasure supplement to the Something For Everyone catalogue is on its way to selected recipients from the master mailing list, with links to the online version sent out through a marketing email. I almost have to physically restrain myself not to hack into the Orders section of our database to see what's selling and who's buying. If anyone is buying anything at all.

I leave work two hours early that day instead of hours late, like I have been the past few weeks. Even though Something For Everyone has a big print deadline coming up, I've been working so hard that I'm up to date on my normal work. And there's nothing more I can do on the special project. I'm absolutely terrified. I'm also excited.

It's the most hopeful I've felt in a really, really long time.

***

As soon as I put my key in the lock, I can tell there's something wrong.

There's a squeaking sound coming from inside somewhere. I'm not sure what it is, but I know it's not normal.

Maybe we have mice. Or intruders! Max is definitely still at work. I said goodbye to him a while ago, outside Chester's office. And Tilly's at a straight-from-work night out with her department – her second in a row organised by Monique, who is dragging everyone out for nightly after-work team-building these days. If it's a person making the sound I can hear, then it's not someone who lives here.

Unless Louis is back unexpectedly? It's possible, though unlikely. The last text he sent me was all about how awesome Paris and Tomas both are.

Just in case, I look around for a weapon – something I can potentially use for self-defence.

The only suitable armoury I can find is a stripy golf umbrella that lives in a corner by the entrance. I pick it up and wield it above my head, chopping it around a bit in a Star Wars lightsaber battle style as I walk down the hallway, stealthy as a Jedi knight. If I wasn't slightly terrified, this could be actually kind of cool.

The source of the sound isn't here. I imagine myself shouting, "Clear!" and totally mixing up my movies as I beckon for the rest of my ninja team to follow me. I head for the kitchen.

As soon as I walk in, I register that there's definitely someone there. *There's someone in our kitchen!*

Luckily, I'm still holding the umbrella aloft. "Aaargh!" I charge towards the outline of the person.

"Aaargh!" a voice echoes. "Ciara, what the fuck are you doing?"

It's Tilly.

Ah.

I put the umbrella down.

"Oh, er, nothing. I thought I heard burglars." I'm almost disappointed. "I thought you were out with work." Then I take a closer look at Tilly. Her eyes are red, her cheeks are tear-stained and she's shaking. I realise she's the source of the squeaking I've heard. She's been crying, and it's a high-pitched sound I'm unfamiliar with because Tilly's always such a happy, positive person.

"Oh my god, are you OK?" I ask.

"Yes," she says. She accompanies this blatant lie with a huge sob.

"No, you're not!" I run immediately towards the sink. This is an emergency coffee situation. "Wait there! Don't move!"

"I'm not going anywhere!" Tilly half-says, half-sobs. "It's you who's running about like a mad thing."

"An umbrella ninja Jedi!" I correct, hoping to make her smile.

She sobs again, even louder this time, but there's a laugh buried in there somewhere.

I want to ask Tilly what's wrong but this thought niggles at me. She couldn't be like this about Max, could she? Maybe she's found out about the nights we spent together and she's heartbroken. If that's it, then I'm the worst person in the world. I'll never forgive myself. I'll...

"It's my gran," Tilly says through sobs.

"Granny Newman?" The woman who gave me the inspiration for 'Treasure'? Now I feel like the most self-centred person in the world. I stop thinking about myself and focus on my poor friend. Turns out it's not all about me after all. Who knew?

"She had a stroke," Tilly explains through her tears. "Last night. While I was out having fun, she was in an ambulance! I can't stand it, Ciara!"

"Oh, no. I'm so sorry! But those two things aren't connected. It's not your fault!"

She doesn't look like she believes me. "My phone died while I was out with Monique. I forgot to plug it in before I went to bed because I'd had one too many. I only found out about Granny Newman after I charged my phone at work today!"

"Oh, Tilly." I want to tell her not to be so hard on herself. "How is she?"

"Mum says it's bad. I have to get to the hospital in Leeds, Ciara! And if I don't hurry, I might never see her again!"

I stop my coffee making, practically screeching to a halt. "Oh no! Why aren't you on your way there right now? Can I help?"

"I *am* on my way. Look, I'm all packed."

I notice she's wearing her coat and has a small, business-like black wheelie case at her feet. "I bought a train ticket and booked a taxi on my phone. But the taxi hasn't arrived and I'm going to miss my train and –" She sobs again. "I don't know what to do! I can barely see this thing right now!" She holds up her phone. "All I can think about is my granny!"

"Tilly, please don't worry!" I take the phone out of her hand and try to see what app she's used. "When's your train? Is it from King's Cross?"

She nods and says, "In an hour and a half. Less now. I'll never make it."

I find the app and cancel the cab, which gives an estimated arrival time that's too late anyway. I pick up Tilly's case. "It's too slow by road. There's a direct train from here to St Pancras plus a walk, or you can connect to the tube from Victoria."

"I know, but I can't do it, Ciara! I'll never get the right connection while I'm in this state. And I was going to use the taxi time to calm down. I can't let people see me like this. I'm a mess!"

"You're not! Even if you were, nobody would notice." I touch her arm. "Besides, I'm going with you. I'll see you onto your train at King's Cross. I'll instruct some friendly Northern passenger to make sure you're OK on the way up. Or I can travel to Leeds with you if you want me to?"

"You can't come with me!" Tilly says, hurrying after me as I head for the door. "You're not even talking to me! You've been ignoring me for ages. You don't even like me anymore!" She sobs.

I stop. Oh my god. "Tilly, that's rubbish! Of course I like you! And of course I'm talking to you! I'm talking to you right now! Where did you get that ridiculous idea? Now, come on!"

I shut the door behind us, put my arm around her and hurry down the road, heading for the least crowded entrance of East Croydon Station. She keeps pace as I rush her to the right platform and all the way to her train for Leeds, saying as many reassuring things as I can think of on the way.

More than once, I tell her to stop blaming herself. There's nothing she could have done. It's not her fault.

"Thank you, Ciara." Tilly gives me a big hug as she gets on the train. "I'm glad you don't hate me after all!"

"Tils, I love you! I really hope everything's OK. Please let me know?"

She promises.

I wave as her train leaves the station.

I sort of hate myself a bit more.

☼

NOW: Louis's New Low

The next day, Tilly texts from the hospital in Leeds.

Not brilliant here, but she's stable, Tilly's text reads. *I made it. Thank you for helping me, Ciara, you're the best.*

I realise with a twinge of guilt that I still haven't spoken to her about Max, but now is definitely not the time.

Let me know if you need anything, I text back. *Anytime. I mean it. Love and hugs.*

I call Louis to tell him about Tilly's granny and he promises to call Tilly as soon as he can. "I miss you and the Tilster!" he tells me. "It's all so boringly glamorous and gorgeous here! You've no idea."

"Sounds tedious," I agree. "There's an uncomfortable red stool here in the kitchen waiting for you. It's gone a bit more wobbly while you've been away."

Louis laughs. "Idyllic! All this wandering down the Champs-Elysee, love-locking on bridges and eating mussels in chic restaurants near Montmartre... Sometimes a guy just wants to sit in a cold, damp kitchen in Croydon putting the world to rights with his besties, you know?"

"Yeah, I totally get that. You must be so jealous of me."

"Oh, yes." He sighs. "Lucky you." He laughs again. "How's it going with Max, anyway? Now that you're all alone together?" His voice is all suggestive. It's a good thing he can't see the deep blush I'm feeling, thinking about being alone with Max.

"Oh, you know," I say lightly.

"Yeah, I know." He chuckles. "You're as loved up as I am. We're a pair of lovestruck fools."

"Louis, it's not like that with Max," I lie. I lower my voice even though nobody's around. "Besides, I think Tilly likes him so I have to stay away from him." My heart sinks at the thought.

To my surprise, instead of getting annoyed with me like I was worried he would, he laughs, loud and long. I have to hold the phone away from my ear.

"What?" I say eventually. "Why are you laughing?"

"I told Tilly you'd fall for that! We know you so well!"

"Er... what?"

"Oh, come on! We both knew from the very start how you felt about Max. It was obvious after our very first comments about his sexy sax, and the way you scuttled off with your phone that night. You should have seen your face!"

He should see my face now. I think I've gone even redder, but from rage this time. "Are you telling me Tilly was only pretending to like him?"

"Oh no, she likes him all right! Just not like that. Like *you* do. Oh, and yeah, when he first moved in, she was vaguely interested in him. But she says she asked you whether there was anything between you, and your answers didn't convince her at all."

I can't believe what I'm hearing. Tilly didn't believe me! "You knew about that?"

"Yes. Apparently you gave her your blessing! You idiot! She called me and told me about it. She said she couldn't think of anything worse than doing a Jess on you, and she wasn't really that bothered about him anyway. She said he wasn't really her type, and it was just a thought. She also said that Max was clearly not interested in her anyway because he only had eyes for you. Apparently he never stops talking about you. Scintillating conversation, I'm sure."

No way. "Why didn't she tell me any of this?"

"Ah." Louis sounds guilty. "That will be my fault. I suggested she shouldn't. Just to see what would happen. I thought it might... encourage you."

I grip my phone. "*Encourage* me?"

"Yes, you know. To make a move on Max. To get in first!" He tuts. "That's what you were supposed to do. But then you didn't, and Tilly got really worried because she said you'd started avoiding her. You've been missing Flatmate Fridays and everything. That was excessive, Ciara. We need to talk about that. Flatmates forever, you know." He pauses. "Hello? Is this thing on?" The phone makes a noise like he's tapping it. "How do you respond, Ms Ryan? Flatmates forever...?"

I'm not saying the end of our stupid catchphrase. I'm too angry. "We need to talk about you two telling me the truth! How could you lie to me?"

"Ah," he says lightly. "We're all as bad as each other."

"No, we're not! I haven't been lying to anyone!"

Louis puts on a silly voice. "He means nothing to me, Tilly. You go right ahead and bone the love of my life, Tilly!"

"Seriously? And I didn't say that!"

"Not in those words, no. Besides, you didn't have to." He laughs. "You just went ahead and boned him instead."

"Louis!"

"I know you did!"

"How? Who told you?"

"Ha! *You* did, right this second. All I can say is, you'd better be doing it in your bed and not mine." He coughs. "And promise me you're using protection. But not in my bed."

OK, these are new lows, even for Louis. He has officially rendered me speechless.

He fills my silence. "I only have your best interests at heart, my friend!"

Right! I recover the power of speech. "When are you back, Louis?"

"Soon, Ciara. I know how much you miss me."

"Oh, I've just remembered. That's the date I'm MOVING OUT FOREVER."

"As if!" Louis laughs. "You love me! You can't live without me! Say it! Say you love me! You know you do!"

I hang up on him.

A smile creeps onto my face despite it all.

Louis is infuriating.

He's also sort-of right.

☼

NOW: Omelette

If I let myself think too much about the way I'm living at the moment, I panic. Anyone who didn't know better would think Max and I were a proper couple, one that had chosen to live together, rather than two relative strangers with a load of history and an inability to keep their hands off each other. Two people who haven't exactly admitted there's anything going on, to anyone including themselves.

We keep our separate rooms as some kind of pretence that we don't spend most of our nights together in the same bed – usually mine, especially after that conversation with Louis. It's not like we have an audience now that Tilly's away, so I'm not sure why we're doing it, but Max still disappears to his room before I wake up, and we always leave the building separately. He's expected in much earlier than I am, but also we don't want anyone at work to get suspicious. Including Chester.

One morning in the kitchen, when Max has decided to make me a cooked breakfast and go in late, I finally tell him what my deal is with Chester.

It crosses my mind that he might get annoyed – or possibly even jealous? – but he laughs. "Ciara, you're nuts."

"In a good way?"

"In a nutty way." He roots about in the fridge. "I've located cheese and two eggs, but that's about it. Cheese omelette?"

"Sure." He could do anything and I'd be happy. "Is that all you're going to say about Chester?"

"I think so," he says. "Why, what did you expect me to say?"

"I don't know. Don't you mind that I've been chasing after your boss?"

"If I thought you really were? Sure. But I've been in a room with you both, and you look like you're laughing at him the whole time. And not in a good way, either. You act like you think he's a hilarious jumped-up arrogant management type." Max pulls a bowl out of the cupboard. "Which he is. Though please don't repeat any of this to the man who pays my salary." He laughs.

"OK." I'm a bit put out by his reaction. "But what about my secret to eternal happiness? I know the thing about making everyone love you is ridiculous, don't worry." I knew that as soon as I'd said it, really. And definitely the morning after, when the tiny amount of alcohol wore off. "But I still want Chester to like me. I want people to care about me. Isn't that essential for happiness? If people don't give a shit about me, I feel bad. I don't think that's weird."

"You're right. It's not weird."

"So... Yeah."

"So... OK. Let me try something." He stops what he's doing and walks over to me. He pushes my hair behind my ears and strokes my face.

What's he doing? Whatever it is, he keeps doing it until I can barely focus on anything. Except him.

"How do you feel?" he asks.

"Um... nice," I mumble.

He nods. "Are you happy?" he murmurs. It gives me butterflies.

I try to snap out of the trance he's putting me in. "What are you, a CHAPS test?"

He smiles at me. "Ssh. I asked you a question. Are you? Happy?"

"Sometimes, maybe." I shrug. It's impossible to answer. It's incredibly complicated. I wouldn't know where to begin.

"OK. But I mean, are you happy *right now*?" He looks deep into my eyes. His eyelids lower. He whispers, "Right this second?"

My stomach flutters. "Yes," I admit.

"Are you happier right this second than you were, say, a minute ago? A month ago? Last year?"

"Um..." The way he's touching me. "Yes?"

"So... there you go, then. There's your answer!"

I keep looking at him, wondering what I've missed.

Eventually, I swallow my pride and say, "I don't get it."

He shrugs. "You're happier right this second than you were before? But you think you need people to care about you so that you can be happy?"

"Yeah..."

"OK. Well, just use me as an example. I care about you right this second."

I gulp. "OK..."

"But I also cared about you before. A minute ago, a month ago. Last year. Nothing has changed about the way I feel."

Oh?

"The only thing that's changed is the way *you* feel."

Oh.

"So, well, never mind me. What I think I'm trying to say is... it's how you think about yourself that matters. Not what other people think of you. You're in control of your own happiness, you know?"

Ohh.

"But even so, I've always cared about you. So... anyway." He lets go of me and goes casually back to the cooking, like he hasn't just thrown a love-bomb into my world and shattered everything I thought I knew.

I stay quiet, watching him finish and dish up the cheese omelette carefully.

"Max?" I say as he brings the matching plates over and settles next to me at the breakfast bar.

"Yeah?"

"I feel awful now."

He laughs. "Oh, great! Well, that's the opposite of what I was going for! I was just trying to explain how I see it – how you can be happy no matter how other people treat you." He hands me a fork. "Don't feel bad!"

I wave my fork at him. "How do you know all this stuff?"

"I've just thought about it a lot. I've had a lot of people in my life who haven't cared much about me, I suppose. Right from the start. I've had to develop coping strategies."

I wonder if he's talking about his dad. I remember the serious little boy Max was, and how relieved his mum was to send him to ours after our eighth birthdays.

"It's life, though, isn't it?" Max continues. "It's hard not to let it get you down sometimes. Maybe some people have a harder time of it than others. There's stuff that can make things more difficult, or easier, I suppose. But I think you adjust to what you have. Even when things are terrible, you find some bits of happiness. I definitely don't think it's all about everyone loving you, or whatever. Or if it is, it's only part of it."

I listen. I don't think I've ever heard Max talk so much. I should ask him more questions, listen to him more.

"Anyway, it doesn't matter. I want you to enjoy your breakfast. And be happy..." He moves his hand lightly over mine in a tantalising touch. "Or I'll have to *make* you happy!"

You do, you do, I sing inside, and I'm tempted to ditch the breakfast and drag him into my room, making us both deliciously late for work. But at the back of my mind, I'm hanging onto his earlier comments, realising how little I know about him, even after all this time. I move his hand, holding it in mine.

"No, tell me what you meant about before. Tell me about your life." I want to know everything.

He nods in the direction of our plates. "We need to eat now and get to work! Some other time."

"How about Saturday night? We could go for a meal." This slips out of my mouth before I think about it. We're not supposed to be going out together. He still doesn't want a relationship and

I'm still scared of how close we're getting. Nothing has changed.

"It might take more than one night. I've had a complicated life. There's so much I need to tell you."

I'm relieved he doesn't seem to have minded my suggestion.

"Max?"

"Yeah?"

"When did you get so wise and grown-up?"

He laughs. "I'm not! I'm still that boy you've always known, only with tons more adult experience."

'Adult experience'? The double meaning lands with us both at the same time and he gives me a shy smile, accompanied by a look that sends shivers around my body.

I noticed, I think.

☼

NOW: Success

The sales from Treasure are better than anyone could have hoped. I get some positive updates by email, and a few days later Chester summons me to his office. I pass Scary Cathy on the way and she doesn't scowl at me, so I already have a good feeling about it all.

"The call centre have been turning customers away," Chester tells me. "The warehouse sent out most of the stock last week! I know a lot of the garments were one-off white elephants, but even some of the larger stock items are nearly gone. I really think you might have pulled it off!"

"That's great!" I beam. "I'll tell Amit." And Max, who helped too.

"Yes, do that. Good work."

I start to leave.

"Oh, and Ciara?"

I pause in the open doorway. Out of the corner of my eye, I can see Max looking at me from his desk.

"Lunch today?" Chester asks.

"Oh, er... Yeah, sure."

"I've only got two weeks to go here now," he adds conversationally. "I'm coming to the end of my contract."

It's like a ticking time bomb. I really should tell him I'm not interested anymore. But then I never exactly said I was interested in the first place, and what if he's not suggesting anything anyway? It's a minefield. A minefield with a ticking time bomb in it.

Alternatively, it's nothing at all and I should stop being so dramatic.

"Great!" I say. "I mean, oh no, that's sad! Er, bye."

As I close Chester's door, Max leaps out from behind his desk. He moves to stand right in front of me, way too close for workplace etiquette.

He leans over and says in my ear, "I've changed my mind. I'm jealous." He brushes his thumb across my bottom lip, his eyes lingering there. "And I want to eat you for lunch."

I laugh and give him a gentle push. "Max. Ssh. It won't happen, anyway. He's been promising me lunch for weeks and he's always too busy."

"Have lunch with me instead. I need to talk to you, anyway. There are things I need to tell you. I've been putting it off for too long."

This is intriguing. I haven't had that conversation with Max yet about his 'complicated life', and this sounds like part of it.

Still... "Can't it wait until we're home?"

"Yeah, maybe. But something happened this morning and I really need to explain it to you. I think I'm ready now. I don't want to lose my nerve."

Max has always been a serious kind of person, but right now his intensity is off the scale. Whatever he wants to tell me must be important. I think through the logistics of leaving the building with him, of having lunch in one of the Croydon chain cafes without inciting gossip from passing colleagues. I think it could work – lots of people probably know we're temporary flatmates. It would be easier if we could ask Tilly along, though. We could pretend it was a flat meeting. It would also be better if I wasn't worried about Chester getting to hear about it.

I realise I'm overthinking everything again. And Max is getting ready to say 'forget it' – I can see it on his face.

"Meet me in the storeroom at one," I say.

Max raises his eyebrows at me but he replies, "OK."

I spend the morning thinking about how the three months are nearly over. Chester will be going soon, leaving horrible redundancies in his wake and turning people's lives upside down. Max will be moving out and Louis returning. Then Max and I have a week at CHAPS, and then... Nothing. We'll go our separate ways, live our lives without each other the way we were always supposed to. Why does that thought make my stomach churn? What am I doing with him? Maybe I should end it right now. The whole thing is a huge, potentially painful mistake.

☼

NOW: Failure

When I click the storeroom door shut firmly behind me, Max is already there, leaning against the side wall and scrolling on his phone, looking utterly irresistible.

My resisting days are over. There is no way I'm ending anything, not today, not the way my heart leaps at the sight of him. I walk over and kiss him, full-on. He responds immediately with a passion that's definitely inappropriate for this time of day and place of work. I return it, and more.

"Ciara," he breathes when we finally break apart. "You're so gorgeous. I wish we were at home." He eyes the floor, which has grown dusty again now that we've stopped sitting on it, working together on my project. My highly successful project! This thought, combined with the fact that we're on borrowed time, makes me reckless.

"Why wait?" I remark. "Let's do it right here." I push myself against him.

He groans and steadies himself with the wall. "Argh. I know you don't mean it. But you're killing me, I swear. Not that I mind." He kisses me more, one hand wandering wonderfully.

I crane towards his touch.

After another long, dizzying kiss he says, "You are the best thing that's ever happened to me. You always have been."

The rebellious feeling courses through me. "But you still don't want a relationship?" I ask.

He freezes, pulling away from me.

He looks at me. "Do *you*?"

The pause after that goes on forever. Some of my boldness drains away.

Why can't I answer him? This is awful.

He speaks again, his voice low. "So, anyway... There's something I need to talk to you about." Max looks so serious. "Can we... sit down, or something?"

Dread sweeps over me. I can't imagine what he's going to tell me, but the way he's behaving is giving me a horrible feeling.

"On the dusty floor? Sure." I'm pretending it's an issue when I was perfectly happy to roll all over it two minutes ago.

"Never mind. Stay there." He reaches for my hand. "I can do this. I just don't want to get it wrong. Please don't freak out!"

Too late. "Shit, Max, what is it?"

"It's..." He shuts his eyes. "I don't know where to begin." He takes a deep breath. "There's so much I haven't told you."

There's so much I haven't asked, I realise. I talk, Max listens. It has always been that way. I stay quiet, watching him struggle with choosing words. Waiting.

"I've... you know CHAPS?"

I nod. Of course I do. We'll be there in two weeks' time. Together. Before we go our separate ways for another seven years. The more I think about that last part, the worse it feels.

"There's something you need to know, and I've been putting off telling you." He sighs. "I've booked a family room there. We weren't sure it would be possible, but it was confirmed this morning."

"What?" A family room? What family? Is he taking Carol, when he told me they're barely on speaking terms? Or does he want to share with me? But that would be like admitting we're together, and...

"For me and... Well, there's this girl. Woman. And a baby. A toddler now. She's... I can explain."

A girl? And a *toddler*?

I look at Max, challenging him.

"OK, so you know I was in a band?"

"Yes." I think back to the pictures I saw before I forced myself to stop following on Facebook. Max with his arm around a dark-haired girl. My mind's already racing. Did he have a baby with her? Is *this* the bad breakup he's been talking about?

"And you know the band split up?"

"You mentioned it." It was literally just a mention, during that phone call after he texted me out of the blue. "Why did you split up?" Is it to do with the child? Why does he need me to prompt him?

"Well, our singer, Grace... She... she got pregnant."

My heart thuds.

"And everything went wrong. It was a nightmare. I didn't know what to do. I felt responsible. We all ended up fighting over it – me and Grace, Dan and Jack too. All the band members. I couldn't handle it –"

I can't believe what I'm hearing. Is he telling me his girlfriend got pregnant and he 'felt' responsible? And *he* couldn't handle it?

"Stop. I don't think I want to hear this."

He looks at me and frowns. "Oh shit, Ciara, I think this is coming out all wrong!"

I step away from him. "I'm not sure there's a right way for it to come out."

His expression changes. His eyes flash. "Wait. Stop right there. What are you doing?"

"Me? What am *I* doing?"

"You're blaming me! Judging me. I can see it all over your face!" He glares at me. "It's obvious what you really think of me!"

"What am I supposed to think?" I hiss. "You're telling me we've been... You've been... with me. While you have a baby and... a girlfriend?" I think about the family room. He's booked a family room at CHAPS. "Oh my god, you're still together, aren't you? You and Grace?" My head thumps. "You're cheating on her with me!"

His eyes are blazing now. "This is exactly what I mean. *Exactly*! I know I'm rubbish at getting my words out, I'm crap at talking about myself... but you're instantly prepared to think the worst of me. You jump straight to the worst conclusions. You don't even give me a chance!"

I blaze right back at him. "I'm not supposed to think the worst of you? When you're telling me you have a baby and a – I don't know. Is she your *wife*?"

"Oh my god, Ciara. And this is why I haven't said anything before. Do you hear yourself?" He folds his arms. "You know what? I'm not even going to try to explain."

"Good," I say. "Because if you try to wriggle out of this one, you'll only make things worse."

"Wriggle out?" His expression crumples. "Wow. It really is over, Ciara. Whatever it was. You and me. I've been fooling myself. You never cared at all. It was never going to work." He stares at the ceiling, his face scrunched with emotion.

He's not going to get any sympathy from me. "Course it wasn't. Because you're not looking for a relationship anyway, like you said! Because you already have one – like you *didn't* say! And a child!" I can't believe how bad this is. Worse than anything I could have imagined. "And... now what? You expect me to be happy for you?

"Think what you like. I can't stop you." His voice is unsteady. "But we had *something*. And you know it. Only you've been looking for an excuse to throw it away, haven't you? I hope you're happy now you've found one."

"It's not an *excuse*, Max!" I feel like breaking things. I kick a dust ball across the floor instead – the best I can manage in this stupid storeroom, where I got to know Max again, where I thought we were reconnecting. "I can't believe I let you in! I can't believe I trusted you!"

"Oh, that's a joke!" His eyes flame. "You obviously don't trust me at all!"

There are voices in the hallway outside, but I'm too angry to pay much attention. And Max is too intent on defending himself by attacking me, or whatever pathetic trick he's trying here, because he doesn't notice when the door opens and two people walk in, just as he shouts, "It's been all about sex for you! That's all you ever wanted from me!"

It's the change of light in the room that makes us both look round.

Chester is standing there with Amit.

They both look shocked. There's no way they didn't hear what Max said.

Chester clears his throat and turns to Amit. "So, er..."

"Amit," says my Design friend in a small voice.

"Yes. As I was saying, this is where we kept the items from the Treasure catalogue, previously known as the Scrap Heap, I believe. So the returns can all go here. Back where they belong."

"Returns?" I mumble.

Amit shoots me a concerned look and mouths, "Are you OK?"

I nod half-heartedly, but it's not true. I am definitely not OK.

"Yes. Returns." Chester doesn't look at me. "I've heard from the relevant department. Nearly everything that got snapped up from your supplement is winging its way straight back to us. I tried to find you to break the news, but I could only find..."

"Amit," she reminds him in a sad voice.

"Yes. Our customers found that the items weren't right for them after all. The call centre is getting annoyed. It seems that whoever wrote the catalogue copy used the old returns policy, the pre-austerity one where we cover all costs of returns. And it's in print. We have to honour it."

Oh, shit. I didn't pay much attention to that side of things. I copied and pasted it from something I found in a rush, and we were so short-staffed that I didn't ask anyone to check. It's not exactly my field – I'm more about the fashion copy.

"So it's going to cost more in return postage than we can make, considering the items have no re-sale value," Chester continues. He takes a deep breath. "You know, it seems you can talk things up in a way that makes them sell – that makes people believe they're worth having. But, if you'll pardon my French, you can't polish a turd." He directs this at Amit. "Am I right?"

"Er," she replies.

"Things aren't always what they're cracked up to be. And the truth always comes out in the end. Now, it's lunch time..." This is the only time he even glances in my direction. "But I won't have time to get lunch with anyone as I have work to do." He looks at Max. "Can you see me in the office, please? Now."

He doesn't look at me again as he stalks away.

Max follows, not looking at me either.

When they've both gone, Amit says, "That was the guy? The one you were having hot daydreams about?"

I nod.

"Do you want to talk about it?"

I shake my head and try not to cry.

☼

NOW: A Conflict of Interest

Amit leaves, which I insist on even though she hovers at the door looking worried for a while. I stay in the storeroom for ages, thinking and fuming. How could he? How could Max do this to me?

And my project is a failure! Worse than a failure. I've ended up costing the company money. I've put everyone's jobs in jeopardy, not just my own. I might be single-handedly responsible for the collapse of Something For Everyone.

And Max has a girlfriend and a baby.

I trusted him. I let myself be happy. I should have known it wouldn't last.

I check the time on my phone. It's the end of my lunch break. But so what? I'm losing my job anyway. There's no way I'll make Employee of the Quarter now, even though it seems to have been forgotten under the cloud of possible redundancies. There's no way I'll survive Chester's cull.

I glance around the dusty storeroom. Soon it will be filling up with scrap heap items, returning to their squalid home. They had a chance, a brief moment of being wanted, but it's all over. There's no such thing as happiness. We are all fooling ourselves. Slapping glitter on our wounds and wondering why it hurts instead of sparkling.

I'm getting sick of my own thoughts so I wipe my eyes and head for the door.

I march straight to Chester's office, determination shooting through me.

I knock quickly and barge in.

He's at his desk, scribbling away at some papers. Signing someone's job away, probably. He's so calm, so business-like. What did I ever see in this heartless man?

Maybe I'm not being fair. He's only doing his job. But I can't stand it anymore. I'm not scrabbling about trying to impress him. Those days are over.

"Chester?"

He barely acknowledges me. Is he going to forget my name now? Not give me the time of day because of what he overheard in the storeroom? Men are pathetic.

"One second," he says.

I wait.

Many seconds later, he looks up. "Yes?"

"I'm going to make this easy for you," I say. "I resign."

A flicker of surprise shows on his face. "There's really no need. Mistakes happen. I've made decisions on where this company needs to streamline, and you're not on the list."

What is he, some kind of corporate Santa, with a 'naughty' and 'nice' list? A few more months of employment for all the good children? Lumps of coal and severance pay for the rest?

I don't care anymore.

"When you say 'mistakes', are you talking about the Treasure supplement? Or Max?" I'm speaking my mind. Nothing can touch me.

He frowns. "Feel free to report that man to HR. He's no longer an employee – we've let him go. But we still have procedures. He's admitted to everything, anyway."

"Admitted to what?" Having a secret girlfriend and baby he didn't think to tell me about?

"Bothering you. He said he was obsessed with you. I'm sorry I didn't see it. I would have done something about it immediately if I'd known, believe me."

Oh, please. Super-Chester to the rescue. Hitting offenders over the head with a P45. And what has Max been saying? Has he lost his mind? My anger at him flares.

Chester clears his throat, looks at me. "Ciara, listen. I'm afraid I can't accept your resignation."

What? Can he do that? Can I reject his lack of acceptance? "Why not?"

"I'll be honest. You've impressed me over the past few months. I've noticed your dedication to your job and the long hours you work. Not to mention the way you speak up with exciting ideas in the first place. Your project might not have worked out, but your spirit and determination could be just what this company needs."

I nearly roll my eyes. Is this all about the lunch we've nearly had every other day and the possible date after he leaves? He confirms it with the next thing he says.

"Now, as you know, I myself am leaving the company soon. And the offer still stands, if you'd like to meet up sometime. Here's my number."

He holds a card out to me. I stare at it.

What am I doing? I suppose I could have some kind of rebound fling with this man.

But do I want one?

I really don't think I do.

"Chester, I'm sorry," I say, not taking the card. "I'm not looking for a... a relationship." Oh god, I sound like Max now.

He withdraws the card, looking startled. "I'm sorry?"

"No, *I'm* sorry. It's just not a good time for me." There. I've said it. At last. "Even though you're great and everything." Phew – I'm glad I remembered to add that.

"I see." A pained frown crosses his face.

Oh no, have I wounded him deeply?

"I'm not quite sure whether to say this, in case I'm mistaken," Chester says, "but I'm worried you might have got the proverbial wrong end of the stick here, Ciara."

"The... what?"

His cheeks have gone a bit red. "I seem to have given a misleading impression somehow. I can't say this has ever happened to me before, but I'm starting to see why this sort of thing can be such an issue for Human Resources."

"Uh... what?"

"What I'm trying to say is that I'm interested in you..."

He's really confusing.

"...in a strictly professional capacity." He goes redder. "Not that you're not extremely attractive in other ways, of course. But I wouldn't dream of crossing those kinds of lines."

OK, *what*? "I thought you wanted to see me after you left?" I mutter. "And you kept offering me lunch!"

"Yes, I did. I wanted to discuss a proposal with you."

A proposal? And he wonders why I misunderstood him? I give him a suspicious look.

He coughs and shuffles some papers on his desk. "It's really something I should talk to you about when I'm no longer working here, so I think that's one reason I never quite managed the lunches. The more I got to know you, the more impatient I became about discussing it. But when it came down to it, I was worried I might be acting inappropriately."

OK, so now I'm wondering whether I misunderstood at all.

"The thing is, there's a conflict of interest," Chester says.

"A conflict of interest?"

"Yes, because... You see, Ciara, I'm here on a temporary contract to help Something For Everyone turn things around. So at the moment, of course, my loyalty lies with this particular endeavour. But the rest of the time, when I'm not contracted out, I run my own consultancy. I help small businesses, basically. And I spotted something in you. An entrepreneurial spirit, so to speak."

So Chester was actually after me for my business skills? Now I've really heard it all.

"Obviously, I think you're an asset to the company and I'll be making that recommendation to Catherine. But I did want to mention that if you ever wanted to start up on your own, I could help you."

Wow. "I don't want to stay here," I say. And it's true – I don't. When I resigned a minute ago, I felt a huge sense of relief. Plus I have a gut feeling that Something For Everyone is not going to last much longer, whatever happens. Maybe that's my newly acquired business acumen popping up.

"If you truly feel that way, Ciara..."

"I do." I really do.

"...then I will request a redundancy package for you as part of my final recommendations before I leave. I think Catherine is still in a position to make a fairly sensible offer."

Well. A silly one sounds better, but I'll settle for any offer at all, seeing as I was going to resign and get nothing. "That would be great."

"And if you wanted to use your severance pay to start your own company, please give me a call." He holds the card out to me again.

This time I take it, mumbling my thanks. Start my own company? Is he crazy? What could I offer – professional knicker-describing services for every occasion?

"Can I leave right now? I mean, is it OK if I go home now and never come back?"

Chester nods. "If that's what you want, I'll start the ball rolling with the paperwork. I'll be sorry to see you go."

"Yeah. Thanks." I hesitate by the door. "Um, but before I go, can I ask a favour?"

"Please do."

"Can you keep Tilly and Louis on? And Steve and Amit? And..." I rattle off a list of my colleagues. My ex-colleagues now, I suppose.

Chester listens to me with an amused look on his face. "I can't promise, but I'll note your recommendations, Ciara. I respect your opinion. I realise the outcome of your project wasn't what any of us had hoped for, but I really do admire your spark."

My spark?

I thank Chester and leave, clutching his card. I walk straight out of the building and head home. I'll ask one of my ex-colleagues to collect my stuff, I think. I don't want to stick around for another minute. I want to disappear.

I feel about as sparky as a damp firework in a rainstorm.

At least Chester's business weirdness has distracted me from thinking about Max and his betrayal for a few minutes.

☼

NOW: News

I travel home, my heart heavy and my stomach filled with bricks. I'm dreading seeing Max, but I realise he'll probably be at the flat now that he's been fired. We'll be there together as neither of us have jobs. It's going to be unbearable. He has two weeks to go in Louis's room and then we have a week at CHAPS. I don't know what I'm going to say to him.

The flat's silent. A quick glance down the hallway shows me that Max's door is wide open. I approach tentatively, scared of talking to him again. I'm not sure I can contain my anger at him right now.

The room is empty, apart from Louis's stuff under the plastic sheets. The mattress is bare. There's no sign that Max was even here.

I look around and check the kitchen. No note, nothing. Max has completely cleared off without any contact at all.

Then again, what did I expect from him?

I worry briefly about Louis, then realise the rent for this month is already covered, paid in advance. Max was leaving anyway. He's just gone a bit early. And without saying goodbye.

Well, good.

It's eerily quiet and I long for the return of Tilly. I feel terrible about having avoided her for so long before she went to Leeds. I wasted valuable time with my friend.

I text her first to ask about Granny Newman, in case it's a bad time. Tilly replies sounding a lot happier and saying things are going well, so I call her.

She answers right away with, "Ciara, I was just about to ring you! Monique says you stormed out!"

"Not exactly..." I should have known she'd have heard. Gossip travels fast at Something For Everyone.

"Oh my god, what happened? Are you OK? Did Chester turn out to be a sleaze?"

"Chester? Oh no, perfect gentleman. Max, though..."

"Ha, right! Wait, you're not joking?"

It feels weird to say any of this. I've had it stuck in my head for so long that I shouldn't talk to Tilly about Max. But I know now how ridiculous that was – and I shouldn't have avoided Tilly anyway.

"Max... yeah, he broke my heart."

"No way! I'm so sorry. He seemed so nice. You got together, then?"

"Um... sort of."

"Louis said you would!" She hesitates. "I honestly didn't mind, if that's what you were worried about."

"I know."

"I wish I'd never asked you about him. For someone who prides herself on her people skills, I was really dense about that one. I shouldn't have listened to Louis about it, either."

"No! God, no, it's not you. It's definitely me. I'm really sorry. Sorry about the last few months, in fact. Things have been weird for me. I think seeing Max again stirred up some difficult memories."

"I should have known."

"How could you have known?" I've been pretending everything's OK when it isn't. "I've never told you about any of it."

"Well, I wish you had. I've been worried about you. You stopped leaving your room, except for work. Once or twice at the weekend I peered in to talk to you and you were asleep, with your curtains closed. At, like, three in the afternoon. I suppose you were really tired from all the extra work?"

"Yeah..."

"Or avoiding me? But it seemed a bit..." She pauses. "Louis told me not to worry, but..."

"Oh." I didn't realise. I shouldn't have shut Tilly out. "I'll tell you all about it sometime, I promise." I've never talked about that kind of thing. It would be too heavy for Flatmate Fridays.

"Yeah, please. I want to help if I can."

I ask more about her granny and Tilly says she's out of hospital and doing well, though she needs round-the-clock care. She hesitates before adding, "Listen, Ciara, it's not completely firmed up but now seems like a good time to tell you. I'm leaving too. That's why I was talking to Monique."

"You're leaving the catalogue?" Wow. Major changes among the Croydon flatmates. "Have you found a better job?"

"Anything would be a better job!" She laughs. "And that place isn't going to last much longer, is it? Even with Chester's good and terrible work. I guarantee it will shut down within a year. Monique thinks so too. That's why she's been spending all her budget on staff nights out lately."

I agree with her. "So where are you going next?"

She hesitates. "The thing is..." she says. "I'm staying here. I'm going to help my mum look after Granny Newman for a bit, and then I'll find something in Leeds. Being home has made me realise I don't really want to leave."

"Oh." Her words sink in. "Oh no! I'm going to miss you so much!"

"I'll miss you too," Tilly says. "And Louis, and the flat. I'm paid up for the rest of the month, and then I hope you find someone good quickly. I'll come back for my stuff soon, OK?"

I want to cry. "It's never going to be the same!"

"I know. I'm sorry, Ciara! And, er, have you heard Louis's news?"

"No." Where have I been?

"Call him. You have to hear it from him."

"OK."

"Ciara?"

"Yeah?"

"Please keep in touch, OK? Flatmates forever! Even if we don't live together!"

We say sad goodbyes before I hang up and call Louis. What a day I'm having. This had better be good news.

It rings for ages before I hear his sleepy voice, which I recognise from Saturday lunchtimes after particularly boozy Flatmate Fridays.

"Huh?" He loses all his wordiness when he's like this and goes monosyllabic.

"Louis? You awake?"

"Uh-huh. Ciara. Got news."

"Tilly said."

"Tilly told you? I expressly told her not to!"

Ah, he sounds a bit more awake now. "No, calm down. She told me to call you."

Louis lets out a sigh of relief. "Well, in that case... Do you want to know the news of the century?"

After the day I've had? Nothing could surprise me.

Louis shouts, "Well, get ready for the wedding of the millennium!"

"What? You mean Tomas proposed?"

"No. *I* did!" He radiates pride down the phone. "Me! I went for it even though I was terrified. But it was worth it! I did this whole cheesy proposal on the Eiffel Tower – and Tomas said yes!"

"Oh, Louis, that's huge! Congratulations!"

"I know! Thank you! You and Max have to come to the wedding!"

"Er..."

Before I can explain, he adds in a sad voice, "But Ciara, I'm afraid there's a downside. Tomas got offered another contract after this one and, well, they've offered me something too. It's too good to refuse, so... I'm staying in Paris. I'm leaving Croydon. I'm sorry. I hope you and Tilly find someone as entertaining as me! If such a thing is possible. Hey, maybe you could ask Max to stay?"

"Er..." It seems wrong to talk about my misery at a time like this. "Tilly's leaving too. She wants to stay in Leeds."

"In *Leeds*?" He sounds incredulous. "Why? Oh, well! Two new flatmates, then! Or just Max," he says in a suggestive voice. "I've always thought it would be a good place for a couple."

"Um, no. I'll explain soon, Louis. But in the meantime, wow. I'm happy for you and Tomas, I really am!"

After we say goodbye, I put the phone down in the empty flat.

From next month onward, I'll need to cover three people's rent. With no job.

And all I want to do is cry.

I wallow for ages before I force myself to text Olive and Sophie: *Help!*

☼

NOW: Sophie's Again

"Ciara! Wow, you look tired and miserable."

"Sophie! Honesty can be a bad thing."

She hugs me. "I'm glad you *sound* OK, at least."

It has taken us nearly a week to get together. Partly this is because the weekend is a better time to meet up, but also it's because I've cancelled a couple of other times Sophie suggested. I've been weirdly unable to face leaving the flat. Both Sophie and Olive offered to come to Croydon to see me instead but I put them off. Then Sophie suggested that we should stay at hers as her dad is away, and I couldn't think of any reason to say no. My parents are away on their big cruise and they're not due back for another couple of days, so they don't even know I'm near their house right now.

We huddle in Sophie's living room and everything feels normal and nice, like when we were teenagers. Sophie grew up with just her dad, and it was always a good, relatively parent-free house to meet in before a night out.

I'm not ready to talk about myself yet, though. I insist Sophie and Olive bring us up to date on their lives before I launch into my tales of woe.

Sophie goes first, telling us all about the new love of her life, who's a yoga teacher with two kids. It's only been a couple of weeks but she is definitely The One.

"Betsy's amazing," she crows.

"And bendy?"

She smiles. "That's none of your business, Ciara."

"What's it like being an instant mum?" Olive wants to know. "What are the kids like?"

"I haven't met them yet," Sophie admits. "But I know I'm going to love them. I love her more, though."

I'm happy for her, but I tease her anyway. "It's way too soon for the l-word, surely?"

Sophie huffs and tells me I have no idea.

Then Olive declares she has given up men forever and found a new passion for politics instead. Disability campaigning, to be exact. "I'm never introducing you two to my new friends," she says bluntly.

Sophie acts offended. "What? Why?"

"A lot of them think it's wrong that I use my voice to make things easier for hearing people. I should sign all the time."

"You could do that with us," I point out. "We could sign back. You taught us when we were little."

Olive laughs. "Yeah, right. You're too slow. I'd die of boredom waiting for you to remember the most basic words."

Sophie throws a lemon slice at her. "Your turn, Ciara."

I don't know why I've been putting this off. My friends are great. We all make sure our drinks are topped up before I launch in.

I tell them all about work first. About how I made a big mistake with the supplement and tried to resign, before Chester offered me redundancy. And how I'm taking some time to decide what to do with my life.

"So you talked up some stuff nobody wanted and it all sold out because you're so good?" Olive summarises. "And then people saw the stuff was actually shit after all and sent it back?"

"Pretty much." I sigh. "It has to be a metaphor for something."

"Something about life?" Sophie suggests. "Or love?"

"It's my life!" I warm to my theme. "It's my relationship with Max. That turned to shit, too."

"Oh no! He seemed so besotted with you," Sophie says. "What happened?"

"Don't get me started," I reply, though that's the whole reason we're here, of course. I should have discussed this with my friends long ago and I wish I hadn't put it off. I relay a quick summary of the past three months.

Olive is super-smug. "Aha! What happened to the five-year love-plan?"

Oh, yes. Chester. "It fell through."

"And why didn't you tell me you and Max were together when I asked?" Olive asks accusingly.

"You didn't ask."

"I did! I asked if you were having sex. You made a point of not answering!"

"Oh. Well, yeah, we were," I admit.

"I knew it!"

"But we weren't *together*."

Olive looks sceptical.

"Anyway, now I wish it hadn't happened. Because he's a cheating, lying loser," I finish. I rest my case, and my drink.

"Yeah, that sounds like Max," says Olive. "Except it doesn't!"

Olive can be so annoying. "What do you know?"

"What do *you* know? How well do you know him anyway?"

"Really well! I've known him since I was seven!"

"Time isn't everything. What do you know about his history or potential as a cheater and a liar?"

"Not much," I admit.

"How much did you trust him?"

That's the thing, I think. He accused me of not trusting him at all. But that's not how it felt to me. I opened up to him in a way I never have with anyone except my closest friends. "I don't think I've ever trusted any man as much."

"Ciara finally lets someone in enough to get hurt – shocker!" Sophie mocks gently.

I pretend to aim a lemon slice at her. "What do you mean? Are you saying I'm closed off? When I'm baring all to you right now?"

"Yeah, Soph. Give her some credit. Ciara's letting it all hang out."

"To us, yeah. How many, you know, *partners* have you allowed anywhere near you?"

"What, you're asking for my 'number' now?"

Sophie shakes her head. "I knew you were going to take it that way! I don't mean getting down and dirty. I mean... emotions. Being vulnerable. Exposing yourself."

Olive giggles.

Sophie rolls her eyes. "Grow up, Olive."

"Max has a baby," I say miserably.

"So what?" Sophie says.

"What?"

"You heard me. So what if he has a baby? Betsy has two. It didn't stop me falling in love with her. The baby's not an issue. The girlfriend is more of a problem. Are you sure he's with her?"

"Not exactly. But he booked for her to stay with him at CHAPS. So..."

"Yeah, that sounds bad," Sophie admits.

"And he didn't tell me. I didn't even know he was with her, or that they had a baby together. The issue is that he lied to me! By omission."

"That's also bad."

"Yeah." Damn. I half wanted my friends to tell me I was being unreasonable. But I know I'm not, and they're confirming it. I pour myself another drink.

Olive's tapping away at her phone like a fidgety school-kid.

"Are we boring you?" Sophie takes the words out of my mouth.

"Ha! Always. Ssh."

"Olive, come on. Ciara needs your support."

"Yeah. And she's getting it. Something about this whole story doesn't add up. Didn't you bump into Max a couple of years ago, and he was with some French girl?"

"She was Belgian, and that doesn't prove anything," I say miserably. "Maybe it was before. Or maybe he was cheating with her, too."

"Yeah, maybe. And maybe not!" Olive swipes and taps a bit more.

"All right, Detective Abiola," says Sophie. "What are you up to?"

I peer over her shoulder. "Are you on Facebook?"

"Nope. I'm on this site that archives old social media pages, including Facebook. Makes it really easy to scroll through years of posts."

"What are you trying to prove, Olive? Max doesn't do social media. He's not going to put stuff like that online, is he?"

"No, but hold on. The band was called Four Part Cure, yeah?"

"Yes. They were big in the Netherlands and Belgium a few years ago."

Sophie sips her drink. "Four Part Cure? I recognise that. It's Epicurean philosophy, isn't it? Tetrapharmakos!"

"Tetra-what?"

"It's an ancient philosophy of happiness. Four cures, like four ingredients in a recipe. Basically..." She counts on her fingers. "Fear no gods, don't fear death, pleasure is simple to obtain, pain is easy to endure. And I'm the one who didn't go to university!"

"Which of those four is Max?" Olive wonders out loud, still focused on her phone.

"Pain," I say without hesitation.

"Easy to endure?" Sophie doesn't smile at me. "The point of it is that happiness is achievable. It doesn't have to be so difficult. And," she adds, "it's the entire meaning of life, according to Aristotle. Though personally, I think that's love."

I roll my eyes, but Olive looks worried. She's committed to the single life and loving it.

"Self-love counts," Sophie tells her.

Olive sniggers happily.

"How do you even know all this philosophy?" I ask Sophie. "Is it from dating a bisexual yoga teacher?"

Sophie frowns at me. "She practises Kundalini Yoga. There's no such thing as bisexual yoga."

"Are you sure? It sounds like fun."

"I'm serious, Ciara. Don't define Betsy by her orientation. She's a person, not a sexuality."

"OK, OK."

"And I know about Philosophy because university isn't the only place anyone ever learns anything. Despite what you two clearly think."

Oh shit. I have officially touched the chip on Sophie's shoulder.

"Ingrid studied Philosophy, didn't she?" Olive mumbles from behind her phone.

I nod. "And Sophie studied Ingrid."

Sophie bristles. "I didn't learn this from Ingrid. I got it from being alive and open to the world around me. You know what? Forget it, Ciara. I'm tired and I can't stay up all night sleuthing with Olive just because you're upset that your boyfriend has a child. As if that's a crime! I'm going to bed. Make sure all the lights are off before you go up."

Well, I've definitely upset Sophie.

I watch her leave, then try to catch Olive's eye, but she's still busy.

"Found some archives!" she announces. "Four Part Cure, band, originally from Manchester. Vocals, Grace Templeton."

I try not to worry about Sophie. "That's her. Grace."

"Drums, Dan Bridges."

"Dan and... Jack? I think that's what Max said."

"Lead guitar, Jack Bridges."

"Yeah, that's it. Do you think they're brothers?"

"Probably. Bass and second guitar, Max Renzo."

"It's definitely them."

"Have you ever heard them play?"

"Er, no."

"Must be loud for you, living with a musician." Olive keeps scrolling, distracting me from a niggling thought in the back of my head. "There's quite a lot here. Hold on..." She swipes around and reads, "Dan Bridges is in a relationship with Grace Templeton, heart heart... It's about six years ago. How old did you say the child was?"

"A toddler. I don't know – two or three? Did she go out with two people from the group, one after the other?"

"I can only see Dan on Grace's profile. Loads of pictures of them together – years of them. Two or three years ago? That was definitely when you saw Max with that girl at the train station. You went on about it for ages."

"I did not."

Olive rolls her eyes. "If you say so."

"Are you suggesting that Grace was cheating on Dan with Max? And Max was cheating on Manon with Grace?"

"Have you been watching too many soaps?" Olive asks. "There's actually a much simpler explanation."

I frown. "Is there?" I can't think of anything.

"Ciara, come on."

"What?"

"Dan was going out with Grace. Max was going out with... the French one."

"Belgian."

"Whatever." She keeps tapping away. "Grace shares everything. There are pictures of her and Dan almost every day."

"She wouldn't share anything about having an affair, though, would she?"

"I don't know. She sounds properly in love. Here's Grace with her newborn. Aw, cute! It's a girl. She's called Elsie! Grace has written a really soppy post about giving Elsie everything in the world and how Dan's the best dad ever. That's sweet. Oh no! This is only a few weeks later. Grace Templeton is single." She switches to another tab. "Dan Bridges is single. Huh. Tough dealing with a new baby."

"Especially if it's not yours," I mumble. "Maybe you should stop. It's like stalking through someone's entire life."

"You give me no choice. There's still no mention of Max."

"Well, yes, but there wouldn't be. He's not even on Facebook. Stop it now, Olive."

"No, wait – oh, oh! Listen to this. 'Going to visit Uncle Max today.' Elsie's wearing an adorable rainbow cardigan."

"Uncle Max? Max is an only child."

"Maybe it's 'uncle' as in the baby's parents' friend. Or the baby's parents' bandmate."

"Or uncle as in 'I'm not admitting he's really the father'."

"You're really sticking to this, aren't you? Why?"

I don't reply. I'm not wrong. I know I'm not.

"Did Max actually say Grace was his girlfriend? Or ex, or whatever?"

"No, but..."

"Did he say he was the father of Grace's baby?"

"No. I said both of those things myself. But he didn't correct me."

"Because he was angry with you. Because he thought you didn't trust him. Which you displayed by jumping to conclusions, accusing him of cheating and lying to you about the whole thing."

"No." I'm sure of myself. "No, I'm right. Otherwise how do you explain the family room at CHAPS? You don't take your bandmate's ex-girlfriend and baby away with you and stay in a room with them. It doesn't make any sense. Why would he do that?"

"I don't know. Maybe you should ask him?"

☼

NOW: Three Things

I think about it all night. I don't sleep at all.
I realise Olive has a point.

She's sleeping soundly in the twin bed next to me in Sophie's dad's spare room. I'm dying to talk to her.

I wish I could talk to Sophie about it too, but she's probably not talking to me after yesterday. Why do I always make such a mess of everything?

Olive will know what to do.

It's nearly nine so it should be acceptable to wake her up.

"Olive!" I whisper. What am I doing? She can't hear me! I shake her shoulder. "Olive!"

She stirs. She signs rapidly, "I don't want to go to school!" She turns over, wrapping the quilt around her. Oh, honestly.

I shake her again. "Olive!"

This time she sits up and signs, "Where's the fire?" At least she's properly awake. "Oh," she voices, bleary-eyed. "Ciara. You've probably woken me up because you want to talk about what a terrible friend you are. You probably haven't slept at all."

"I slept! A bit. Maybe."

"You didn't. You've been stressing all night. Worrying that that I was right about Max."

I nod, admitting it.

"And you'd rather talk to Sophie, but you think she's not talking to you after yesterday."

"I wouldn't rather talk to Sophie," I say. "I want to talk to both of you. But she's probably not talking to me after yesterday."

Olive yawns. "You hearing people are terrible at communicating."

"Olive! That's... ableist, or something."

"Nuh-uh. It doesn't work that way round. You don't get to claim about things like that."

"Olive!" My heart sinks. "Am I the worst friend in the world?"

"Sometimes." Olive is always so honest. "And other times you're the best friend. It's like most people, really. Even me, sometimes!"

"You're always the best."

She laughs. "OK, you need to stop lying to me, Ciara."

"I –"

"I know I'm not perfect. Neither are you. It's as if we're both human beings! Amazing, huh?" She laughs. "I accept your apology."

"Wait – I didn't say anything."

"But you were about to. Weren't you?"

I can't deny it.

She gives me a look. "Sophie's right. It's worrying."

"What is?"

"You. You're worrying us. You've been more and more... miserable. Blaming yourself for everything."

"You accused me of –"

"Yeah, but old Ciara would have just told me to shut up, without wanting to say sorry immediately afterwards." Olive shrugs. "I mean, I probably deserve it. But now you're all... W*oe is me! Olive says I'm sometimes a crap friend, so I must be the worst person in the world!*"

I can't keep up. What's Olive suggesting?

She sighs. "You know what? I know things are tough for you right now. So I'll let you off, with a full lecture on disability rights to be held some other time, if you promise me you'll do three things."

I eye her warily.

"Don't worry, they're easy. Number one is apologise to Sophie. She's probably fine this morning anyway. She's probably downstairs eating toast and thinking she was too prickly with you last night. True friends forgive their friends all the time." She nods sagely. "And then... go and talk to Max. Get him to explain. Find out what's really going on before you chuck away your soulmate."

I don't react to her use of the word 'soulmate'. She might be right. "What if he won't talk to me?"

"What did I just say? Don't make me repeat myself! But I will anyway, since it's you." She nods. "If he won't forgive you, then he's not a true friend. But he will, because he is, and because I say so." She's so sure of herself. "Go get your man. Go. Go!" She waves her hand at me. "Why are you still here? I said go!"

"I'm waiting for the third thing."

"Oh." She laughs. "There isn't one, but 'three things' sounds better. More mystical. I'll tell you what, you can figure out the last one by yourself. Discover the meaning of life, the secret of eternal happiness! Save the world!" Her hand waves again. "Go, go!"

I leave to follow her instructions.

Sophie's downstairs eating toast, just like Olive said she would be.

As soon as she sees me, she scrapes back her chair and launches herself at me.

"I'm sorry!" She hugs me. "I'm so sorry, are you all right?"

I can't believe it's this easy, after the way I've been panicking all night. "I came to apologise to you!"

"No, no. I shouldn't have been so..." She steps back, sighing. "Sometimes I get so frustrated..."

"With me?"

"Not with you."

Phew.

"With the way you get sometimes."

Oh no. "That's with me!"

"No, I just mean... You're so down on everything. I wish you could... Oh, forget it. I know you've been getting more and more stressed about..."

It's not like Sophie to be so hesitant. I give her a confused look.

She sighs. "Look, are you sure you should go to your social study thing?"

"To CHAPS? Yes, I have to go!" It's like a part of me now. I don't want to give it up.

"I know, but... I'm worried about you. I think it's going to be so tough since... you know. What happened last time. I think it's been stressing you out."

I know. And she's right. I thought I'd been hiding it really well, though. I should have known my friends would see through me.

"I think that's why you've been so... down lately. And so quick to get angry with Max, maybe?"

"Olive is pretty sure the baby – and the girlfriend – isn't his," I tell her.

"I knew she'd find something like that."

"She thinks I should speak to him. Make things up..."

"You should. Apart from anything else, I'd feel better if I knew he was looking out for you there. I made him promise, you know. When I saw him. I said I was concerned about you and I asked him to make sure you're OK."

"Sophie! I don't need anyone to look after me!"

"I didn't say you did." She hugs me again. "Anyway, Olive's right. Sort things out. And call me if you need me. Or text, or whatever. Anytime, yeah?"

I nod before we say goodbye.

Then it's time to go and get Max.

☼

NOW: Calling Max

I'm so buoyed up by my friends and excited at the thought of putting things right, at the chance that it was all just a big misunderstanding, that I call Max at the earliest chance I get. I don't think things through at all. It turns out to be a huge mistake.

My calls go to voicemail.

I send a text that says: *Max, can we talk?*

When he doesn't reply, I try again. I add: *I'm really sorry. I didn't let you explain. I haven't been fair. Please can we talk?*

Two hours later I get a reply: *I don't want to ignore you or delete your texts. How did you manage it for so long, Ciara?*

Then: *Forget I asked. I know the answer.*

Why did I think for a second that this might be easy?

I try calling again. And again.

The next time he answers, barely even saying hello before getting to the point. "What do you want to talk about? If it's work, then I'm really sorry about getting you into trouble. I lost my temper... Nobody should have heard that. I shouldn't have said it. I tried to tell Chester it was just me being crazy. I said I was obsessed with you. It wasn't far from the truth. I told him it had nothing to do with you."

Oh god. And I hadn't given work a second thought. "Thanks, but I walked out."

"You resigned?"

"Yeah, but then Chester insisted on giving me redundancy."

"Why did you do that? You loved that job."

"It was OK. The whole place is going down the drain anyway. But I'm sorry you lost your job there." I didn't defend him to Chester, though, the way he did for me.

"It was temporary. I'll survive."

"Listen Max... I think I got the wrong idea about Grace, and I'm sorry."

He doesn't reply, so I plough on.

"And the baby isn't yours, is she? I'm sorry I thought –"

"No, I'm not Elsie's dad. But so what?"

"I know. I'm sorry. I thought you were cheating on Grace –"

"And now you know Grace was never my girlfriend anyway? How, Ciara? It's not like you've asked me about her."

"I know." My heart's sinking. This really isn't going well. "Olive found Grace's profile on Facebook. It said –"

"Facebook? You need to consult social media before you can make up your mind about whether to trust me or not?" His voice gets quieter. "And – wait – Olive did it? You didn't even care enough to search by yourself?"

"Olive loves that kind of thing," I mumble.

"Did you ask her to look?"

"No, I..." I believed the worst of him. "...I didn't want to invade your privacy."

He lets out a tiny laugh. "Oh god, what am I asking? You're right – I don't want you to stalk me anyway. It would be nice to think you cared enough to give me a second thought, but I should know by now that's not how it works with you." He sighs. "Look, Ciara, I'm not sure why you called, but right now I'm... Well, I'm kind of a bit heartbroken."

I nearly ask who has broken his heart.

"And talking to the person I'm trying to get over isn't helping."

Can I be in any doubt at all now that he means me? That he was talking about me all along?

"But we weren't together!" I protest. "Not properly."

There's a massive pause. "Yeah, OK. You're right, we weren't." His voice goes really quiet. "I'd better go."

"Wait! Max?"

He hesitates. "What?" he whispers.

"Can I see you again? Can we talk more?" I want to explain! I want to hear about his complicated life and find out about Grace and the baby. I want another chance with him. We are so right together, me and Max.

The pause that follows is even longer.

"I'll see you at CHAPS," he says finally.

He hangs up.

It's goodbye. I know it's exactly what I deserve. It hurts like hell.

☼

NOW: The Cavalry

I wallow for ages.

I realise CHAPS is only a week away, and it could be the last time I see Max for another seven years. And that's if he'll even talk to me while we're there.

Now that I have no job and no life, I barely get out of bed. When I do, I wander aimlessly around the shops in Croydon, feeling sad and lonely and missing Max more than I ever thought possible. Everything I see reminds me of him. A cafe advertising cheese omelettes, a charity shop selling orange slippers, a guitar in the window of a shop called Instant Cash 4U. All I can think of is Max, Max, Max. What am I going to do?

I walk past a construction site. That makes me think of Tomas instead of Max, at least.

That's it! I need a grand gesture! It has to be worth a try.

But it has to be just right.

I call in the big guns. It's the only way. I know for a fact that harnessing the combined strength of my friends and their crazy ideas is the only way I'll have another stab at happiness with Max.

I start at the top, with the king of grand gestures. Mr Nude Long-Johns Construction Vehicle Paris Proposal himself.

"Louis, is Tomas there?"

"Ciara? No, he's filming all morning. Are you planning on stealing my fiance?"

"As if he'd ever let himself be stolen. No, I need him because of his PhD in Grand Gesture Studies."

"Let me guess! You upset Max? You need a grand gesture to win him back?"

I begrudgingly admit that he's got it in one.

"Let me help! Please please please, Ciara! Tomas might be the master, but I put all the thoughts in his head with my long-johns request in the first place. I can do this, I can!"

"OK." I give him a chance.

"Hurray! You won't regret it. OK, here goes. First question. Did Max like anything unusual in bed?"

"Louis, seriously?"

"I'm deadly serious! It's a genuine question. I'm not sure I want to hear the answer..." He pretends to shudder. "But it's a good starting point. I know men."

Yeah, no. "I think we're barking up the wrong tree." Especially when Max accused me of only wanting him for his body.

"So... barking? Trees?"

"So I'm not answering your question."

He tuts. "Ciara, don't be like that! I'm helping!"

"Can you help me by asking Tomas to ring me when he has time? Thank you! Bye, Louis!"

Sophie's next. She's at work in her health food shop, so she has to pretend I'm a customer whenever her supervisor is within earshot. "Have you tried vitamins?" is her first piece of advice after I explain.

"Should I call back later, Soph?"

"No, no. She's gone. OK, so you've basically trampled all over Max's heart for no good reason, and...."

"Ouch, Sophie!"

"I'm just summarising." Her voice changes. "Also, we have a special offer on Ginseng tea."

"I'll call you later," I tell Sophie. "Thank you!"

Who else? I still feel weird asking Tilly but I can't leave her out of this. I'm making lots of effort to talk to her and send her messages in general, trying to make up for the past few weeks. Her phone goes to voicemail, though. That means it's Olive's turn.

Olive! I need you! I text.

At your service! she replies instantly. She works at a research lab and she'll have dropped all her life-changing discoveries to help me. I explain the situation, which she mostly knows, of course.

Words, she replies. *You're good with words. Write him something.*

I could, I suppose. It doesn't seem quite right. *Some catalogue copy?* I joke.

Ha. No. Changed my mind. That's you, not him.

Yeah.

Music! Olive sends next. *He's a musician, isn't he? Reach him with music. Personal stuff. Perform it yourself.*

I can't play! I can't sing! I reply, panicking.

So learn? Learn one of his songs? she writes.

Oh god. Could I? It would definitely be the grandest of gestures. Would it even be possible in a week? What if I was terrible – would it make things worse?

I realise something and my heart sinks.

I don't even know any of his songs, I write. *I've never listened to his band.*

Why not? OMG Ciara, do you actually like this man?

I love him, I type back, admitting it to Olive and myself at the same time. *I'm the worst!*

You're not, she texts. *You're just scared. You've deliberately switched off your feelings. You won't let yourself love him. Soph and me figured it out. We love you. You can do this.*

Oh, wow. I love my friends very much.

What can I do? I ask her.

Find his music online! Or remember what he played at home? Did he cover famous songs? Any favourites?

Do I remember what he played at home? No. Not at all.

I think back to the silence in the flat when Tilly and Max were in their rooms. My signal that the coast was clear and I could dash to the kitchen, or whatever, avoiding them.

He didn't play anything, I type.

He's a musician and he didn't play anything? she writes. *That's impossible.*

I remember the niggle I felt when Olive was talking to me at Sophie's house. This time it screams in my brain. "It must be loud living with a musician," she'd said.

I remember Max arriving with his guitar. It was the main thing that made him recognisable as the Max I used to know. The case had stickers on it that spelled 'Max', and a torn Four Part Cure sticker.

This rings alarm bells too.

Olive, you are a genius, I text. *I have to go. Bye!*

I didn't think I'd get recognition in my own lifetime, she replies.

I run out of the flat, slamming the door behind me. I reach Instant Cash 4U within minutes and stare at the shop window display, out of breath but excited.

It's there. The guitar that reminded me of Max. I look closer. It's perched in front of its case, looking flashy and expensive. I peer through the grease-smeared window. The stickers on the case spell 'Max'. There's a torn Four Part Cure sticker.

It's Max's guitar. He must have sold it. Why? To pay the rent? That night when he wanted to take me to dinner, he said he'd come into some money. How does someone like Max, whose family have largely disowned him and who were never wealthy anyway, come into money?

He sold his guitar.

Why, why?

Whatever the reason, I think I've found my grand gesture. I can't believe Max wouldn't want this back. It must have felt like losing a limb. Like when he broke his leg and gave up his dreams of becoming a footballer. Only this time there's a fix! I'm squinting through the window, looking for the price tag, when my phone rings. Louis.

I answer with, "Please don't ask me that kinky thing again!"

Someone clears their throat. "Have I got the right number? Ciara?"

Oops. It's not Louis. "Tomas! Sorry about that. I can explain..."

"No need. I know the explanation must be Louis. Now, he asked me to call you? Something about grand gestures?"

"Yes! But –"

"The best advice I can give is that you should speak to him from your heart. Whatever form that takes. I wish you luck. It's a gamble, but it paid off for me. Grab happiness where you can!"

I gaze at the guitar. "OK. Thanks. Send my love to Louis."

After we say goodbye, I go into the shop to ask about the guitar. The price makes me gulp. It is extortionate. It's unaffordable. I'd have to leave the flat, that's for sure. I'd have to move back into my parents' house. It would use up my entire redundancy cheque, the one Chester insisted I should have.

I ring my landlord to hand in my notice. I couldn't have covered the rent for much longer anyway, not now Tilly and Louis aren't coming back. It all makes sense.

"Oh, great!" is my landlord's reaction. "I can ask for a lot more if I put it back on the market. I was only keeping it low as a favour to Monique."

Low? OK, if he says so.

"Move out as soon as you like!" he says cheerily. "That area's in high demand. I could find new tenants tomorrow!"

I ring my mum and tell her I'm moving back. She only moans a little bit. "I'm glad we got our cruise, at least," she says. "We're never child-free for long."

I promise my mum it's temporary.

I am buying that guitar back for Max.

When I get home, I finally look up Max's band and listen to hours of their music, watching wobbly live performance recordings made by fans on YouTube and trying to catch glimpses of Max. The chemistry between the singer and the drummer – Grace and Dan – is obvious in a couple of the clips I find. She keeps glancing over at him, and in one of the videos he winks at her cheekily. Max is usually tucked away at the side, firmly in the background, concentrating on his guitar.

I want to reach into my phone for him.

☼

CHAPS: Twenty-eight – part 1

Moving out of Croydon and back to Northwood takes much longer than I expected. I have to put Louis and Tilly's stuff in storage for them, which they agree to, both issuing me with specific and complicated instructions. Then I have to make what I estimate will be a hundred trips across the entire Greater London train and tube network to get back and forth between my flat and the house I grew up in.

After the first hundred trips – well, after the first one, in truth – I moan to Mum so much that she sends Dad off to Croydon in the car to get the rest of my stuff, lock up the flat and deliver the key to the landlord's cleaner. Parents are great, especially when you're supposed to be too old to rely on them.

All of this makes me late for CHAPS, though. And I have extra things to pack this time, like a guitar and a heavy, hopeful heart.

Dad, reprising his old role as Taxi Driver of Many Daughters, drops me at the gate to the adventure park I'll be staying in for the rest of the week. "I remember taking you and your mum to this thing when you were fourteen," he says fondly. "Feels like yesterday." He gives me a long look. "Are you sure you'll be OK, Ciara? I know this must be tough after –"

"I'm fine, Dad," I insist.

"Well, OK. Call me if you need me. Anytime. I mean it."

I thank him and wave as he leaves, a pile of luggage including Max's guitar at my feet. Then I trudge up to the reception area.

It's strange to think that Max is at CHAPS before me. I don't think that's ever happened before. I remember knocking at his door when we were fourteen and he hadn't arrived yet. I remember waiting for him when we were twenty-one, and Amelia directing me, blind-folded, to walk into him.

This time he's already here. In a family room, whatever that's about. I need to listen to his explanation.

And I have to find him and tell him everything I realised when I was talking to Olive. That I want to be in his life too. That I'm his friend, at least.

That I want to be his girlfriend again, if he'll consider it.

I settle into the cabin I've been assigned – a cosy single – before heading off to the part of the residential area where the family rooms are. As I approach, hoisting Max's guitar on my shoulder, I can already see children running in the direction of a large adventure playground in the distance. They're probably the sons and daughters of some of the people I've been coming here with since I was little. I'm not sure I'll ever get used to the fact that we're in our late twenties now.

I see them before they see me. A cute and chubby little girl, absolutely adorable in a bright blue dress, toddling down the pavement hand-in-hand with a man whose smile makes my heart leap. Max.

Behind them, wheeling a pushchair, is a tall woman with long dark hair. I vaguely recognise her from the picture I saw years ago, but she looks older, of course. Max turns to her and says something. They both laugh.

As I walk towards them, he spots me. He stops laughing. He mumbles something to the woman.

Suddenly I'm a bag of nerves. I want to turn and run in the opposite direction. What if he won't speak to me? What if it's not his guitar? What if he doesn't want it – or not from me? I can't do this. I can't, I can't. I stop walking.

Grace is watching me. She leaves the pushchair and strides over, holding out her hand.

"Ciara, right?" She shakes hands with me. "Max has told me a lot about you. Hi, I'm Grace. And that's Elsie."

Elsie takes a few steps towards us, her arms stretching out to Grace. Max focuses on her, ignoring me. Oh god.

"So... yeah, me and Elsie have to..."

"Wing! Wing!" Elsie shouts.

Grace laughs. "We have an appointment with a swing. Excuse us." She picks Elsie up, gets the pushchair and wheels it one-handed towards the playground, leaving me alone with Max.

"Hi," I try. Is he going to reply at all? My heart pounds. I don't think I can take this.

"Hello, Ciara," he says quietly, looking at the ground.

"Hi."

"Grace has heard about you from other people," he says. "Not me. Not lately."

This is worse than I expected. Why is he saying this? "No?"

"It turns out we're a bit famous at CHAPS. You and me."

"Oh, er.."

"I think people must have seen us together last time, or something." He still doesn't meet my eyes. "Grace was talking to this woman yesterday and she recognised me and asked about you. Apparently we were the only CHAPS couple, as far as she knew. Apart from a few one-nighters."

We were a couple?

We were, we were.

Max shrugs. "Do you want to guess who the woman was?"

What? "Er... no. I don't know."

"It was Ali Rashid. Can you believe it?"

"Ali Rashid is a woman after all?"

"Yup. And she knew who we were. So we've finally found her. Well, Grace did."

"We should talk to her," I say. "About the birthday cards."

"I know." Even this doesn't make him smile. There's a silence.

Max takes a deep breath. "You missed the tribute to Amelia," he says. "At the introductory meeting. They made an announcement. A message from the researchers."

"Oh." My heart sinks. "I didn't know..."

"Doesn't matter. You would have hated it. It didn't sound like they knew her at all."

"Oh."

I should have been there, though. I am the worst person in the world. It's official.

And he still hasn't looked at me.

"Listen, Max, I, er... brought you something." I pull the guitar case off my shoulder and show him. "It's yours, right? I thought you might want it back."

His eyes widen, staring at the case. "Where did you get that?"

"Where you left it, I think. One of those cash shops in Croydon."

"I was going to buy it back," Max says. "Eventually, if nobody else got there first." He sighs. "I was hoping they wouldn't."

"Well, now they can't, can they? It's yours again." I hold it out to him.

He doesn't take it. "How did you pay for it?"

"My redundancy money," I mumble.

He looks at me at last, his eyes blazing. "It's not right. I have to pay you back."

"No, I –"

"I will." He frowns. "It might take me a while – I have other priorities now." He glances in the direction of the playground. "But I'll do it."

"No. I got it for you. It's a present! I want you to have it." I hold it out further, practically shoving it at him.

He shakes his head. "I can't take it until I've paid for it."

Frustration rises in me. "For fuck's sake, Max! I got this for you to say sorry! To show you what you mean to me!" Oh no, this is wrong. I've never seen a movie grand gesture where the gesturer loses it with the gesturee.

There's a silence. He looks at the ground.

His voice is so quiet that I barely hear what he says next. "What *do* I mean to you, Ciara?"

"Everything!" I actually stamp my foot, I'm so frustrated. "You're my best friend, and that's saying something, because I have awesome friends. And I'm sorry! I'm sorry I treated you so badly. I'm sorry I accused you of cheating without letting you explain! I'm sorry I didn't read any of your texts for years! I'm even sorry about blocking your MSN account when we were fourteen! I understand why you hate me. I've treated you like shit! I would hate me too."

"I don't hate you," he says quietly. "And you haven't –"

"I have! And you should. I keep hurting you! You mean the world to me and I'm sorry I can't make you happy. I just wanted another chance. But I get it, I do." My voice wobbles. *Don't cry, don't cry*, I tell myself. "Keep the guitar. Please." I put it on the ground in front of him. I can't look at him.

I walk away.

"Ciara!"

I keep walking.

I tried, but it's no use. It really is over.

☼

CHAPS: Twenty-eight – part 2

I manage to get through the next two days on autopilot. I keep my head down and go through the motions, hiding at the back at of any meetings and doing the bare minimum. I don't make eye contact with anyone, let alone Max. I'm not even sure whether he's at any of the activities. I arrive late and leave early, keeping myself as far apart from the others as I can.

After that, I spend a day in bed, knowing nobody will miss me. I sleep a lot, but it doesn't help.

The next day it's nearly the end of CHAPS, so I make the effort to drag myself out of bed, but I can't face the activities. I walk around the adventure park aimlessly for hours, not knowing where to go or what to do with myself. It's different from the place we went to when we were fourteen – bigger and more modern, but also more earthy and less plastic, with lots of wooded areas and zipwires trailing Tarzan-like from tree to tree. In other ways, it's the same – there are rollercoasters, water slides, all the thrill rides Amelia would have wanted to go on again and again.

I can't stand it. Where is she? Where's my wild friend from CHAPS, my partner in crime? She should be here. I can't do this without her. I knew it would be hard, coming here. But I underestimated how much everything about the residential would remind me of her.

And she's not here. She'll never be here. Not just here. Anywhere. It makes no sense. I can't deal with it. And I'm annoyed with myself not being able to, which makes me feel worse.

I go back to my cabin. There's an envelope waiting for me, pushed under the door. It has my name on it next to a scribbled smiley face. Nice touch. I tear it open and find a standard happiness questionnaire, the kind I've filled in loads of times now for CHAPS. I could laugh at the irony of it.

I pick up the special flat pen they've thoughtfully provided and angle it above the questions.

"I am confident about myself."
Rate agreement on a scale of 1 to 10.
"I am optimistic about the future."
Rate agreement on a scale of 1 to 10.
"My life is satisfying."
Rate agreement on a scale of 1 to 10.

Should I tell the truth? Zero, zero, zero.

The reverse questions are there too. They are equally bad.

"I do not feel contented with my life."
Rate agreement on a scale of 1 to 10.
"I do not feel I am achieving what I want in life."
Rate agreement on a scale of 1 to 10.
"I am not looking forward to the future."
Rate agreement on a scale of 1 to 10.

Eleven, eleven, eleven.

Should I tell the research team that I am not happy and I will never be happy again? That there's no point to anything, that life is empty and meaningless and I've just been playing at being a person all this time, pretending everything's OK when it's not, and it never will be? When my friend wanted to kill herself and I let her? I let her go – I didn't even try to save her? And then I pushed away the only man I've ever really loved? And even when he came back into my life and showed how much he still cared about me, I kept pushing and pushing until he cracked and left me forever, with good reason? That I'm not surprised he doesn't want me, because I don't want me either? That I know I have the most amazing friends, that I love Tilly and Louis and Olive and Sophie, but I don't think I deserve them, any of them? That even when I sit around laughing with them and having fun on the surface, deep down inside I am hollow, an echoing void?

I turn the pen in my hand, stare at the paper.

Oh shit, oh shit. I can't do this. I can't.

I should tell the truth. I should write it all over these forms, and the others I was supposed to have filled in this week. I should scratch it out in huge lettering and press too hard with my pen, I should scrawl outside the boxes. Maybe they'll suggest I should leave the project, like Amelia. And then... And then...

An almighty sob shakes through me. I can't do this. I can't live like this. I can't.

But I don't know how not to, either.

And a wave of realisation washes over me.

I am like Amelia.

This is what she was talking about, that day when she came to say goodbye. Seven years ago, almost to the day. Seven years I've gone on without her, pretending everything is fine. Seven years of feeling numb, like the world's spinning without me. Seven years of grief. Seven years of going through the motions.

Seven years of hiding. I didn't want anyone to see it. I wouldn't let myself see it. A depth of nothingness I would never admit to in a million years.

And before that? Before Amelia left? I don't know. I've always been tentative – pushing happiness away. I've never been sure of myself. I've never been happy being myself. Not really.

I wanted to be Amelia.

I cry and cry, turning my back on the world, hoping it will go away. Ignoring the knocking at the door. The voice saying, "Ciara? Ciara, please let me in. Ciara, come on!" Waiting for it to stop.

It doesn't.

"Ciara, it's Max! Please let me in!"

I walk to the door in a trance. The tears are pouring down my face and I'm watching them land on the grey flooring. They don't seem connected to me. I don't feel connected to anything.

I open the door.

"Ciara." Max steps into the room, takes one look at me and pulls me into his arms. "I got your cabin number from reception. I haven't seen you for days – I was worried about you."

I shift away and look at him, confused. "Are you here because you promised Sophie?"

"What? No. No, I... Anyway, I promised *you*."

"Me...?"

"I said I'd be here for you. And... and I haven't been. But, no, I came to tell you I'm sorry too. I'm sorry for being so stubborn. I'll get over myself. Thank you for buying back my guitar. Thank you for what you said." He puts his arms around me again.

"You can't save me, Massimo the Monster Slayer," I state, blinking. "Please don't try."

"OK, I won't. Just let me stay with you?" His voice is low. "Until you can save yourself? Please, Ciara." His arms tighten around me as I sob. "I'm here, I'm here."

He holds me as I cry seven years' worth of tears.

☼

CHAPS: Twenty-eight – part 3

I wake up next to Max, morning light streaming through the small window of my cabin.

We're fully clothed, entwined on my bed. My head is resting against his shoulder. His t-shirt is still damp from my tears.

So I didn't dream it. I really did cry myself to sleep in Max's arms.

It's a new low.

Or maybe not. Maybe I'm grateful he was there.

He stirs and strokes my hair away from my face.

"Ciara," he whispers. "How are you? Are you OK?"

"I think so," I say.

"I'm so worried about you. Are you sure?"

I mentally check myself over. The despair I felt last night is like a dull ache in the back of my head. It's less vivid, less insistent. But it's still there. And so familiar. Now that I've acknowledged it, now that I've felt its full force, I can see that it's been there for a long, long time.

"I think I might have a problem," I say.

Max is quiet.

Eventually he says, "I know you've been struggling."

"I don't think it's depression," I say. "Not like Amelia." It still feels strange to say her name so freely. "I think it's something else. Squashed grief, or something..."

"I don't know." Max shifts a bit to look at me. "I know you have trouble letting yourself enjoy life because you're scared. Because you feel bad about being alive when Amelia... isn't."

Survivor guilt. It's not like I haven't read about it, thought about it. I've been fully aware of it. And... "I haven't been feeling bad, though. I've been feeling..."

"Like there's no point? Like you don't want to invest too much in anything, just in case? Like it's better to skate along on the surface, never letting people see the real you?"

"Meh," I say, that one little sound that sums it up. "I've been feeling meh. Indifferent about life, about love, about... everything." I look at Max. Nearly everything.

"OK, well, I'm no expert. And I think people are all different, like with everything. But I do think you've been going through... Well, a lot. You don't need to label it, but you probably should talk about it. And maybe you could do with some professional help?"

I reel at the thought.

But he might be right.

"You know, feeling like this now doesn't mean feeling like this forever." Max's voice is so soothing. "I think everyone in the world experiences something like this at some point, and most of us pull through."

"Yeah," I mumble.

"Yeah. Life definitely isn't easy. But it's worth holding on for the good times. And asking for help if you need it?"

He's right, he's right.

Max shifts in the bed, moving to comfort me. "It's understandable, though. The Amelia thing hit you really hard. And I bet you think it's too long ago, but I don't think it works that way. It's tough, losing a friend like that. And depression can be part of grief."

I know this. I know and I still never connected it with anything in myself. "So is anger," I realise. "I'm still angry with Amelia, too. Mostly about you."

"About me?"

"She wanted me to be with you, Max. It was practically the last thing she said to me. She insisted." I remember the conversation like it was yesterday, I've replayed it that many times in my head. "It was like she was offering me *you...* instead of her." I can't believe I've never thought about it in these terms before. Not explicitly. "I wanted both." And if I couldn't have both, I'd have neither. I didn't want to be with Max... because it was what Amelia had asked me to do.

I was angry with her for that. And I refused to let it happen.

"Max," I wonder aloud, "how do you do it?" How could he be so patient with me last night, the state I was in? And now? Why isn't he running a mile away from me? "How are you so good at... life?"

"I'm not!" Max replies. "I'm really not. But I've had to think about stuff a lot, I suppose. My life's been kind of complicated."

"You never did tell me what you meant by that. Was it Carol?" I remember Max's lateness for CHAPS and some of the things he'd told me at the time. It makes me ask, "Did she have depression too?"

"Not Carol, no. She had a different illness. Chronic Fatigue Syndrome. It makes life very tough for her, on and off. She has good days and bad days. The bad days were particularly hard when I was little, I think. But she still soldiered on, looking after me, giving me everything. She was amazing. One day soon, I'll call her again. I miss her. It's why I can't get properly angry about Malcolm – my step-dad. He's been brilliant for her – really supportive. He's just a bit traditional, that's all."

"And that's why he threw you out? Tradition?"

"Well, yeah. I was eighteen. People like him don't support fully grown adults. Especially when they're not yours... you know, by blood."

"But you're Carol's. His girlfriend's. She's your mum."

Max sighs. "Yeah, but... not by blood."

What? "Max?"

"Carol's not my birth mum. Never mind. It's a long story."

"You know what?" I sit up. It's about time I listened to everything he has to say. I want to hear it all. "I've got time."

Max insists on getting breakfast for us first. He makes me promise I'll be all right for a few minutes on my own before he runs down to the free cafeteria provided for CHAPS. While he's gone, I get up, wash and change, avoiding glimpses of my tear-stained face in the mirror.

He comes back breathless, holding a tray of food and two lidded coffees. We eat at the little desk in the corner of my cabin, mostly in silence. Then we move back to the bed because it's the most comfortable place, really. I settle with his arm around me as he talks.

☼

CHAPS: Twenty-eight – part 4

Max tells me about his birth mum, a woman called Maria Renzo – Carol's childhood best friend. About how Maria got pregnant when she was nineteen and the father didn't want to know. And how she had severe post-natal depression, to the point where she couldn't take care of Max. Her parents were mega-religious and wouldn't help, so Carol and Carol's parents stepped in, on instructions from Maria and with the approval of social services and courts.

Max's birth father eventually came back into the picture, but only for long enough to make promises and then disappear again several times as Max grew up, hurting Max in the process. Max has mentioned his useless dad before, but now I see it in context and I understand why Max was such a serious little boy.

I understand it even more when he explains the next part.

"Maria got better, though, while I was still small. She got treatment, she stuck to it and it worked. But even so, she decided... not to have me back. Carol told me it was nobody's fault – it was an after-effect of her illness. Maria just didn't feel... attached to me. She couldn't cope. But sometimes I can't help thinking she didn't even try." Max's voice wobbles slightly but he continues. "Carol didn't mind – she loved me – but she didn't get why Maria wouldn't want me in her life at all. She and Maria completely fell out over it. They still don't really speak."

I place my hand over his.

"And then my grandparents – Carol's parents – died. One after the other, in the same year. They weren't even old – it was bad luck. Cancer, and an unexpected heart condition. But Carol and I had each other, and we got through it. And eventually – and it took years and years, because everyone wanted to be sure it was the right thing to do – Carol adopted me. She became a young single mum out of love for her friend. And for me, I suppose, by that point. That's why I don't blame her for wanting Malcolm – she kind of missed out on a lot and she deserves some happiness, you know? Even if we don't speak much now, I still love her for wanting me."

I don't know what to say. "Wow. Max."

He squeezes my hand before ploughing on. "Anyway, a long time before I was officially adopted, Maria got pregnant again and had her second baby."

I connect the dots. "Grace?"

"Grace," he confirms. "This time she got loads of help and everyone watched out for her. It was completely different. Plus my dad was a transformed person with Grace. I don't know why." He sighs. "I still won't talk to him. He hurt me too much when I was so young. I talk to Maria occasionally. It feels weird, but I think I accept it now. It wasn't her fault."

"So Grace really is your sister?"

"Yeah, technically – we have the exact same birth parents. Different surnames because I have my birth mum's – Carol thought we shouldn't change it after so long – and Grace has our dad's. Grace is only three years younger than me but there's kind of a lifetime between us."

"Did you know Grace? Growing up?"

"Not really. Our mums weren't talking. We had a strange sort of relationship for years – I mean, we knew about each other, but only from a distance. She didn't feel like a sister at all – just some little girl with a vague connection to me. But then one day, when she was only sixteen, she turned up on my doorstep, asking to move in with me. She'd had a fight with her parents, found my address and made the train journey all by herself. It was dangerous, really."

"But she stayed?"

"Yes, because she fell in love. With Dan – who I'll never, ever forgive."

I wonder about that. I think about what Olive said about friends and forgiveness. Maybe there are situations it doesn't stretch to. Max and Dan. Carol and Maria.

"Dan was seventeen at the time – he's Jack's little brother. So in a way, it worked out. Jack and I both had our younger siblings with us and we could keep an eye on them. Grace's parents weren't happy about it, but at least she was safe. Plus Grace could sing – beautifully. It gave our band an extra dimension." He smiles, remembering. "Especially because we had the word 'four' in our bandname, thanks to Jack's Philosophy studies, but only three members, until Grace! That was a major reason Grace stayed, to be honest."

"And then she got pregnant?"

"Yeah... She and Dan had been together ages by then. They lived together. They're young but not exactly kids or anything, and it didn't feel like the end of the world, you know?"

I nod.

"I don't even think it was unplanned. That's Grace for you – she was always in a hurry to grow up. But it was the beginning of the end for our band. Dan fell apart when the baby was born, and before, too – drink, drugs, you name it. Other women. It was awful. I couldn't stand seeing it happen. Grace kicked him out eventually, but I was worried about her. With her... our family history. I moved in with Grace and tried to be there for Elsie."

"To be like a dad?"

"No, not at all. I know single-parent families are fine. Better than that, in many cases. I'm from one! But I want to protect Elsie from the feeling you get when you have a crap dad – that horrible rejection." His face is grim. "I'm not going to stand around and watch history repeat itself, not if I can help it."

"Oh, Max."

"No, don't feel sorry for me. I've been a bit crap too. A while ago, it all got too much and I met this girl and followed her to Australia. I mean, I couldn't have gone much further from Grace and Elsie if I'd tried! But Grace insisted I should go, and we kept in touch. Anyway, it didn't last long. Also I managed to get some useful training and save some money so I could come and live in London, where Grace has been planning on moving with Elsie. She's got a brilliant job in admin for a chain store and they're transferring her to head office – starting after her leave this week. I said I'd go ahead of her and find accommodation for the three of us, but I... got a bit distracted." He glances at me.

It's all falling into place now – why Max needed a temporary place to stay. Why he came to London in the first place.

"Anyway, she managed it from a distance and we're moving in soon. And I asked the CHAPS team if Grace and Elsie could come with me this week. They're family, after all, and I thought they needed a holiday. I explained it all to the research team and got the approval... the day I tried to tell you."

I look away. "Why didn't you tell me any of this before?"

"I tried, once or twice. But you were... you kept your distance, and it's a complicated situation to explain. I was worried about how you'd take it, especially the fact that I'd invited them here. I didn't want to upset you. I knew how hard CHAPS would be for you."

He was right to be worried. When he did try to tell me, I'd twisted it all before he'd even finished speaking.

"Stop it, Ciara, I know what you're thinking. Don't. Stop bashing yourself."

He's right. And I should be focusing on him, anyway, and on what he's telling me. "How long do you think you'll live with Grace and Elsie?"

"As long as they need me, I suppose. I want to help Grace financially, and also with Elsie if I can. I want to be the best uncle in the world! This is why I had to get a safe and boring job... I needed to give up music and grow up. So selling my guitar made sense." He gives a sad smile. "It was about time, don't you think?"

I really don't. "You don't have to give up music! And look what happened with the boring job you just had. The whole company is doomed. Soon there won't be anyone left there. There's no such thing as 'safe'. I've been made redundant twice in the past six years. Well, three times now! The sensible business-to-business magazine I worked on before folded even quicker than the knicker-describing job at the catalogue. I know I left that but –"

"Chester would never have sacked you."

"Ssh," I say. I feel uncomfortable whenever I think about Chester. "Turns out he only liked me professionally, anyway."

Max makes a face. "Yeah, *right*. I don't believe that for a second. I bet he only said that after he found out about us!"

I get back to my point. "Look, what I'm trying to say is that there's no security in any job. You might as well do something you love – it's equally risky! And loving what you do makes it more likely to succeed anyway." I think. "Though that didn't work with my Treasure sales, did it? Nearly everything got returned!" I go for the same jokey tone I used with my friends, repeating what I said to Sophie. "It has to be a metaphor for something!"

Max doesn't hesitate. "Yeah. For being awesome even if you get rejected," he says. "Because rejection doesn't make you any less awesome."

I feel instantly guilty. Max has been rejected by his family – and by me. "That sounds like you," I mumble.

"No, Ciara, it sounds like *you*. Look at me and tell me you didn't feel rejected by Amelia."

I can't.

"The ultimate rejection. You can't even try to patch things up."

My eyes fill with tears, but I'm not going there. Not again. I think about Max instead. "What about you? With your dad. And then Carol." And then me.

"No, it was definitely Malcolm – not her. I've thought about it a lot since I talked to you about it. It wasn't all one-sided, anyway. I was horrible to him – and to Mum." He thinks. "I always used to call her Mum, you know. It's only after Malcolm arrived that I started calling her 'Carol' – to annoy her, I suppose? But she wasn't annoyed. She put up with so much from me. And she is my mum in every way, really, including all the irritating ones. The only thing she didn't do was give birth to me."

"Did you always know? That she wasn't your birth mum, I mean?"

He nods. "She first told me when I was tiny – I don't even remember when – and lots of times afterwards. She didn't want me to find out later and be upset. I knew it before I understood it."

A memory pops into my head of the first time I met Max at CHAPS. He'd said that confusing thing when I spoke to him.

"You told me," I realise. "When we were seven. I said your mum was calling you, and you replied that she wasn't your mum."

"She wasn't, officially. Not then. She was my legal guardian. I suppose I did call her 'mum'. But I had this weird need to tell you the absolute truth!"

I think about it. "You said you didn't tell the truth to just anyone." I remember it. "I wanted to be that person."

"You always have been, Ciara." Max takes a deep breath. "So you have to believe me. What happened to Amelia was tragic and terrible, and I know you wish you could change things. But unfortunately you can't. Nobody can."

He takes my hand.

"It wasn't your fault," he says. "Or mine. It wasn't Penelope's, or Hugh's. Or the doctors who were treating Amelia. Or even Amelia's. It wasn't anyone's." He pauses. "Amelia had a serious illness. Lots of people have the same one and pull through. My birth mum, for a start. But Amelia didn't. And it's awful, but it is nobody's fault. *Nobody*."

I stare at him for a long moment.

"And something else," he adds. "You are allowed to be happy."

I see what he means – finally. And anyway it's not about being off the scale for stratospheric, unbridled joy at all times. It's about letting myself live and enjoy the good moments when they come.

"OK," I say at last, blinking. "I believe you."

"Great. But there is one thing I haven't been completely honest with you about."

☼

CHAPS: Twenty-eight – part 5

I look at Max. "When haven't you been honest?"
"When I said I didn't want a relationship. You kind of cornered me into saying it! Then you kept repeating it. But the first time, you were asking me about Tilly. I meant it about her, about other people. Not about you," he says. "I thought there was no chance with you. You made it pretty clear the moment I moved in, if not for years and years before."

"Oh."

"And I'm not sure whether I should say the rest, but I want to. And this is definitely the truth."

This sounds kind of worrying. "OK," I say, bracing myself for bad news.

He looks into my eyes.

He says, "I love you, Ciara." He touches the ends of my hair. "I've always loved you, and I always will. Whatever you think of me."

"Even if I don't care about you at all?" I can't help asking. It's how I felt for so long, after all. After Amelia died. So utterly numb. About him, about everyone. About life. I've been going through the motions, and now I see it. I see the difference.

Max can light up my world.

But I have to let him. I have to let the light in on myself first. It's down to me. My ability to be happy is in my own hands. And I'm going to work on it.

He swallows. "Well, yeah. It doesn't change how I feel about you. Nothing could. Believe me, I've tried. But it's fine if you feel that way. I'll –"

I interrupt him. How can he doubt it, after all this? Still, I don't mind spelling it out for him if that's what he needs.

"I love you too, Max," I say. "And I always have, even when I had a funny way of showing it. And I'm pretty sure I always will."

A smile grows on his face. His eyes spark at mine. "I can't believe you just said that."

I can't believe he didn't know. I lean towards him, desperate to kiss him.

Max hesitates. "We can't... Ciara, I can't take advantage of you."

I frown. "What do you mean?" I remember our argument in the storeroom. "Didn't you say *I* was the one using *you*?"

His cheeks redden. "I told you I should never have said that! I was hurt, and lashing out. It was wrong. I'm really sorry."

"Max. It's OK."

"No, it's not." He shakes his head. "I mean it. And I mean this, too. I don't think we should jump into this, however much... I want to. I think you should have time by yourself. Get better. Then if you still want to –"

"I still want to," I tell him without hesitation. "Right now."

"Give it time. Then see how you feel?"

"I know how I'll feel." I sweep my eyes over his face, his body. "I feel it now."

"Ciara..." He sighs. "I want to be with you. You've no idea how much. But, even more than that, I want you to be happy."

"I'm happy with you," I state.

"Happy by yourself. Happy for yourself." He brushes at a tear stain on my cheek. "And then with me, if you still want. OK?"

I suppose I see his point. These past few months have been about more than Max. I started my own happiness project, I made myself try. I threw myself into Treasure at work with a passion. It didn't work out, but I'm glad I gave it a go. I forced myself to banish indifference – I let the emotions in for the first time in years. It hasn't been about Max. Or at least, not all of it. I can do this. I can get through it.

I reluctantly agree with Max.

We spend the rest of the day talking. Maybe I'm still avoiding the world, or at least avoiding CHAPS activities. But I'm no longer avoiding the truth. I'm no longer lying to myself. Instead, I'm telling myself – and Max – everything. And he's doing the same with me.

It feels like a start.

***

The next day, it's the end of CHAPS. Grace and Elsie head to the playground for one last swing, leaving me and Max to say goodbye before we go our separate ways for another seven years.

Or less. Max suggests a year before we meet again. A year for me to sort my life out, find myself, recover. See if I still want to be with him.

I make a counter-offer of a month.

Max smiles but he says, "That's not long enough, Ciara. You need to focus on yourself."

I know he's right. "Three months?"

"Three months is nothing."

"Three months is ages. It's three months since you moved into my flat." It was the time limit I secretly gave myself for my Operation Happiness. Three months to sort myself out before CHAPS.

"Yeah. OK, then. Three months," he agrees. "And if you change your mind about me, I'll understand. I won't like it, but I'll get it. I promise."

"I won't change my mind." I stare at him.

He holds my gaze. "OK. Well, good."

"Though I swear," I murmur, "if you don't kiss me right now, before you go, then it's over. Forever." I'm so sure of myself, and of us. I can say anything to him.

Max touches my face. "As if it could ever really be over between us," he says in a low voice. "I found that out a long time ago. No, if we're going to do this, I'm not going to let you ruin it." The look he gives me makes my heart pound. "Not this time. Or next time, either. Because I know you – I know *us* – and I know there will be next time. And whatever it takes... Whenever you're ready to have me in your life, I'm there. I'm not going anywhere."

He pulls me into his arms to say goodbye for now.

I find his mouth with mine and kiss him forever.

☼

EPILOGUE

It takes Louis and Tomas more than eighteen months to plan their wedding, but the big day finally arrives. The reception is massive and extravagant, set in the grounds of a grand castle in Kent, and it's bursting with models and glamorous fashion types. Everything about the surroundings and the abundance of beautiful people should be intimidating, but I'm having the time of my life.

Louis and Tomas are gorgeous grooms. I wouldn't have been surprised if Louis had asked Tomas to wear the nude long-johns that were so significant in this new phase of their relationship, but Tomas is too much of a fashionista for that. He's wearing a designer suit that looks extremely expensive, and he probably should be paid to wear it. He looks so amazing that there must be hundreds of men here making a mental note to buy the same one. Louis stands with him proudly. He's shorter, scruffier and less shiny, but nevertheless radiant and beaming.

There are hundreds of people here, of all ages. Louis doesn't have much family and Tomas's family couldn't make the journey from Iceland, demanding another ceremony over there later in the year. So Louis asks all his guests to bring whoever they want to, emphasising that we should bring 'old people and children', too. He says weddings should always have plenty of them. "A wedding needs to be attended by lots of grumpy older people who complain about the food and fall asleep on plastic chairs," he insists. "There should also be millions of children running wild. At least one child should wail through the speeches, and another one has to throw up on rented clothing after eating too much sugar. Promise me you'll bring the entire Ryan clan. Promise me they'll be badly behaved and knock all the plants over."

I promise, truly understanding why Louis gave up the wedding photography.

I invite Olive and Sophie, and Sophie brings Betsy and the kids. Sophie's so sweet with the little ones. And it's lovely to see her so happy, after all the heartache she's been through over the years. She decided not to go to Ingrid's wedding in the end, which was a relief for everyone.

Olive doesn't bring anyone because she's still 'right off men', so we get to spend all our time together, just the two of us, like in our Beyoncé 'Single Ladies' days. We gossip about the guests' outlandish outfits, especially some of the snootier people I remember from last time I met Tomas's friends, the ones who look us up and down and decide we're not stylish enough for them. Olive and I conduct our conversation in sign language for privacy, but we freeze when one of the guests walks pasts and quickly signs, "I understand you. Stop discussing my friends!" before marching away, laughing.

Olive gazes after him with a stunned look on her face.

"Talk to him," I suggest.

"Nah. I'm not chatting someone up just because we speak the same language."

"Or because he's really hot and seems to have a sense of humour? And keeps glancing back at you?"

"I can't leave you all alone," Olive says nobly.

Tilly chooses this moment to come over and say hello, removing Olive's excuse. She's with a shy-looking tall man who gazes adoringly at her every two minutes when he thinks we're not paying attention. I find out they're living together in Leeds and have launched their own recruitment business. I try to use my eyes to communicate with Tilly without him seeing, along the lines of, "He seems all right, Tils. Hang on to him!"

Tilly asks me how things are going. We've kept in touch online, but not chatted as often as either of us would like. I tell her about working from home on brochures and documents for various charities, thanks to a glowing reference from the voluntary work I did at The Amelia Fund. Penelope's charity helped me in more ways than one – I ended up using its contacts and advice for my own issues, as well as working on their literature. I hope I'll find a more permanent job eventually, but right now life is good.

Olive mumbles something and slinks away from our catch-up to speak to the good-looking guy who seems fascinated with her.

My conversation with Tilly is interrupted by the arrival of my parents. I invited them at Louis's insistence, but I never thought they'd make the far-eastward journey from Northwood. They say hello and then disappear onto the dancefloor as the DJ plays a track that's far too young for them. Mum bumps hips with Dad while he throws his arms around to denote various sizes of fish and a cardboard box.

I am officially disowning them.

My sisters are also here, also avoiding our parents. Instead, Alannah and Brigid are busy chatting to each other while my twin nieces dance crazily around some chairs. Louis will be happy. OK, they might have had too much sugar, but they should be old enough now not to destroy many plants.

The DJ finishes his set and the live music starts – the band Louis and Tomas booked. It's an up-and-coming brother/sister duo called Elsie's Socks, with Grace Templeton on vocals and Max Renzo on guitar.

Max and Grace play weddings and teach music to kids in their spare time, when they're not too busy working on their debut album. Grace left her retail job to do this because she was missing music so much. The lessons take place in the spare room of the East London flat we share: me and Max, Grace and Elsie. Max and I help out with childcare whenever Grace needs us. I've suggested they should contact Chester for business tips but so far Max has rejected that idea. Instead, he's asked Carol for advice, what with all her experience of self-employment. It's good to see them on speaking terms again.

Elsie's Socks tempt everyone onto the dancefloor. They are amazing.

I dance with the band's namesake, little Elsie Templeton, twirling her around as we groove to the beat. My nieces run over to join in, and Betsy's children appear beside us too. Elsie's clearly impressed with all the exciting big kids.

From the stage, Max catches my eye and smiles.

My heart swells with happiness.

Almost everyone I love is here.

☼

Also by Luci Beach – coming soon!

i'll Give you the moon

Luci Beach

Thank you from Luci Beach

Hi! Thank you so much for reading Ciara and Max's story. I hope you enjoyed it! Please leave a review on any site you like – I would be extremely grateful!

My email address is lucibeachbooks@gmail.com

Find me on Twitter and Facebook @LuciBeachBooks

Please sign up for giveaways, news and more at LuciBeach.co.uk

Printed in Great Britain
by Amazon